FALLING

OTHER BOOKS AND AUDIO BOOKS
BY CLAIR M. POULSON

In Plain Sight

Checking Out

Framed

I'll Find You

Relentless

Lost and Found

Conflict of Interest

Runaway

Cover Up

Mirror Image

Blind Side

Evidence

Don't Cry Wolf

Dead Wrong

Deadline

Vengeance

Hunted

Switchback

Accidental Private Eye

FALLING

a novel

CLAIR M. POULSON

Covenant Communications, Inc.

Cover image: *Helicopter in the Sky* © Pavel Tops

Cover design copyright © 2014 by Covenant Communications, Inc.

Published by Covenant Communications, Inc.
American Fork, Utah

Printed in the United States of America
First Printing: August 2014

20 19 18 17 16 15 14   10 9 8 7 6 5 4 3 2 1

ISBN-13: 978-1-62108-686-4

To Nick Stevenson, Jet Ranger pilot extraordinaire, who flew me to places I needed to go when I was sheriff. Nick was a great help, and never once did he even hesitate when I called him for assistance. Despite his scaring me a couple of times, I always had great confidence in Nick's ability to get me where I needed to go and home again.

Prologue

HEAT WAVES ROSE FROM THE bleak valley floor as the Black Hawk helicopter I was flying skimmed swiftly along not far above. My copilot, two crew chiefs, and eight Army Rangers had just taken out a dangerous nest of Taliban soldiers that had been launching rockets toward our base for several days. Mission completed, we were headed back to base.

I am US Air Force Major Corbin Daniels, and I've flown dozens of missions similar to this one both here in Afghanistan as well as in Iraq. This mission, unlike others, had me stressed out. It was the presence of the woman I loved that did it to me. Angie, my copilot for this mission, was also my fiancée. Captain Angie Brower was also an experienced pilot, though not as experienced as me. She normally flew as copilot to another major, but in the predawn hours as I was preparing for the flight, she'd showed up. "Angie," I said with a sinking feeling in the pit of my stomach, "what are you doing here?"

"I've been ordered to fill in," she said.

I had requested a backup copilot when the man who normally flew at my side had become ill during the night. It hadn't dawned on me that my commanding officer would send Angie. "I'm as capable as anyone," she teased with a grin.

I couldn't deny that. But this had been pegged as a very dangerous mission, and the previous evening, Angie had told me she was worried about me flying this morning. I reminded her of that, but all I got was that grin that I liked so well and the statement, "I'll worry less about you if I'm with you. Now, let's get ready to fly. The rangers will be here in a few minutes."

Much to my relief, the mission had been completed without a single hiccup. We were on our way back when we suddenly came under fire. Despite desperate evasive measures, the Black Hawk took a hit that I knew was serious the moment I felt the jolt. However, I didn't lose complete control and was able to get it almost to the ground before losing all power. We hit hard, but not hard enough to cause any serious injuries.

"Away from the chopper," I ordered urgently the second the damaged aircraft came to rest. If the enemy put another rocket into the helicopter now, it would almost certainly blow up and kill us all.

My crew followed the rangers, and we took what cover we could behind a small ridge just a couple hundred feet away. It wasn't much, but it was the best we could do. Several minutes passed as we called for assistance and waited anxiously to see if any enemy combatants would appear. Apparently the men who shot us down thought they'd done a better job than they had, for when they appeared over a steep ridge beyond the downed Black Hawk, I heard shouting and laughing. About a dozen heavily armed Taliban soldiers approached the downed helicopter. The Black Hawk was badly damaged but not a complete loss by any means. If we could get help to secure the scene, we might be able to salvage the chopper.

We were doing our best to stay out of sight, but the ridge simply didn't provide adequate cover. The young ranger lieutenant whispered that he and his men would take out the enemy. At the very moment he gave the order for his men to open fire, one of the Taliban spotted us, shouted at his comrades, and opened fire. They all dropped to the ground, some already hit and others fighting back. We had at least some protection behind the small ridge, but they had foolishly approached the aircraft without cover of their own. The battle was fierce but short. The rangers advanced to make sure all resistance had been eliminated.

The lead soldier made it about fifty feet when three of the wounded enemy soldiers suddenly opened fire from where they lay scattered on the barren sand. Another squad of Taliban appeared, shouting and firing their weapons, from the same ridge the others had come over only moments earlier. One of our advancing soldiers was dead before he hit the ground. The three downed Taliban soldiers and the new squad continued their onslaught while our men returned fire. I was shooting, as were Angie and our two crew chiefs. I felt a burning sensation across my left cheek. I knew I'd been hit, but it wasn't a serious wound. The last soldier looked me right in the eye just before I took him out.

The dust and smoke settled, and the lieutenant began barking orders. Two rangers ran, hunched over, to the tall ridge the enemy had been hidden behind. As they reached the ridge, I heard a whimper from a few feet to my left. I turned and saw Angie, bleeding into the blistering desert sand. With a cry of anguish, I rushed to her. Blood was gushing from a hole in the center of her chest. I knew an armor piercing round had hit her. I pulled her close and applied pressure to the wound while I called for help.

But it was hopeless. She opened her dark green eyes for just a moment. Then with a small, tight smile, she relaxed in my arms. I couldn't get myself to let go of her, even when the lieutenant told me she was gone. Her blood saturated the ground beneath us. Finally, I removed her helmet, smoothed her short, dark hair, closed her eyes with my fingers, and wept like a baby.

Other rangers had taken hits, but besides the one who had been killed instantly, none of their wounds was life threatening. Two more Black Hawks arrived within twenty minutes, and the accompanying soldiers secured the scene. The bodies of the two who had died—a young soldier of about twenty-one and my beloved Angie Brower—were loaded into body bags and flown back to our base.

* * *

Angie and I had both loved our military assignments. At thirty, I'd been in the army for eight years, having enlisted just a few months after returning from an LDS mission. Angie had joined at age twenty-one, much to the anguish of her parents. Both Utah natives, we had felt a duty to serve our country as well as a yearning to fly. We'd found both as combat pilots. Angie's latest enlistment would have been up in two years. I still had three left. We had planned to marry in the Salt Lake Temple following our present deployment.

Since that would never happen, I simply volunteered for another year in Afghanistan. My heart was not in it like it had been, but I was a good pilot, or so I was told, and continued to fly mission after mission.

After my latest enlistment was up, I continued to serve, but no longer full time. I became a member of a National Guard unit in Utah and served once more overseas with that unit. After that, I resigned my commission and gave up military service. In my civilian life, I trained for and was licensed as a private investigator. At the passing of my father, I sold our family ranch and bought a helicopter, a Bell Jet Ranger, and started a business flying clients just about anywhere they wanted to go.

I moved my business to scenic Moab, Utah, and began to transport oil field workers to and from some new, controversial oil rigs that were drilling on private land quite a distance out of town. The money was good, the scenery was great, and the flying was enjoyable.

I was tired of combat, but flying for my new business was pure pleasure.

Chapter One

IT WAS A WARM MONDAY afternoon in early May. I was flying three tired men from an oil rig they had been at for the past week back to Moab. They had been replaced by three other workers that I had flown out there. We had been talking about the swirling debate.

Being new in the area, I wasn't embroiled in the drilling controversy, but I supposed it would only be a short while before I was. However, I wasn't too worried. There had been no violence, only protests, editorials, and cries of foul from those who didn't even live in the area. Those people thought the distant wells were polluting the scenic variety by their very presence. And perhaps they were, but it was helping me make an enjoyable business quite successful.

One of the workers, Devan Rish, a young man in his midtwenties, was particularly vocal about those who opposed drilling, an activity that made him a decent living. I think he took it as a personal affront. "You realize that you're one of us when you fly us to work and back the way you do, Major?" Devan said. He was in the seat next to me, but I could see his grin as he spoke into his headset.

When the workers had learned that I had been a major in the army, they had taken to calling me "Major." I'm not a major anymore; I'm just Corbin Daniels, a single, forty-two-year-old helicopter pilot and private investigator trying to make a living. "Yes, I suppose you're right," I said. "But it doesn't bother me. With all the years I spent in combat, I've developed very thick skin. I don't care what people say or think as long as they don't actually interfere."

Devan changed the focus of the conversation. "Which do you spend more time at, flying this chopper or investigating?"

I was doing more flying, and I told him that. "I not only fly you men, but I do some tourist flights over the area."

"Hey, what's that down there?" Devan suddenly asked as he pointed out the window of the Jet Ranger. We weren't very high, and it was possible to see things on the ground, even though we were flying at nearly a hundred miles per hour.

"I'm not sure what you're talking about," I said. "What did you think you saw?"

"I know this sounds crazy," Devan said, "but I'd swear it looked like some guy was lying on his back on the ground. That would be suicide in this hot sun."

"We better check it out," I said as I cut my speed and banked to the left, dropping elevation.

The men in the backseat began to hoot and laugh. They were all talking at once, so I couldn't tell what was being said, but I was pretty sure I heard something about the Major flying like he was in a Black Hawk. I just chuckled and studied the ground as I leveled. "There! Right over there," Devan shouted, gesturing wildly.

I looked in the direction he was pointing and saw what he was looking at. It was ahead of us and to the left. I slowed more, turned again, and then hovered just a few yards from the object. "That looks like a man all right," I said. "And he doesn't look okay either. I'm going to set this thing down and take a closer look."

"I think he's dead," Devan said. The others chorused their agreement. I said nothing, but I was quite certain they were right.

Finding a fairly level spot to put the chopper down about two or three hundred feet from the body, I told my passengers, "I'll take a look. You men stay put. I don't want to leave any more tracks than we need to. We don't want to mess the area up in case the sheriff wants to come out here, which I'm sure he will."

None of them argued, so I stepped out, ducked, and ran, sheltering my eyes until I was out of the dust the rotors were creating. I approached the body slowly, watching the ground each time I put a foot down. I didn't want to disturb any tracks the fellow might have left getting to the spot where he was lying.

Once I was within a yard or so, I stopped, bent over, and peered at the man. There was no doubt he was dead and had been for several hours, since, I guessed, well before sunup that morning. His face was badly burned from the sun, his eyes closed. His body was twisted badly. I could see the end of one femur poking through his pant leg, and it appeared other limbs were also broken as none of them were lying in normal positions. Even his head was bent badly to the side. Blood had flowed from his mouth and nose and was now just black goo covered with flies. I straightened up and continued to examine him with my eyes. It was hard to be sure, but I estimated that he was several years older than me and about my size. At least he was probably my height, an even six feet, but I guessed that he outweighed me by twenty pounds. At 180, I wasn't overweight, but this man was.

Without moving, I carefully examined the ground around him. I couldn't see tracks of any kind. So far, the vultures and other creatures hadn't done him any damage—but that's not to say he wasn't damaged. He was—terribly so. He had to have died violently to have broken his leg like that and caused all that bleeding. This was most assuredly a matter for the county sheriff. I pulled my cell phone out, but I didn't have a good signal, so I stepped back quickly and returned to my helicopter.

Devan, the talkative one, asked, "What happened to him?"

"I think he fell out of the sky," I answered. "Cell phone service is limited, so I need to use my radio to call the authorities."

I relayed to the airport what we had found and gave them our location. I waited while the information was relayed to law enforcement. A couple of minutes passed before I heard back, at which time I was told that the sheriff and a detective would come out, but because of the remoteness of the location, they would need me to come and get them. I agreed but said, "I can't leave this body unattended. What would the sheriff like me to do? I have three passengers. I could leave one of them and pick up the officers after I let my other passengers off."

When I received my answer in the affirmative, Devan spoke up. "I'll stay, Major."

"Okay, let me give you some water; it's going to get hotter out here before I get back," I said. "And stay here near where the chopper is. Don't go any closer to the body unless you have to chase off a vulture or something."

"You can count on me, Major," he said.

I instructed the man at the airport to have the officers meet me there so I could get fuel before we came back out.

I flew the rest of the way to Moab, let my passengers off, and then flew to Canyonlands Field Airport several miles north of town.

I had finished the fueling process when an unmarked police car came speeding into the airport. It parked some distance away, and then two persons started running toward me. Having only been in Moab for a short time, I had yet to meet the local sheriff or any of the deputies. The sheriff was not what I expected, nor was the detective.

"Major Daniels," she said, holding out her hand in greeting. Apparently, she knew who I was. "I'm Sheriff Lisette Statton."

"It's nice to meet you," I said as we shook hands. Sheriff Statton was an attractive woman of maybe thirty-seven or thirty-eight. She was only a couple inches shorter than me but a lot better to look at. She was trim and fit, with dark brown eyes that seemed to be studying me as closely as I was assessing her. Her short, dark blonde hair was partially covered by a gray, short-brimmed Western hat. Her uniform was neat and clean and fit her perfectly.

"Thanks for calling us," she said as she turned to her deputy, another very pretty young woman of something not far under thirty. Her eyes were light blue, and they were also studying me closely. I was used to people's eyes lingering on the left side of my face where there was a pronounced three-inch scar from the bullet that had grazed me in Afghanistan. "This is Detective Jarbi Patterson. She's as smart as she is pretty," the sheriff said with a grin.

"It's nice to meet both of you," I said with a nod. I know I shouldn't have been surprised when it was women—attractive women. After all, my late fiancée was also an attractive woman in a position traditionally filled by men only. "I'm a former major; it's just Corbin Daniels now," I added. "Let's get you ladies on board, and I'll fill you in on what we have out there."

Sheriff Statton climbed in the front seat next to me, and Detective Patterson got in the back. Both women were carrying purses large enough to hold all kinds of equipment, such as cameras. They could also have held pistols, though both officers had 9mm semiautomatics strapped to their belts. After helping the officers get their headsets on and offering quick instructions on their use, I started the helicopter; in a couple of minutes, we lifted off.

I headed southeast. The sheriff spoke after I had leveled out. "I'd heard we had a new private investigator in town," she said. "Is it true that you used to fly Black Hawks?"

"More than I care to remember," I said.

"I guess you saw a lot of combat," Deputy Patterson said from her seat in the back.

"Yeah, lots," I agreed. But I didn't want to talk about me. Whenever I did, someone inevitably asked about the scar, something that brought back terrible memories, something which, even after all these years, I didn't like to talk about. So I said, "I've only been here a few weeks, but business is good. I didn't expect to find what we did out there."

The sheriff agreed. "All I was told is that you found a dead body, a man?"

"That's right," I said.

Before I could explain further, Detective Patterson asked, "Was it some hiker that got lost?"

"I'm afraid not," I said. "The man died a violent death."

"Was he shot?" Sheriff Statton asked, adjusting her headset slightly.

"I don't know if he was or not," I answered as I read my instruments and set as straight a course as I could to where Devan and the dead man were waiting. "He's lying face up, and of course, I didn't touch him. I tried to preserve the crime scene. I suppose there could be a bullet in his back, but if so, it didn't go all the way through his body."

"If he wasn't shot, do you have any idea how he died?" the sheriff asked. "You did say it was violent."

"His body is badly broken, as you will see," I explained. "And I couldn't see any evidence of tracks around the body."

"So how did he get there?" the detective asked.

"I know this will sound crazy to you ladies," I began, "but it appeared to me like he fell out of the sky."

"Goodness," the sheriff said. "I wonder if he was a stowaway on some jetliner. I've heard of people climbing on the tires, riding there when the wheels are pulled up, and then falling out when the landing gear is lowered."

I shook my head. "That's not what happened here," I said. "No jetliner would have been lowering landing gear out here. Anyway, they fly several miles up, and a body falling from that distance would have sustained even more damage than this poor guy did."

"So what are you suggesting?" Sheriff Statton asked.

"I don't know what happened, but I would have to guess that he fell from or was pushed out of a small plane," I said.

The sheriff twisted the hat she was holding on her lap. "Are you suggesting murder?"

"It did occur to me," I said, looking at her with a short smile. "Either that or some kind of daredevil stunt gone bad, and this guy didn't look like the kind to be walking on the wing of a plane or something equally stupid."

"What do you mean by that?" she asked. "I wouldn't think you could tell much just by looking at a dead body."

"The guy is about my height, I would guess, but he's heavier. I just don't picture heavy guys doing stunts like that," I explained. "No, I think you have a murder on your hands, Sheriff."

Detective Patterson spoke up. "If he was thrown from a plane, then somebody was flying it. I wonder if they filed a flight plan."

"I would think not, but we'll check," the sheriff said. "First we've got to figure out who he is and where he's from."

The ladies and I visited for the next few minutes as we streaked toward the remote crime scene. I found that I liked both of them, especially when they didn't disparage me for working as a private investigator. The sheriff asked me where I had worked last and why I had moved to Moab. "Opportunity," I said. "There's plenty of work for an experienced investigator in the Salt Lake area, and I very much enjoy the work, but it was the chance to do more flying that led me down here. That is my first love, I guess you could say."

"I see. Well it makes sense," she agreed. "It's nice to have you here. I trust we'll have a good working relationship."

"I would hope so," I said. "I certainly hold law enforcement officers in high esteem."

"Have you moved your family here yet?" she asked.

"I'm not married."

"That makes three of us," she responded, flicking a thumb toward the backseat. "Some gal is missing out."

"Or a couple of good men are," I countered.

The three of us shared a laugh.

We flew without discussion for a few miles, and then I said, "We're almost there. I'll set this bird down and let you officers take it from there."

Devan waved at us as I took one pass over the scene to allow the officers to take a look at it from the air. "I trust you've had some experience at crime scenes," the sheriff said.

"Yes, some."

"Good, because we may need some help."

"Whatever you need," I said. "I just don't want to get in your way."

Once I shut the helicopter down, we got out, and I made introductions. "Devan and I will wait here." He nodded in agreement. I added, "The only tracks you can see near the body are mine."

The women walked to the body, stopped where I had, and did as I had done, studying the body and the surrounding area. I could tell that they were talking, but I had put the helicopter too far away to hear what they were saying. The sheriff pointed to the body, gestured a couple of times, and then turned toward us. Detective Patterson pulled a digital camera from her oversized purse and began to snap pictures while Sheriff Statton returned to where Devan and I were standing.

One look at her told me that something had disturbed her. "You okay?" I asked.

"Yes, I'm fine, but I know the victim," she said.

"Oh my, I'm sorry," I said.

"Yeah, his name is Edward Jones. We ran against each other last fall when my old boss retired."

I couldn't come up with a good response to that, so I made none.

She went on. "He used to work for the sheriff. He actually retired a couple of years ago but kept his certification up. I think he's had his mind set on replacing Sheriff Dunham for years. He wasn't a bad police officer but not a great one either."

Now I had something to say, even though I wasn't sure she would like it. "Was it a contentious election?"

"Not really," she said. "He was a nice man. The only thing he made a big deal out of was the fact that I was a woman trying to do a man's job. That didn't go over real well with a lot of people, and I beat him two to one. Don't get me wrong; he wasn't a bad sort of guy. He just had that one hang-up."

"That's not the only reason Sheriff Statton beat him," Devan said. "It looked to me and a lot of other people like she was a far better police officer and a lot smarter than him. His being a decent man didn't compensate for that."

"Thanks, Devan," the sheriff said. "At any rate, I can't imagine who would do this."

Chapter Two

WE ALL STOOD OVER THE body of the dead man. After a moment, Sheriff Statton took a deep breath. "This is not going to be fun. Would you men mind giving us a little help?"

"Whatever you need," I said.

"Yeah," Devan agreed. He looked a little too eager, but I figured I could keep him from messing anything up.

"Jarbi is taking some photographs. As soon as she's done, we'll need to move the body—turn it over, see what we find there—and then decide what to do about getting him to Salt Lake for an autopsy," she said.

For the next half hour, we examined the body from every angle. There were no visible wounds that couldn't be accounted for by a fall from the sky. "I hate to think he was alive when he fell . . . or was pushed . . . from a plane," Jarbi said with a shiver. "That's too horrible to even consider."

Finally, the sheriff was finished. "Okay, now we need to get him moved out of here. I don't suppose you have a body bag, Major."

"No, that's not something I've ever needed before," I said.

She gave me a tired smile. "I guess it didn't hurt to ask. If we had one, could you haul the body in the helicopter?"

"That's not a problem. My cargo area is plenty large enough for that."

"Okay, let me get on my radio and see what it'll take to get a body bag. That's not something we cops carry around with us."

She spoke on her handheld police radio for a minute or two, and when she finished, she had a plan. "I know Devan needs to get home," she said. "Major, I'll fly in with you and Devan, and then you and I can bring a bag back. Jarbi will need to stay with the body."

It was getting quite warm now, and I left Detective Patterson a bottle of water. She flashed me a pretty smile and said, "You guys hurry back. I'm not particularly looking forward to spending time alone with Edward."

"He was nice to Devan while they were alone, Detective," I joked.

She punched me playfully on the shoulder. "I think we've been together long enough that you can call me Jarbi."

The sheriff chuckled and said, "She's right, Major. We aren't too formal in my department. Not under the previous sheriff and not under me. So you can call me Lisette, if you don't mind."

"And you ladies can call me Corbin. I haven't been Major anybody for several years," I said.

"But we all call him Major," Devan said. "I mean, how many guys get to ride with a Black Hawk pilot?"

"I'm a Jet Ranger pilot now," I said. "Devan, why don't you get in, and we'll be on our way."

On the flight in, Devan talked almost nonstop. From time to time Lisette and I would look at each other and smile. This was a tragic, horrific case for Lisette, but it was all a big adventure to Devan. "Hey, let's do this again sometime, Major," he said when we dropped him off.

"You'll be riding out to that rig enough that I suspect you'll get tired of it," I responded.

"Never. And if there are any more bodies, I'll spot them," he said. With a cheery wave, he ran from under the rotors, and we lifted off again.

"Where to?" I asked Lisette after we were back in the air again.

"The airport. A mortician was dropping a body bag off there for us, and he'll meet us when we get the body back."

When we landed with the body back at the airport, Lisette thanked me and told me how to bill the county for my services. The rest of the day was relatively uneventful. When I left the officers and the body at the airport, their work had really just begun. For me, it was a drive back to the office in town to see what work, if any, my secretary, Crystal Burke, had for me.

Crystal is a cheerful young woman of twenty-five. She's not only my secretary, but she's also my cousin. In fact, she's really more an assistant than a secretary. Crystal was invaluable to me. She followed the job and me from Salt Lake to Moab. She was enthusiastic about the change, and I was grateful she'd agreed to come. Mostly, she'd told me, she wanted a different look in eligible bachelors. She is an attractive girl who is in a constant battle with her weight, or so she says. I think she looks just fine, but she never thinks so. It doesn't affect her personality, though, and that's as big a plus to my business as it is to her social life.

When I walked in the door, she greeted me with a cheery, "Hi, Corbin. How's your day going?"

I told her about the dead man, and she gasped. "What an awful thing for you," she said.

"Not so much for me as for Edward Jones," I commented dryly.

"Who's Edward Jones?" she asked.

"The dead man."

She stuck her tongue out at me, a favorite gesture of hers, and then said, "Sounds like you need something to do."

"What have you got?" I asked, pausing beside her desk.

"A possible insurance fraud case," she said. "The client is a local realtor, seems like a nice woman. She's in a bind but doesn't want to turn it over to the cops if she doesn't have to. She's hoping you can help her."

It was a day for nice women, I guessed, and a nice, but very dead, former sheriff candidate. I took the woman's contact information and entered my private office. I made a call, told the client, Nora Briggs, to come in and tell me what she needed, and I would then see what, if anything, I could do for her.

* * *

Nora turned out to be a woman of about fifty, with short, black hair and very dark eyes. A sturdy woman and not too tall, she had a pleasant face and nice personality. She explained that if I could dig up some information on a client who was trying to sell some business property, she might be able to convince the man to come clean on his insurance claim so that she could either proceed or let him find a new realtor. "I don't want him prosecuted. He really is a nice guy. I think he's just been given some pretty bad advice. A little scare might bring him around," she said.

"If it's scary you want, you've come to the right place," I said. She chuckled, signed a simple contract, left me a retainer, and headed back to her office.

I worked into the late afternoon on that case—not a complicated matter, and one I believed I could complete in a couple of days, barring any major interruptions. I did have some flights booked, but nothing that would take too much of my time.

I was just ready to leave the office and make a couple of visits on the case when Crystal buzzed. "Call for you," she said. "I think it's the sheriff. I guess it's the sheriff. Anyway, it's a woman who says she's the sheriff."

"I guess I didn't tell you that," I said. "Yeah, the sheriff is a woman."

"She sounded really nice and not too old. And she sounded pretty. Is she single?" Crystal asked.

"Yes to all of the above; now transfer the call."

"So she really is pretty?"

"Yes, quite, as a matter of fact. Now transfer the call," I repeated.

"You don't have to get testy," she said with humor in her voice and did as I instructed.

Crystal is a great girl, loyal, sweet, efficient, and very concerned that I wasn't actively looking for a woman in my life. She kept telling me that she was going to help me change that. So far, she hadn't had any more luck finding me a wife than she'd had finding herself a husband. I was pulling for her, but I was doing just fine single. I'd nearly been married once and ended up with a shattered heart. I wasn't anxious to try it again.

I picked up the phone. "Hi, Sheriff. I hope your day has improved."

"Fat chance of that," Lisette said, sounding both tired and stressed.

"I'm sorry to hear that," I said. "Is there anything I can do to help?"

"That's why I'm calling. I went to Edward's home to deliver the bad news to his wife," she said.

"I suppose she didn't take it too well. That's normal, I'd guess," I responded.

"That's not the problem. She didn't take it at all. She's missing. A neighbor told me that Edward and his wife left last night in their pickup and didn't come back. Of course, we know why Edward didn't."

"Have you contacted their children or other relatives?" I asked.

"I met with his daughter and talked to his son on the phone," Lisette said. "They both claimed that they hadn't heard from either parent for a couple of days, and they didn't have any idea where Edward and his wife might have been going."

"I assume the son and daughter know their father is dead?"

"They do now," was the sheriff's response. "And now they're worried about their mother."

"I guess that makes sense," I said. "So what do you need me to do?"

"I know this is asking a lot, Major," she said. Apparently, she hadn't got the message that I was Corbin, not Major, but I let it go. "I was wondering if we could do a little more flying."

"And look for another body?" I asked.

"You read my mind," she said. "Jarbi found their pickup in the airport parking lot. If we'd had any idea, we could have found it when we were all there earlier."

"Do they have another vehicle?"

"It's in the garage at their house."

"Okay, so what time do you want to go?"

"I'm sorry to give you such short notice, Major, but could we go soon? We don't have a lot of hours of daylight left, and I thought it might be good to use what we have."

"Sure," I said. "Meet you at the airport?"

"I could just swing by your office and pick you up, save you some driving," she suggested.

"Sure, let me give you my address." I told her what it was and then asked, "How long before you'll be here?"

"Five minutes. Ten at the most."

I hung up, then stepped out of my office and said to Crystal, "Do you have a hot date or anything in the next couple of hours?"

She chuckled. "I wish. Is there something you need me to do?"

Crystal was more than a secretary and receptionist. She also did some of the leg work that went with my investigation practice. She was quite good at it, and with all the flying I did, I relied on her a lot. I often referred to her as my associate. "I was going to make a couple contacts for our new client, but Lisette and I have to do some flying," I said. "I was wondering if you could make the contacts. I'll tell you exactly what we need to find out from the people you'll be visiting."

"Lisette, huh?" she said. "That was fast."

"Sheriff Statton is informal, and she insisted I call her by her first name, if it's okay with you," I said in mock severity. "Can you take care of this for me?"

"You know I can," she said. "Give me the names and addresses and tell me what to ask."

"I'll write it down," I suggested.

"Or you can tell me and I'll write it. That way I can read it later," she countered.

She had me there. My handwriting was not the best. So I dictated, and she made notes. We were just finishing when the door opened and Sheriff Statton walked in, glancing around. "Not a bad office, Major," she said. "Thanks for helping on such short notice."

"Not a problem. Meet my secretary, receptionist, and very able associate, Crystal Burke," I said. "Crystal, this is Sheriff Lisette Statton."

They exchanged pleasantries, and then I said, "Crystal helps out from time to time in my investigations. She's also looking for a man, like your detective is." I grinned at the sheriff.

"Corbin," Crystal said with a red face. "I just like to meet guys."

"Yeah, right. Well, go meet a couple now. Of course, one of them is married. Anyway, you can report back in the morning on what they tell you," I said, pointing at the notes we had just made.

"I will," she said, grinning. "But don't get your hopes up, Corbin. I've never met one of your clients yet who would have made good dating material. Anyway, you and the sheriff have a good time."

Lisette and I headed for the parking lot.

"She seems like a nice girl," Lisette said, steering me toward her patrol vehicle, a silver, unmarked SUV—a Ford Expedition, I noted when we got closer.

"Crystal's my cousin," I said. "She's almost like a sister to me. And she really does keep my office running. She does double duty, taking care of both of my phone lines—one for my flying business, one for the investigations—and she does a lot of the leg work as well. I'm not sure what I'll do if she actually finds a husband and he won't let her work anymore. It would probably be a disaster."

On the way to the airport, the sheriff filled me in on the situation with the late Edward Jones and his wife. "They were apparently having marital trouble," she said, "which comes as a total shock to me. I didn't see any sign of it during the campaign, but both her kids told me that this afternoon."

"I see," I said evenly. "Was divorce imminent?"

"Apparently so," Lisette said. "And apparently, I'm to blame."

"What? Who told you that?"

"Well, nobody, exactly, but both of her kids said that she had blamed Edward for losing the election because he was so negative about me, using my gender to tear me down."

"I don't see how that means you are to blame," I said.

"Well, maybe it doesn't, but both kids told me that their mother and dad had argued bitterly over the way he was making his entire campaign about my gender. She apparently didn't think he was being fair about women. His kids think that if he'd based his campaign only on his experience and expertise, he would have won."

"I doubt that, and so does Devan, the young rig worker." I glanced over at her. "You seem quite competent to me."

"Thanks. I'd like to think I'm better qualified," she said. "I'm sure there were other problems the kids didn't know about. They're both grown, married, and have families of their own. The daughter and her family live here in Moab but all the way across town. The son lives down in Blanding. So I'm not sure how much they really knew about their parents' relationship of late."

"Either way, I guess your first priority is to see if you can find Mrs. Jones. Marital problems aren't an issue anymore."

Lisette shrugged. "But it may have a bearing on my investigation into his murder."

"That's not a pretty thought," I said. "I guess I should have said there won't be any more marital problems for the two of them."

"I still hope I can find her alive. I don't want two bodies to deal with. And if anyone can help figure out who killed him, I think it would be Mrs. Jones."

A few minutes later, we were in the Jet Ranger. I was letting it warm up for a moment before taking off. "Any particular route you'd like me to take? I mean, do we have any idea about the plane they were flying in—if they were in a plane?"

"No idea. There was a plane that flew out in the middle of the night, but who was in it and where they were going, we have no idea."

"So should we just sort of take a direct path from here to where we found Edward and then straight on from there?" I asked. "There's some pretty rough terrain out there, so I'll have to either get high in places or do some flying around the high points."

"You're the pilot," the sheriff said. "Frankly, I'm not expecting to find another body, but the Jones kids sort of insisted. So at least I can tell them I tried."

"What about search and rescue?" I asked when we were airborne. "Were you planning on involving them?"

"Maybe later, if I need to. In the meantime, I'm hoping that either the son or the daughter will be able to make contact with Mrs. Jones and we can forget about all this," Lisette said hopefully. "Her cell phone isn't at the house, so if she's okay, she's probably just being stubborn and not answering it. Her kids are sort of leaning toward the worst, though, especially the daughter. That's why I had to bother you."

"I suppose they have a reason for that?" I asked. Lisette hesitated. "If it's none of my business, that's okay," I added.

"No, it's not that, Major. I was just thinking about what you asked. Apparently, Edward had applied with the drilling company to do some security at the wells. He was notified a few days ago that he had been hired. Edward's son, Trace, told me that. He doesn't think his mother knew anything about it. I don't think the daughter knew either, but I need to ask her specifically about that later."

We flew for a couple of hours, and I was about to ask if we should be getting back when Lisette suddenly said, "Hey, I think I saw something down there."

Indeed she had. I circled around for a moment and spotted a dark object in a deep crevice quite a ways below us. There was no place to put the helicopter on the ground near there, so I set us down on top of a ridge.

"I'll hike down and have a look," she said.

"I'll come with you, if you like," I offered.

"Do you dare leave your helicopter unattended?" she asked. "It might take an hour or so to get down there, see what it is, and get back up here. By then we'll be losing our daylight."

"Who's going to bother it?" I grinned as I swung my arm toward the miles of beautiful but empty scenery surrounding us. "I'll shut it down and come with you."

The hike was steep, but we made it in about twenty minutes. We had to search for another five minutes before we found what we had seen from the air. "At least it's not another body," Lisette said with relief as we lowered ourselves into the ravine.

What we found was a large brown suitcase. It had broken open and spilled its contents, but because of the narrowness of the ravine, things hadn't scattered far. It only took a minute to figure out who the suitcase belonged to. The label read *Johanna Jones*. The clothing that was scattered about, however, was men's apparel not women's—Edward's stuff. There was also a box that had been tightly taped shut and hadn't broken open.

The sheriff pulled a small knife from a pocket of her pants and carefully slit the tape. "Will you look at this," she said, as she pulled one of probably five hundred pamphlets from the box. "This is anti-drilling literature. I saw one the other day. I'm not sure where it came from, but one of my deputies gave it to me."

"An interesting thing for a new security officer of the oil wells to be carrying in his suitcase," I said.

"Very," the sheriff agreed. "I wonder if he had become involved with both sides of the drilling dispute. That doesn't seem like a very smart thing to do. It makes me wonder if this could be a motive for murder, one way or another."

Chapter Three

PUTTING EVERYTHING BACK IN THE suitcase, we took turns lugging it up the unforgiving ridge. I tried to do most of the lugging, but Lisette was not a lazy woman. And she reminded me that it was her job. "I'm grateful for your help, Major, but you don't have to do all the work."

On the flight back in, darkness overtook us. Not that I minded flying by only my lights and instruments. I'd certainly done a lot of that in my military career and even in my Jet Ranger. I was totally comfortable, but I think it must have made the sheriff a little nervous. "I'm sorry we're so late," she kept repeating. "I know you have things to do besides helping me."

"Lisette, I am really quite enjoying your company," I said truthfully. "I hope that you won't hesitate to call on me in the future."

"Do you mean that?"

"Of course I mean that. I'm not someone who says a lot that I don't mean."

"I appreciate it," she said. "There's another fellow who's helped out from time to time. Sheriff Stuart used to use him a lot, but he always complains. To be honest, after taking so much of your morning, I called him before I called you. He said he didn't have time. I get the feeling he shares Edward's opinions about a woman sheriff. I know he supported Edward during the election."

"Where does he keep his chopper?"

"He has a private hangar outside town. His name's Earl Bassinger. As I'm sure you know, there are several outfits here that fly both helicopters and fixed-wing planes on sightseeing tours," she said. "He does some of that."

"Yes, I knew there were others around here that flew for hire. I guess I was taking a chance coming down here. But, even though I've only been in town a few weeks, I've got plenty of business."

"I hope you do well," she said. "Do you plan to move your helicopter closer to town?"

"When I find a place to keep it, I will. I won't leave it out in the weather, so I rented a hangar at the airport. I sold the farm to buy this machine, and I intend to make it last for a long time."

"Sold the farm?" she asked.

"That's right. I suppose I could have taken over and run it when Dad died, but that's not my thing. Flying and investigation are my life. I sold the place—a very nice place—split the proceeds with my sister, and bought this helicopter."

We talked about other things on the way back to the airport. I found Lisette easy to talk to. I was glad about that since, on the Wasatch Front, I hadn't always been able to develop such an easy relationship with many cops. I'm sure it wasn't their fault. I know I'm not an easy man. I'm headstrong and determined, and that doesn't go over well with a lot of police officers. I hoped that I could keep from letting that get in the way of a good professional relationship with Lisette and her deputies.

At one point, Lisette asked, "Have you found a permanent place to live yet?"

"No, and neither has my cousin. We're both in small apartments and are looking for something better."

"There is a house for rent just a short distance from me. In fact, that house is my closest neighbor. I live out of town a few miles, in an unincorporated area of the county. A local realtor manages the property for the out-of-town owner," Lisette continued. "The previous tenants moved to Salt Lake. And I'm told the rent is reasonable. The house is quite large. The basement has a kitchen and all. There's also a lot of acreage attached. You and your cousin could probably both live there and have room to spare."

"Thanks, I'll look into it," I said. Crystal and I had considered adding an extra office if I found a place large enough and if she found one nearby. "Do you have the name of the realtor?" I asked.

"I sure do. She's a nice lady. She's in my ward. Her name is Nora Briggs. Her husband is in the bishopric," Lisette said. "I'll call you with her number when I get back to the office if you'd like."

"Thanks, but that won't be necessary. I know Mrs. Briggs. I'll call her in morning."

"You know her?" Lisette asked, a little surprised. "Have you already talked to her about helping you find a place?"

"No, I just met her this afternoon."

"Oh, is she a client?" Lisette asked. But before I could respond, she blurted, "Don't answer that. I shouldn't have asked. Sorry."

"That's okay," I said, knowing Lisette had figured it out, not that it mattered. But it wasn't something I was likely to discuss with her, and I was grateful she didn't appear to intend to pursue the matter. If Nora had wanted Lisette aware of the situation, she'd have gone to her in the first place.

Thanking me once again, Lisette promised to ask for my help again whenever she needed it. She waited in her silver Expedition while I fueled up the Jet Ranger and put it in the hangar. Then we rode back to Moab together. While she was driving, she got a call from her dispatcher. "The son of Mrs. Jones says he found his mother," she told me after the call was complete. "He wants me to call when I get back to town. Too bad he couldn't have found her earlier and saved us both a lot of time."

"At least you'll be able to talk to her about her husband," I said.

Lisette sighed. "I told the dispatcher I'd call as soon as I get back to town." Then she looked over at me in the murky light of the SUV. "I suppose it'll be a night with very little sleep. But I'm not complaining." She had a smile on her face. "I ran for the job. And I sure wouldn't want to trade places with Edward Jones right now. Tomorrow, I'll put more of my people on this case. My chief deputy is hardworking and smart, as is Jarbi. We'll get this case solved."

After Lisette dropped me off at my office, I went inside and checked to see if Crystal had left any notes for me. She had. She'd written: *Corbin. Call me on my cell phone. I'll be at my apartment. It's very important. It's not about Nora Briggs's case. It's a prospective client that I think you'll want to talk to right away. Crystal.*

It was getting late, but I decided it wasn't too late, so I sat at my desk, picked up the phone, and dialed my cousin's cell phone number.

She answered right away. "I know you're probably tired, but this woman was insistent that I have you call her tonight. She said it can't wait until morning."

"Did she tell you what it was about?" I asked.

"No. She said you were the only one she would talk to and that it was very, very critical that you call her tonight."

"Okay, give me her name and number," I said.

Crystal gave me the number first and then said, "Her name is Asher Grady, and she lives here in town. She's really upset over something."

"All right, I'll give her a call. How did it go with those men I needed you to contact?"

"Pretty well, I think. I'll fill you in on that in the morning."

I disconnected and called the number for Asher Grady. It rang twice, and a woman answered, "This is Asher Grady."

"Mrs. Grady, my name is Corbin Daniels."

"Major Daniels, thanks for calling," she said quickly. How did she know I was sometimes called Major? "I need your help. Are you in your office?"

"I am, but I—"

She interrupted. "I'll be right there. I know where your office is. You've got to help me."

The call was cut off, and I assumed she was already heading out the door and to her car at a dead run. I wasn't sure that I was going to like this visit at all. I had a feeling that this could only be about Edward Jones and the missing, but presumably located, Johanna Jones. If it was, Mrs. Grady must know something the sheriff didn't. I wondered why she was asking me for help instead of the sheriff. I guessed I would know soon enough . . . if it was about Jones, that is.

I expected that right about now the sheriff was getting an earful from the brother, Trace Jones. And if my hunch was right, I was about to get an earful from Asher, the sister.

A few minutes later, a young lady of about thirty stormed through my door. I had to do a double take. She had short, spiked hair that was black with wide streaks of bright purple. She was fairly tall, probably five-nine or so. Her face was dark, and her eyes flashed with anger.

"You must be Mrs. Grady," I said.

"Yes, I am," she responded. "Major Daniels, I need help."

"Come into my office, and let's talk about it," I suggested, gesturing for her to precede me. She did so and sat down right where I would have asked her to had she given me the chance.

I hadn't made it around my desk to my chair when she began to speak again. "I'm pretty sure my brother had something to do with my father's murder. And I think he might have killed my mother too. You've got to find him."

"Whoa, slow down," I said. "Let's take this from the top and take it slowly. First, who is your father?"

"You should know," she snapped. "You found him this morning and brought his poor battered body back in your helicopter."

"Your father is Edward Jones?" I asked, not wanting to let on that I'd already figured that out.

"Yes, or at least he was until my brother killed him or had him killed or something like that," she practically shouted.

"Okay, Asher. Let's slow down. First, I need to decide if I'm even going to take your case. Then we can get into details about your allegations," I said calmly.

For once, she didn't blurt anything out. Big tears formed in her eyes, ones so shrouded in eye shadow that I had a feeling she wouldn't be recognizable with a washed face. "Asher, I'm not saying I won't take your case, but I need to make sure we understand each other. First, I'd like to know why you came to me."

She sniffled, wiping the big tears from her eyes and smudging mascara all over her cheeks in the process. "My husband told me about you after the sheriff came to tell me about my dad. My husband works on one of the oil rigs, and he told me that you do investigations as well as fly."

Now I understood why she had called me Major. Her husband had flown with me. "Okay, thanks for telling me that. Now let's discuss how I work. First, I don't work for free," I said.

"I know, and we will pay you," she said. "My brother has got to be stopped. He should be in jail." She sounded slightly calmer.

"Let me ask you this," I said now that she was not quite so agitated. "You already mentioned that Sheriff Statton was at your house today.

Why don't you talk to her about your brother? She's in charge of the official investigation."

Asher's face darkened. "She won't help. She only came to rub it in. She hated my dad. She took the job that should have been his!" she railed, making me wonder why she would say such a thing. I was sure Lisette hadn't intended to rub anything in Asher's face.

I raised a hand while shaking my head. "Asher, if you want my help, you have got to remain calm and listen to me."

"The sheriff—" she began again.

"The sheriff is my friend." I cut her off sharply. "If you want my help, you will not accuse her of anything. You will keep an open mind. Do I make myself clear?"

"Yes," she said in a clipped voice. "But she took my dad's job."

"No, she and your dad ran for the job. Sheriff Statton defeated your dad in an open and fair election. The office of sheriff is a public position. By a large margin, the voters of this county voted for Sheriff Statton. That means she won. Your father—a good man, according to Sheriff Statton—lost. That election is over, and you have got to move on. If I'm going to look in to your allegations, you must understand that I will be working with the sheriff, not against her."

Asher stood up, turned, and took a step toward the door. "Are you leaving then?" I asked, feeling some relief, for I didn't relish the prospect of working for this extremely emotional young woman.

She stopped and turned back around. "Will you help me?" she asked.

"On my terms, I will consider it," I said, slightly disappointed I hadn't scared her off. "I just need to make sure you understand where I am coming from."

She moved back to the chair and sat down again. Oh boy, I thought. Here we go. She began to speak again. "Please, someone has got to listen to me, for Dad's sake." Big tears flowed once again. I offered her a Kleenex from the box that Crystal kept on my desk for occasions such as this. Asher made a bigger mess of her face, a face that could be quite pretty if she'd let nature have its way. "Okay," she said when she'd finished wiping at her face. "You do it your way; just promise me that you'll at least look at it from my point of view."

"I will, but what if the evidence I find doesn't support your theory about your brother?" I asked. "Will you let the sheriff do what she has to do at that point?"

Asher nodded slowly, but at least it was an affirmative sign. "I'll cooperate," she promised, quite meek now.

"Okay, let's assume I'm going to look into this matter for you. Tell me about your brother. You're accusing him of something extremely serious. Why don't you explain why you think he is somehow responsible for your father's death?"

She started right in. "He and Dad never did get along. He and our mother did, but I was the one who liked Dad. Don't get me wrong, I like Mom and usually get along with her, but Trace hated Dad."

"Can you tell me how you know that?" I asked.

She laughed mirthlessly. "He's told me so on so many occasions that I couldn't even begin to tell you how many times. But it's more than that. He openly supported that Statton woman for sheriff."

"You mean Lisette Statton," I told her in a voice I hoped she knew was meant as a rebuke.

She nodded and went on. "Trace said Dad wasn't as qualified as she was, but I know it was only because he hated Dad. Trace didn't even know the Statton woman—Lisette Statton."

"I heard your brother doesn't even live in this county. Isn't he down in San Juan County?" I asked.

"Oh yeah, but that doesn't mean he didn't let people up here know that they should vote for Lisette Statton. He was quite vocal about it. He cost Dad a lot of votes," she said, her face red with anger.

"I see. Well then, he got his way. That should have appeased him some," I said.

"It didn't though. He and Dad disagreed about other things."

"Give me an example."

"Okay. Trace is opposed to the drilling that's going on—adamantly opposed. He's against just about anything that he thinks has to do with messing up the environment. He's even against hunting with lead bullets, if you can believe that. He says lead is polluting the water and the forest and, well, pretty much everything." She shook her head in disgust. "Just the opposite of me and Dad."

"I see." I nodded. "But can you point to anything specific where one might infer that he was an actual threat to your father?"

"I told you," she said. "He is against the drilling. He and my husband almost came to blows over that one day. Now they don't even talk to each other. Dad was for drilling, and he supported my husband in his choice of a career. Dad even went so far as to accept a position with the drilling company as a security officer a few days ago. That was the straw that broke the camel's back with Trace. He called Dad and raged. He called me and raged. He said he would see to it that the drilling was stopped even if it meant stopping Dad from doing his job."

"He said that?" I asked. That could be construed as a threat. Asher had my full attention now. "And who did Trace say that to?"

"First to Dad and then to me. Dad told me about it right after Trace called him," Asher explained. "Then I called Trace to give him a piece of my mind, and he said it to me too."

"Did he threaten you or your father in any way?" I asked even as I was thinking about the inconsistency I was seeing here. After all, Edward Jones did have a whole bunch of anti-drilling pamphlets in his suitcase at the time of his death. But I didn't mention that to her.

"Not directly, just what I told you. He said he'd stop Dad from doing his job. Well, he certainly has!" Tears erupted, and I waited while she smeared her face with another of my Kleenexes. "I know he did it. I need for you to prove it," she finally added.

"If I take this job, I'll look into it," I promised. Then I asked her another question. "Do you know how your father died?"

"The sheriff said he was thrown or pushed out of a plane."

"That's likely," I agreed, "but we don't know that for sure yet."

"Oh, he was pushed or thrown all right," she insisted. "And it was from Trace's plane."

"Trace has an airplane?" I asked, surprised and suddenly extremely interested in my prospective client's story.

"Well, he doesn't own one, but he rents one, and he flies some," she answered. "And he wouldn't hesitate to use it to get rid of my dad."

Chapter Four

"WILL YOU TAKE MY CASE?" Asher asked me earnestly. "I would really appreciate it."

I was more than intrigued at this point; I was hooked. So I agreed. We did the formal contract thing and exchange of money, and then I was ready to get down to business.

We talked about a lot more things, and I took several pages of notes. Asher had come prepared with a lot of information: I had to give her that. She even had the wing number of Trace's rented plane and an exact description of it. That was where I'd start first thing in the morning, I decided. I'd see if anyone had seen the plane at Canyonlands Field Airport—sometimes referred to as the Moab airport—check out any flight plans Trace might have filed, and so on.

She told me he drove an older model Ford pickup, brown. She said he'd had a white Dodge Neon, but when he and his wife recently got a divorce, she took that and their two kids and moved to New Mexico, where her parents lived. She couldn't tell me what year model the pickup was.

Asher told me a lot of things her brother had done over the years that were either outright illegal or bordered on it and the clashes those activities had caused between him and their father. As she outlined the list of offenses, I couldn't help but feel sorry for Edward Jones. It couldn't have been easy being a cop with a son who was, at the least, on the borderline of being a criminal, if his sister was to be believed.

I had to be objective here and remain unbiased. The second thing I'd look into in the morning, I duly noted in my notebook, would be to learn all I could about Trace Jones to either prove or disprove what

Asher was telling me. I had learned early in my career as an investigator that clients don't always tell the truth all the time and that some of them never tell it at all. I committed to myself that I would keep an open mind about both Trace and Asher.

Around midnight, Asher left my office. As she walked out, I was thinking that, despite her outrageous appearance, she seemed to be a woman of moderate intelligence and reasonably good sense. I suspected, though, that Trace wasn't the only one who had caused their parents concern. She clearly had a rebellious streak, and I wondered what illegal or borderline illegal kinds of things she may have done. Drug abuse was a possibility.

After she was gone, I locked the outside door, turned out the light in the outer office, and then entered my private one, leaving the door ajar. Another thing I had learned early in my work as a private investigator was to not let my notes get cold before I reviewed them. That way, things would be firmer in my mind, and details I may have failed to jot down could be added. I could also make sure I could actually read everything. My handwriting was not the best, and when I was interviewing a client or a witness, I would sometimes write a few words while keeping eye contact. That didn't make for easily interpreted notes. So as I reviewed them, I wrote over a few words so I could easily tell what they were and even added a few comments between the lines.

I'd been reviewing my notes for maybe fifteen minutes when there was a knock on my outer door. Puzzled about who would be here at this time of night, I shoved my chair back and got up. I was thinking maybe Asher had thought of something else she wanted to tell me. That was the most likely scenario. I also wondered if Crystal had thought about me working late and had come to see if she could be of assistance. Not likely, but possible.

It was neither of them. "Sorry to come by so late, Major," the sheriff began when I opened the door, "but I saw that your light was on. At least, it looked like there was a light in your inner office. And your pickup was parked out front. Is this a bad time?"

"Come in, Lisette," I said. "I suppose it's as good a time as any. You appear to be working late."

"It looks like we both are," she said with a weary smile that looked good on her tired face.

"So what gives?" I asked, honestly wondering why the sheriff would show up on the doorstep of a PI, especially at such a late hour.

"I needed someone to bounce a couple of things off of. Ev is off duty, and there are no lights on at his house. I hated to call and wake him up. It was just on a whim that I drove by your office," she said with that tired smile that I was beginning to enjoy.

"Who is Ev?" I asked.

"Sorry, Ev is my chief deputy, Evan Belgar," she explained. "He's a good man with solid judgment and total loyalty."

"The kind of second in command I'm sure any good sheriff needs." It made sense, and I was glad she had someone like that to help her.

"That's for sure. He was also loyal to my predecessor. He was his chief deputy as well."

"Sounds like a man of experience," I said.

"He is. Ev is the one man that could undoubtedly have beaten me had he run for sheriff. Of course, I wouldn't have run if he had."

"I take it he didn't want the pressure," I speculated.

"That's it exactly. Ev is the one that suggested that I run. The sheriff supported the idea, and so I did, with the understanding that if I won, I'd keep Ev on as my chief deputy. That was a good decision," she said. "He's smart, hardworking, tough, and highly respected in the county."

"I look forward to meeting him," I said, wondering what exactly it was that she would have talked to Ev about if he'd been up at this late hour.

"I'd like you to meet him. I think the two of you will hit it off." Lisette rubbed her eyes. I could see she was exhausted, but then, so was I. It had been a long and rather stressful day for both of us. She sat back in her chair and studied me for a moment. I waited patiently, a virtue I had managed to develop through long waits for assignments in the wars and again when I began doing stakeouts after I had become an investigator.

Lisette finally spoke. "I called and talked to Trace Jones," she began. "In addition to the fact that he and I disagree with his assessment that his father was a first-class jerk, there is something about Trace that makes the hair stand up on the back of my neck."

That was not inconsistent with what Asher had told me. I was anxious to hear what Trace had told the sheriff. It might make my own investigation easier, perhaps streamline it for me. But before Lisette said anything more about Trace, I felt like it was only right that I let her know I'd been hired to investigate him. Asher had agreed to that before we signed the contract. "Before you tell me more about Trace, there's something you need to know."

"Let me guess," she said. "You have been hired by Asher Grady."

"How in the world did you figure that out?" I asked, quite astonished.

She chuckled pleasantly. "I drove by your office about a half an hour ago. I know Asher's car quite well. She shuttled her dad around a lot during the campaign. I don't suppose she had a lot of good to say about me."

"You suppose right," I said. "But she did agree to allow me to disclose to you the fact that she had hired me and to keep you posted on what I learn in the course of my investigation."

"How in the world did you get Asher to agree to that?" she asked. "I know she dislikes me and thinks I'm totally inept. She certainly gave off vibes to that effect when I spoke with her earlier today."

I smiled. "I didn't give her a lot of choice. So we are free to discuss what I learn, and if I get in your way or in some fashion step on your toes, please let me know, and I'll back off."

Lisette nodded her head. "Actually, Major, I welcome the help. Your involvement, under the circumstances, is almost as good as getting another good deputy helping with the case, except without an impact on my budget."

"That's all I want to do," I agreed. "I want to help find who killed Edward no matter who that turns out to be. So, what did you want to tell me about Trace?"

She shook her head and then rocked me with her answer. "Nothing at the moment," she said. "Maybe later."

I really hadn't expected this. I thought she was going to be as open with me as I had just promised to be with her. Maybe I needed to be a little more careful in what I said. "So what did you want to talk about if not Trace?"

"Hey, Major, don't look so disappointed. I'm not trying to keep anything back. There just isn't much to tell. Like I told you, he's a jerk," she said. "No, it was my other conversation tonight that bothered me the most. I had barely finished talking with Trace when Devan Rish came to the office."

"Devan! The same Devan that helped out today?" I asked.

"Yes, the same guy. He's worried," she said.

"About the murder?"

"Well, sort of. He said that he got to thinking after he got home." She paused and rubbed her eyes again. I waited patiently once more, despite the fact that I was anxious to hear what Devan had been thinking about. He seemed like a decent young man, although he was maybe just a little too enthusiastic about his discovery this morning. He'd been the one who'd spotted the body of Edward Jones as we flew over, and I suspected that he would talk a lot about that to his friends and family.

"Devan told me about one of the men he works with," she finally said. "His name is Jordan Yost. I know his family. They're fairly well to do. I would have thought Jordan would have been in college instead of working on a rig. From what I understand, he was always on the honor roll at school. He's bright and would probably do very well in college. I know there's good money out in the oil field, but it isn't something that a person can count on a hundred percent. Of course, what is a reliable profession these days? Anyway, Jordan works on the same crew that Devan does, but he's said a few things that made Devan wonder about him."

"If he works with Devan, then I'd know him, not necessarily by name, but I'd certainly recognize him," I said. "What does he look like?"

"He's the kind of kid that stands out. I say kid because he's only nineteen. He is thin but quite tall, probably an inch or so taller than you, and weighs maybe 150 pounds. He has long blond hair and keeps it in a ponytail much of the time. He's got a very light complexion and a thin, foxlike face."

"Yeah, I know who he is. No wonder the name didn't ring a bell. He seldom speaks a word on the helicopter, and the other guys don't talk to him much. I don't remember anyone ever mentioning his given name," I said as I pictured him in my mind—tall, lanky, awkward. "But he does have a nickname. That's what the guys use when they do talk to him."

"That's right," Lisette confirmed. "They call him Bean, short, I guess, for beanpole. He doesn't like the nickname, but he tolerates it. What else could he do?"

"Not much, I guess. But I'm with you," I said. "He doesn't seem to fit the job."

"That's what Devan thinks too," she said. "He isn't physically strong and is exhausted by the end of a shift. But it's not just that he doesn't fit the job; it's some things he's said after work when they are lounging around the trailer at the drilling site that bothered Devan. That and his reaction today."

"What reaction?" I asked. "I don't recall anything that stood out."

"It was while you were out of the helicopter checking the body," Lisette said. "Devan said something to the other two guys about the guy being dead and how sad it was. He said both he and the other fellow were surprised at what Jordan said."

"What did he say?" I asked.

"Well, Devan said he kind of mumbled, but it was something about maybe it was one of the guys that were financing the drilling that was dead. Then Yost said, 'Wouldn't that be a kicker?' Devan said it wasn't just what he said, but how he said it. He was almost gleeful, Devan told me. But that wasn't the main reason Devan came to me. He said he needed to talk to me because he remembered something else that Jordan had told him."

"Was it also something to do with the drilling?" I asked.

"Not directly. But he has been bragging about his older brother learning to fly a plane. Jordan told Devan that he was learning to fly as well."

"Jordan is?"

"That's what he told Devan."

"So are you suggesting that the Yosts might have something against the drilling?"

"That's what Devan thinks, and he's pretty sensitive about it. He says he's making more money than his dad ever made, and he'd hate to lose the job just because some people are so stupid about it. That was the word Devan used," she said. "He called it stupid."

"Does Jordan's brother have his license yet?"

"To fly?" she asked.

"Yes, his pilot's license."

"Devan says he does, that he got it several months ago."

"Does Devan have anything to back up his concerns about the brother? Clearly, Jordan couldn't have pushed Edward Jones from the plane because he was at the oil rig," I pointed out.

"Yes," she said. "Devan knows about Jordan's brother, which is one of the reasons he thinks there's something hinky with Jordan."

"Why?" I asked.

"He's about ten years older than Jordan and has a degree in something to do with plants and ecology," Lisette said. "Jordan has commented about his brother being worried that all the smoke in the air is killing a lot of endangered plants. Now, Devan did tell me that Jordan never said that he agreed with his brother, but he also didn't say that he disagreed."

I couldn't help but chuckle. My first thought was identical to one I had when Asher told me about her brother's attitude about fossil fuels considering the fact that he was a pilot. I didn't mention Trace to Lisette, but I did say, "I wonder if the Yost brothers know that planes couldn't fly if someone didn't drill for oil. There is something contradictory about the notion of opposing drilling and wanting to fly and burn that very fuel."

Lisette also chuckled. "That does seem rather inconsistent. It's sort of like some of these wealthy environmentalists who curse smoke but fly all over the world spouting their concerns. There is something hypocritical about it."

"That's for sure. Anyway, back to Jordan and his brother. What's the brother's name?" I asked.

"The same as their father's. It's Leon Yost, but they call him Junior. He's twenty-eight or twenty-nine. He lives in Denver and teaches at the University of Colorado–Denver. Maybe that's why he started flying, so he could come back here easier," the sheriff said.

"And offer rides to people who work for the oil companies," I added facetiously. "Fatal rides, I mean."

"You think that could be the case?" Lisette asked. "That's why I wanted to talk to someone. I wanted to know if anyone else would react the way I did, if anyone else would wonder if Junior Yost could be our killer."

"Oh, yes, I think that's entirely possible," I said. "Junior Yost should definitely be viewed as a person of interest at this point. But let's talk about Trace Jones while we're talking about pilots who might have a bone to pick with oil companies and their employees."

"Trace Jones flies a plane too?" she asked, clearly surprised. "He didn't tell me that."

"Asher says he does," I said. "And so far, I don't have any reason to doubt her. It's not as if she would think that I couldn't easily check it out."

"Okay, so does that mean that Asher thinks that her brother might have had something to do with their father's murder?" Lisette asked.

"That's exactly what she thinks, and she wants him arrested," I told her.

For a moment, Lisette sat thoughtfully. "I did call Trace, and he did claim that he'd found his mother. But he wouldn't say where she is or what she's doing. He was really very secretive about it all."

"Then why did he even want to talk to you?" I asked.

"That's exactly what I'd like to know. Like I said, he is really quite a jerk, and that, as near as I can tell, was the only reason he called me—to jerk me around," she said with a touch of bitterness. "You know, Major, I really don't like being jerked around. And you know what else? Asher just might be right about Trace. How can I help?"

"Actually, it's your murder, Lisette. The question should be, how can I help you?"

Chapter Five

I TOLD THE SHERIFF WHAT I had planned for the next morning. "The first thing I want to do is see if I can learn anything about where Trace has flown lately and especially try to determine if he's been at Canyonlands Field here in Moab in the past thirty-six hours or so. I know that might be difficult since the airport isn't manned all the time, but I'll at least try. Then I plan to learn all I can about the guy, both his history as a youth and what he's been up to the past few years, since he got out of high school."

"I can help with that," she said. "I can run a criminal background check on him."

"If you'll do that, I might fly down to Blanding and do a little snooping there if I have time," I said.

"In the meantime, perhaps I can get Ev and Jarbi working on the background of Junior Yost," Lisette suggested. "And I'd really like to find out where Mrs. Jones is hiding out because that's what it sounds like she's doing if . . ." She paused, her eyebrows scrunched. "After talking to Trace, I thought that she was alive, but as I think about it now, I'm not so sure. He may simply be encouraging me to call off the search for her. Which I have already done, but that might have been a mistake. I think I should initiate the search again." She was thoughtful for another moment. "Did Asher say if she had any idea on her mother's whereabouts?"

"If she did, she didn't tell me. She says she and her mother got along okay, but they weren't close like she was with Edward. On the other hand, if she's being straight with me, Trace was closer to his mother but despised his father. I wonder if there are other family members around that could help sort that out."

"You mean extended family?"

"Yes, that's what I mean."

"Let me work on that," she said as she got up from her chair. "Right now all I want to do is go home and get some sleep."

That's what I wanted to do too. And that's what I tried to do. I was doing pretty well at it until my phone rang at around five in the morning, earlier than I had planned to start my day. It was a pilot who had come to fly his plane that morning when he noticed that someone was standing beside my helicopter with a knife and wrench. Whoever it was dashed past him, nearly knocking him down, and fled in a late-model blue Dodge pickup. The pilot didn't get a good look at the guy, didn't see his face at all. All he could tell me was that it was a short guy, well under six feet, and weighing less than 150 pounds. The guy wore a hat pulled low on his face, blue jeans, and a light-brown jacket.

As I bounded out of bed, I asked him if he got a license number off the truck. He said it didn't have plates, just a temporary sticker in the back window, and he didn't come close to getting the number off it.

I asked him if he could see any damage to my chopper. He responded that there was nothing obvious, but he couldn't be sure. He offered to call the airport manager before he took off, but he had a deadline to meet and couldn't wait for me to get there.

I hurriedly dressed and dashed out the door. I drove the sixteen miles as rapidly as I dared. I watched for a pickup that matched the description, but I didn't see one.

I drove into the airport, skidding to a stop in front of the hangar, and ran to the door. The hangar lock had been jimmied. A large crowbar lay on the ground near the door. The pilot who had called me had taken off, so I was alone.

I went inside the hangar, afraid of what I'd find. At first glance I couldn't see any damage to the Jet Ranger, but that didn't mean it hadn't been tampered with. The fact that the burglar had been holding a knife and a wrench was alarming. I could only hope that the other pilot had arrived in time to scare the vandal off before any damage was done.

I was going over my helicopter, inspecting every square inch of it, when the damaged door opened and the airport manager, Gerard

Saxon, stormed in, his blue eyes flashing. Gerard is a short, wiry man with an abundance of energy. "What in the world happened here?" he demanded, as if I knew any more than he did.

"As you can see," I said calmly, "someone busted in here. He was frightened off by Robert when he came to get his plane out."

Gerard calmed down and approached my Jet Ranger. "Robert said someone appeared to be messing with your bird," he said. "Is there any damage?"

"Not that I can see so far," I told him. "But I've barely begun to inspect."

"Did he get inside of it?" he asked.

"No, the doors are still locked, so I don't think he got in the cabin. But I can't say yet if he's tampered with the engine. There could be some hoses or wiring cut."

"I called the cops," Gerard said. "A deputy is on the way."

"That's good," I said, though I was quite certain nothing could be done at this point. What I was interested in now was making sure my helicopter was safe to fly and, if not, to get any necessary repairs made. Then I planned to take steps to keep it safer in the future.

"Can I help you?" Gerard asked. "I do know quite a bit about aircraft. I used to work on them."

"That's great," I said. "Yes, if you'd help me inspect the chopper and see what, if anything, has been tampered with, I'd appreciate it."

We'd made little progress when a uniformed deputy entered the hangar. Gerard turned his attention to the officer, and I continued the inspection alone. I was convinced when I finished a few minutes later that my Jet Ranger hadn't been touched. Robert had appeared in the nick of time.

The deputy did what he could and told us that he would let the sheriff know what had happened. He hadn't been gone more than five minutes when my cell phone rang. "Major," Lisette said. "Are you sure your helicopter isn't damaged?"

"I'm pretty sure," I said. "I've checked it over as thoroughly as I can. But I'm also sure someone intended to do damage, probably serious damage."

The airport manager broke in, "Major, do you have any idea why anyone would target your helicopter?"

I spoke into the phone, repeating the question to the sheriff, and then I answered, "The only thing I can think of is that I'm shuttling oil field workers to and from the rigs."

"That's crazy," Gerard said. "I can't imagine why anyone would take their prejudices out on your helicopter."

"I'm coming out there," the sheriff said. "We'll talk when I get there."

"That's not necessary," I protested. "I'll pull my helicopter out of the hangar and fire it up."

"Wait until I get there. Please."

"Okay, I'll get it outside, and then I'll wait for you."

"Was that Sheriff Statton?" Gerard asked.

"Yes, she's coming out," I said.

"I'll help you pull your aircraft outside."

As we were working, we talked quite a bit. He was clearly worried about further vandalism. "I'll try to make arrangements to move my helicopter," I told him. "I'd like it closer to town anyway."

While we waited for the sheriff to arrive, I decided to see if Gerard knew anything about Trace Jones or Junior Yost and whether either of them had been in the airport the preceding few days.

"Too bad about Trace's father," Gerard said. "I understand he fell from an airplane. Seems like a strange thing to do."

"That's the theory," I said. "Have you seen Trace here lately?"

"Trace comes in all the time. He rents a small plane, although I don't know who owns it—someone down in Blanding, I think. It's a Cherokee Cub. I don't always see Trace, but I do see the plane from time to time."

"Was he here yesterday or the day before?" I asked.

"I didn't see him or his plane," Gerard said, slowly shaking his head. "But that doesn't mean he couldn't have come in the middle of the night."

"If he fueled up, is there any chance you would have a record of it?" I asked as I saw Lisette pull up.

"Actually, we might not. As you know, pilots fill up using a credit card. The credit card company has those records, but all we know is how much fuel was purchased," he said.

Disappointed, I followed him toward the terminal. Lisette joined us when we reached the door. I explained that we wouldn't be able to tell who had fueled up unless someone had actually seen them doing it.

"Of course, not everyone who flies in here needs fuel," Gerard reminded us.

I understood that, as did the sheriff. A few minutes later, as we walked back to my helicopter and out of earshot of the airport manager, Lisette said, "I would suspect that whoever killed Edward would take pains to avoid leaving a trail through the airport."

I knew she was right. "That makes it harder to identify who Edward went up with and who tossed him from a plane."

My helicopter started just fine. The sheriff got in with me, and we took it for a short test flight. "I guess I got lucky this time," I said when we landed a few minutes later. "I think I'll run back to town before I fly to Blanding. I need to see if there's any place I can keep this machine closer to town and perhaps more secure."

"And I'll have Jarbi look for a blue Dodge pickup," the sheriff said. "Who knows, whoever intended to damage your helicopter may be more than an anti-drilling nut. He could be a killer."

That was an unsettling thought, one that I'd already mulled over, but hearing her say it didn't make me feel any better. The sheriff left after that, but before driving back to town, I spoke with the airport manager again.

"Does anyone here regularly drive a blue Dodge pickup?" I asked.

"I've been thinking about that," he said, "and I honestly can't think of anyone."

I asked him if he'd seen any planes lately that he wasn't familiar with. He couldn't think of any.

"Edward Jones or someone else apparently left his truck here," I said. "I know the sheriff had someone impound it yesterday, but did you see who drove it here?"

"I didn't," he said. "But I'm sure it would have been Jones himself. I've never seen his wife or anyone else drive it."

I wasn't so sure it couldn't have been someone other than Jones, but I let it pass. Lisette was having her chief deputy, Evan Belgar, check the truck out today.

On the way back to Moab, I thought about Edward Jones, his missing wife, his angry son, and his strange daughter. I wasn't convinced that Mrs. Jones would ever turn up alive. I couldn't wait to learn more about Trace. If Asher was right, he could be the key to the entire case.

I went straight to the office and found Crystal busy at work. It was nearly ten o'clock, and even though I hadn't had much sleep, I had a lot to do and was anxious to get at it. However, since Crystal had gone to the trouble to help me out on Nora Briggs's case, I thought I better find out what my cousin had learned.

"I think I put the scare into one of the guys," she told me with a grin.

"Which one, the married one or the single one?" I asked. The single man, Jarrett Bloom, was the focus of Nora's concern. He was a young guy of about twenty-five who, according to Nora, had inherited some money and wanted to use it to make more money. She'd said he was a likable guy and she didn't want to see him get into trouble over this insurance matter. The other fellow was simply a witness to what Jarrett Bloom was doing. It involved a property Nora was handling that belonged to Bloom and had sustained some damage. However, it was not, according to Nora, anywhere near the amount Bloom was trying to get out of it.

"The single one, Jarrett Bloom," Crystal said in response to my question. "He was surprised to see me and seemed quite rattled. I think that if you had time to go talk to him, it would rattle him further, and the problem could be nipped in the bud. I'm sure he didn't intend to do anything illegal. He said he was told that what he was doing was completely legal."

"Okay," I said, thinking about all the other things I needed to do. But one of those things was talking to Nora about her rental property. It was outside the city limits, and I suspected that I might, with the permission of county leaders, be able to keep my helicopter there, where I could keep a close eye on it. "Fill me in, Crystal. Tell me what you learned, and I'll see what I can do."

She did, and I listened, but apparently not as closely as she expected. "Corbin, you look like you have something on your mind," Crystal said with a worried look. "Did you hear everything I said?"

"I've got it," I said.

"Has something happened on the Jones matter? You look worried."

I wearily sat down across from her desk and brought her up to date on the investigation. Then I told her where I had spent the morning. "Someone was going to sabotage your helicopter?" she asked, clearly outraged. "What is that all about?"

"That's what I'd like to know."

"Could it have anything to do with the fact that you are hauling workers to oil rigs?" she asked perceptively.

"That thought has crossed my mind," I said blandly. "But I don't intend to quit what I'm doing."

"Okay, so what are you going to do?"

"Well, first I'll follow your advice and go talk to Jarrett Bloom. Then I'll swing by the realty office and speak with Mrs. Briggs. I want to talk to her about a rental property she has out near Sheriff Statton's place."

Crystal stared at me for a moment before saying, "Good grief, Corbin. I think, after what you just told me, that you can wait to talk to Mr. Bloom. You've got to do something about protecting your helicopter. That's much more important."

I stood up, grinning. "You're right, as usual," I said. "So I'll go talk to Mr. Bloom."

"That's not what I just said," she protested.

"I know. Let me explain. It will give me an excuse to talk to Mrs. Briggs. If I can rent the place, the sheriff thinks I might be able to keep my Jet Ranger there. It's out of town, no real close neighbors, several acres of land, and more than enough room to build a small hangar to put the chopper in."

Crystal grinned too. "You had me going, cousin. Yeah, good idea. Let me know what you find out. If the place is big enough, I could sublet from you and help watch the chopper when you aren't home."

"I'm sure we can work something out if you're interested. Now I better get moving."

Only ten minutes later, I was knocking on the door of Mr. Jarrett Bloom's house, hoping that I would find him at home at this time of day. I got lucky, and he answered the door. When I introduced myself, he got a worried look on his face, and he stammered when he invited me in.

I took a seat, looked him in the eye, and said, "My associate, Miss Crystal Burke, explained to you what we are looking into," I said. "I thought, after she briefed me this morning, that it might be a good idea if you and I had a little chat."

"Ah . . . sure. Ah, that's fine," he said.

So we talked. Thirty minutes later, I prepared to leave with his promise to withdraw his improper claim that day. The matter, I believed, was resolved. I stepped toward the door but stopped when he said from behind me, "You might want to also talk to an acquaintance of mine. He's the one that suggested it was okay to do this. It worried me, but he said he'd done it and it worked out just fine and that it would for me to."

I turned and faced him. "It's illegal," I reiterated. "He must have just been lucky . . . so far."

"Well, maybe I better talk to him," Jarrett said. "I wouldn't want him to get in trouble."

"I'm sure you wouldn't."

"His situation has nothing to do with Nora Briggs," he added.

"That's good," I said, again turning to the door. I had ahold of the doorknob when he stopped me again.

"This might not be a good time, though, what with his dad being killed and all."

I let go of the doorknob and faced Jarrett once again. "Might your friend be Trace Jones?" I asked.

"He's not really a friend, just someone I've done a little business with. And yes, his dad was found dead yesterday."

"I'm aware. I was there," I said. "I guess you could say that I found him—me and the men I was hauling in my helicopter."

"Oh yeah. You're the new pilot in town," he said. "Trace told me about you."

"He did, did he? Do you mind if we sit down and talk for a minute longer?"

He nodded. He looked even more worried now, but I made no attempt to put him at ease. We began to discuss his relationship with

Trace, which, he convinced me, was really very limited. But that wasn't all I learned.

Chapter Six

I HAD ONLY SPOKEN WITH Jarrett for another fifteen minutes when his doorbell rang. By then, I'd learned that Trace Jones was far from being an honest man. It was no wonder he and his father hadn't gotten along. I stood while Jarrett answered the door. "Sheriff," he said, when he opened the door.

"I see you already have another visitor," she said. "May I come in?"

"Ah, sure, we were just talking about a guy I know."

"Trace Jones?" the sheriff asked with a raised eyebrow.

"Yeah, that's right. This is . . . oh, I guess you know Mr. Daniels," Jarrett said awkwardly.

"Yes, I do," she said as she caught my eye. I could see a question there. "Corbin's helping out on the case involving Trace's father."

"Yeah, he told me that," Jarrett said.

"In answer to the question you were about to ask, Sheriff," I said with a grin, "I came by to see Mr. Bloom about a separate matter that I'm looking into for a client. I was just leaving when he mentioned that he and Trace had done a little business together."

"Yes, I just learned that myself about thirty minutes ago, and that's why I'm here," she said. "I'm trying to learn all I can about Trace from people he knew here in Moab."

"I really need to get going, but maybe," I said, turning to Jarrett, "you could bring the sheriff up-to-date on what you just told me about Trace. You don't need to waste her time on what you and I discussed prior to that. I think we have that matter resolved, and I'll go report to my client right now." I turned back to Lisette. "You'll find Mr. Bloom's information quite interesting. Maybe when I get back from Blanding this evening—because I do still intend to go down there—we could compare notes."

"I look forward to it, Mr. Daniels," she said quite formally.

Once again, I approached the door, but I stopped before opening it and turned once more to catch the sheriff's eye. I smiled at her, then turned back and left, relishing the smile she had given me in return. I'd never known an officer of the law before who was so easy and pleasant to work with.

I found Nora Briggs at her real estate office. "Don't tell me you already have my little matter taken care of," she said when I came through the door.

"I think it'll be fine now," I said. "Mr. Bloom promised to withdraw the claim today."

"Thank you, Mr. Daniels," she said. "I like that young man, and I was so worried about this. You are a miracle worker."

"Not quite. Actually, while I'm here, there's something I was hoping you could help me with."

"Certainly," she said with an engaging smile. "Are you looking for a house?"

"Yes, as a matter of fact, I am. But right now, I only want to rent. Sheriff Statton tells me that you might have just the sort of place I'm looking for."

"Please sit down," she said, gesturing toward a chair. I took it, and she sat behind her cluttered desk. She leaned forward. "I'm assuming Lisette told you about the house near where she lives. It's a nice house, quite large, has a fully finished basement with a kitchenette. Honestly, I think it might be a lot more than you can use. You are single, aren't you?"

"I am, but I have a cousin who I'm sure would love the basement."

"Oh, well in that case . . ." she trailed off.

"You know her. My secretary and associate, Crystal Burke, is my cousin. We are both paying quite a bit now for apartments in town. It would help us both. But that's only part of the reason I am interested in the place. Sheriff Statton tells me that it's out of town—thus fairly secluded—and covers a number of acres."

"That's right, but they're not developed except for the yard, and the previous tenants let that get rather run-down," she said.

"Crystal and I could remedy that," I said. "But one of the things I'm interested in is being able to put a small hangar on the property and keeping my helicopter there. Lisette thinks I could get that approved by the county since it's secluded enough that it wouldn't be a bother to neighbors."

"Lisette is by far the closest neighbor. I'll have to check with the owners about having a building added. I assume it would be at your expense?"

"Of course," I told her. "It has to be on a concrete pad, but the building itself could be one that I could move if I need to."

"I'll contact the owners. And by the way," she added, "if you like the place, I think I could persuade them to sell it to you."

"I like the area so far, and I'd like to stay, but I need to make sure that I can make a good living here first," I told her.

She settled back in her chair, clasped her hands together, and asked, "Where do you keep your helicopter now?"

"It's out at Canyonlands Field. I rent a hangar there."

"Why would you want to move it?"

I explained, and with a look of concern on her face, she said, "I see. Perhaps some of the antidrilling folks take exception to the fact that you are flying the oil workers around."

"Perhaps," I said.

"Would you like to look at the place now?"

"If it doesn't take too long. I need to fly down to Blanding on another investigation today, and I don't want to be too late."

"I'll get the key," she said as she rose to her feet.

The place was excellent. The house was large and quite nice, although the previous renters had left a bit of a mess. Nora promised that it would be cleaned before we moved in—if we decided to do so. There were almost twenty acres of open ground, part of it up against a hill. There were also some big cottonwood trees on the property. I really liked what I saw. Before I left, I called Crystal, explained a little about the property, and suggested she come out and look at it. She enthusiastically agreed.

"I won't be here when you get here," I told her on the phone. "I need to head for Blanding. But Mrs. Briggs will wait here for you."

"If we like it, how soon can we move in?" she asked.

"Well, first, I want to make sure I can put the chopper here," I said. "I'll work on that as soon as I can. I'll see if I can make an appointment tomorrow to meet with someone to get approval to build a small helipad and hangar. If you like the place, that is."

"I probably will," she said. "Maybe I can work on beginning the approval process for you today."

"Bless your heart, Crystal. You're truly a gem. That would be great."

"Oh, Corbin, how did it go with Mr. Bloom?"

"You laid the proper groundwork," I said. "You must have really got him thinking about what he was doing. Anyway, I think the matter is resolved now. And get this, small world that it is, Jarrett and Trace Jones know each other. Trace is the one who told Jarrett that what he was attempting to do was legal and honest."

Five minutes later, I was on my way back to Canyonlands Field. The drive reaffirmed that, if only for the sake of saving time, I'd really like the Jet Ranger closer to town and especially right by where I lived. It was forty-five minutes before I was finally airborne and on my way to Blanding.

I had previously made arrangements to have a car available for me there, so when I landed, all I had to do was top off my fuel tank, secure my Jet Ranger, get the car, and drive into town. Blanding is small, and it only took me a few minutes to locate Trace's house. If the sad state of the yard was any indication, it was likely Trace wasn't an ambitious or motivated man.

I modified that conclusion, however, when I noticed the back end of a blue Dodge pickup parked in an open two-car garage. There was no license plate on the back, and I could just make out a temporary sticker in the back window. Perhaps Trace was motivated, just motivated in the wrong ways. It looked like he'd traded off his brown Ford. Could it just be a coincidence that Trace's new truck matched the description of the one driven by the guy who had been attempting to tamper with my helicopter? Not likely, I thought.

I followed the short walkway to the door and pressed the doorbell. I waited for a minute, and then I knocked. Finally, the door opened, and a woman of about fifty asked, "What do you want? If you're here to see my son, you'll have to come back later. He's asleep. He had a long night."

Yes, I thought, he probably did at that. As for the missing Widow Jones, she wasn't missing now. And as for Trace's long night, I had no sympathy at all. "I had a long night as well. Wake Trace up. He and I need to talk."

"No," she said. "You'll have to come back later. I promised I wouldn't let anyone disturb him."

"You don't have to; I will," I said forcefully.

"Do I need to call the cops?" she asked, her face growing dark with anger.

"Actually, if you don't mind, that would be nice of you," I said. Her hazel eyes opened wide, and she seemed at a loss for words. I pressed my advantage. "They're looking for Trace's truck and would be happy to know that it's in his garage right now."

Johanna Jones didn't call the cops. Instead, she slammed the door in my face. For a moment, I just stared. And then I did what she had decided not to. I called the cops. Well, I called one cop. I called Lisette. I walked back to my rented car while the phone rang. Finally, Lisette answered.

"Hi," I said by way of greeting. "I found a couple of things here in Blanding."

"Hi, Major," she said. "What did you find?"

"A blue Dodge pickup with a temporary registration in the back window, for starters."

"Well, that explains why we can't find it in Moab. Who does it belong to?" she asked, sounding quite upbeat.

"The son of the woman who answered the door at Trace's house."

For a moment, Lisette was quiet. Then she said, "Do you mean you also found Johanna Jones?"

"Yes, I mean that."

"And the truck belongs to Trace Jones."

"It appears that way. It's in his garage. Of course, it might not be the same truck, but I have a feeling it is."

"Is Trace at home?" Lisette asked.

"His mother says he is but that he had a long night and she won't disturb him. She threatened to call the cops if I tried to wake him up, but she changed her mind and slammed the door in my face instead. So I called you. I'm standing outside his house right now. I have a feeling that Mrs. Jones has probably disturbed Trace's sleep by now. Don't you think?"

Lisette chuckled. "I would imagine." She paused, and I waited to see what else she might have to say. After a moment, she spoke again. "I'll call and have a local officer or two meet you there. In the meantime, I guess I better head that way myself. I'll bring either my chief deputy or detective with me."

"There is probably no need to drive all this distance. Once the local officers get here, I could fly up and get you," I suggested.

"That's a thought, but I'm racking up a lot of hours on your chopper as it is."

"I have a client," I said. "I won't need to bill it to you."

"Thanks. In that case, let me know when you're ready to come up."

"Will do," I said, and we ended the call.

I moved around to the far side of my car. It wasn't a large car, but it would afford at least some protection in case Trace Jones decided to become aggressive with a gun or something. After all, in my mind at least, he was a strong suspect in the murder of his father. If he was the killer, I didn't suppose that he would hesitate to kill again. And if he was the one who'd attempted to tamper with my helicopter, I couldn't be sure he hadn't intended to kill me anyway.

I waited, hoping a cop would soon show up. But after a couple minutes, I heard one door slam and then another and another. Then, the engine of the blue Dodge fired up, and a second later, the truck shot out of the garage, right past me, and into the street. I ducked when I saw the driver reach out of the window with a pistol in his hand. He fired one shot then stomped on his accelerator, fishtailing. I could see two people in the truck, but I didn't have to speculate as to who they were.

I jumped in my rental car, grateful I hadn't been shot, but it wouldn't start. I got out and walked around front. The bullet had missed me, but it hadn't missed the car. I whipped out my phone and dialed 911. I was assured that help was already on the way. I described the truck Trace was driving and warned them that he might be headed for the airport.

When a cop finally arrived a minute or two later, I suggested that we head to the airport. "Let me take a look at your car first," he said after introducing himself as Officer Bobby Beckett of the Blanding Police Department. He popped the hood.

"Gee whiz," Officer Beckett said. "He is either a really good shot or a really bad one," he said as he examined the bullet-shattered battery of my rental car.

"Either way, I want him arrested," I said. "And I'm guessing he's on his way to the airport now."

"Then I guess we'll hurry," he said. We hopped into his car, and he hit his lights and siren. It was a rather nerve-wracking ride to the airport. When we arrived, Trace's rented plane was already on the runway starting to taxi.

There was no way I was going to let him get away now. If he had killed his father in the plane he was in now, there would be evidence. I explained that to the officer, and then I said, "Would you let Sheriff Statton up in Grand County know what I'm doing? I'm going to be too busy flying to use my phone."

"Will do," he said.

"And will you see that my rental car is taken care of?" I asked as I jumped out of the patrol vehicle.

"I'll have it impounded."

"And have that Dodge pickup impounded as well. There is probably evidence in it," I shouted. He exited his car and followed me as I began to jog toward my helicopter.

"Got it," he said. "Be careful, and we'll talk later."

By the time I was airborne, Trace and his mother and his plane were just a dot in the eastern sky. But that didn't concern me. I had a full tank of fuel, and there was no way that Trace's little Piper Cub could match my Jet Ranger for speed. I was determined to catch him and stay with him until he landed. If I had to, I knew I could get help to force him down or to at least chase him until he ran out of fuel and was forced to land.

Within just a few minutes, I had caught up with Trace's plane, and then I simply followed him. I wasn't about to get up alongside where he could take a shot at me. I'd had enough of that kind of stuff while fighting overseas. All I wanted now was to get Trace to land and have him arrested—and possibly his mother as well.

I'd been in the air about twenty minutes when I got a call from Lisette on my cell phone. "So it looks like Asher Grady was right about her brother," she said after I filled her in on the chase.

"Probably," I agreed.

"I'll have Trace's truck and house searched," she said. "I really want to get this thing nailed down, but I also want to be sure we have the right guy, that this thing that's going on right now isn't a red herring."

"I've thought about that," I said. "Maybe his attempt to sabotage my chopper was nothing more than his anger over me hauling those rig workers around. So you're right. We've got to be sure."

"We'll keep digging on the Yost brothers; although right now, I think we need to put most of our effort on Trace Jones."

"Yeah, like getting him on the ground. I'm in communication with all sorts of folks now. A fixed-wing plane will be in the air in a few minutes out of Colorado Springs, where we're apparently headed. I'll let you know how it goes."

My next phone conversation was with Crystal, who called me. "Be careful," she told me. "I heard what happened in Blanding."

"I'm fine," I assured her. "What did you think of the place Mrs. Briggs showed you?"

"Perfect," she said. "I'll live in the basement if it's okay with you. It's really set up nicely."

"If we can work out the—" I began.

"Yeah, about that. It shouldn't be a problem. The owner of the property has already approved that with Nora. And I have things lined up with the county. I'm told it can almost certainly be worked out," she reported.

"Great," I said. "I'll talk to you later."

Trace seemed to have no intention of stopping anytime soon. My fuel was okay, so I decided to stay in the chase even after a Twin Barron joined me. I was really quite enjoying myself. Being in a chase without worrying about rocket attacks wasn't all that bad.

Chapter Seven

EVERY EFFORT WAS MADE BY the proper authorities to get Trace to land and turn himself in. He resisted until the last minute, when he ran out of fuel and crash-landed the little Cherokee Cub on a stretch of dirt road east of Grand Junction, Colorado. By then, another helicopter, one from the Colorado State Patrol, had joined the Twin Barron and me in the pursuit. The Twin Barron couldn't land in the area, but the helicopters were soon on the ground. I let the two officers approach the downed aircraft while I stayed a discreet distance away.

I was glad I had when bullets began flying from the wreckage. Trace was apparently not hurt so badly that he couldn't resist arrest—in a deadly fashion. It only took me a moment to realize that one of the troopers was injured. While the other one returned fire, I pulled the injured man to relative safety behind our helicopters. The other trooper joined me, angry and frustrated. He called for an ambulance and backup, though I was pretty sure the men in the Twin Barron—now circling low overhead—had already called it in.

I began to administer first aid to the injured officer. He'd taken a bullet in his left leg, and it was bleeding badly. The other trooper kept an eye on Trace's plane while I worked. He could see I knew what I was doing and told me he'd try to keep us covered.

Officers joined us on the ground before Trace finally quit firing wild rounds in our general direction. He must have run out of bullets because he was soon taken from the plane. His mother, it appeared, could wait. She hadn't survived the crash.

I finally got a chance to call Lisette after the injured trooper and Trace Jones had been taken to the nearest hospital.

"Are you okay, Major?" she asked as soon as she heard my voice. "Are you on the ground yet?"

"I'm fine, Sheriff, but Johanna Jones isn't," I responded. "She died when Trace crashed after apparently running out of fuel."

She moaned. "That's tragic, but what about Trace? Did he make it?"

"Yeah, he's all right. He crashed, but when the Colorado troopers tried to get him to surrender, he opened fire. One of the troopers was injured—a bullet in the leg—the other one retreated until help arrived and Trace ran out of ammunition. He has a broken leg and a lot of serious cuts and bruises from the crash. There may have been internal injuries as well. I'm surprised he was even able to shoot at us. They took him to the hospital. He is, of course, under arrest."

"What about the plane?" she asked. "I know this is a long shot, but I need to have someone go over it to see if there's anything there that would indicate that Edward Jones had been in it recently or if there's anything to indicate he'd been shoved from the plane."

"I've already alerted the authorities here that you want to do that. They don't have a problem with it and told me they'd help any way they can. But I would suggest that the sooner you can get it done the better since the National Transportation Safety Board will want to investigate as well," I told her. "Their focus won't be the same as yours." I shifted our conversation. "What have you learned there?"

Lisette made a sound that sounded like a snort. Then she said, "I've learned that the Jones family was a mess. The only one even close to being normal is Asher. I really wish that Edward's wife had survived the crash. She could have probably shed a lot of light on things. But at any rate, it seems that Edward had divorce papers served to his wife on Friday, and the medical examiner says Edward was killed sometime early Monday morning. Mrs. Jones's sister came down from Wellington after the papers were served on Friday and took Mrs. Jones back to Wellington. At this point, I have no idea how she got to Blanding. Edward was apparently alone at the house all weekend."

"You mentioned Asher. Did she know about her mother going to Wellington? She didn't mention it to me," I said.

"Ev talked to her. Apparently, she doesn't have the same problem with my chief deputy that she does with me. She was very open with him," Lisette said. "She repeated much of what she had already told you. She said she hadn't talked to her mother for several days and had no idea where she might be."

I thought about it for a moment. "But Mrs. Jones's sister clearly knew, at least until Johanna went down to Blanding."

"She did, and I talked to her, but after I finally got her to admit that Johanna had been there, she told me she hadn't told anyone else about it."

"But she should know when and how Johanna got to Blanding," I said.

"I'm sure, but she won't say. She didn't even admit that Johanna was gone. She was being quite elusive. I'll talk to her again or have Jarbi do so. Once the sister learns of Johanna's death, I expect she'll be a lot more forthcoming," Lisette speculated. "At the very least she'll have to admit that her sister left her place and went to Blanding with Trace."

"What about the Yost boys?" I asked. "What have you learned about them?"

"Not much. But now that we have Trace in custody, I think we need to concentrate on him. I know I can't assume anything, but I'd say at this point that Trace is our number-one suspect."

I couldn't disagree with that, although I personally wanted to know more about the Yost brothers since I was going to continue shuttling Jordan, the younger brother, to and from the oil rig he worked on. But that was my problem not the sheriff's. I made a mental note to talk to Devan Rish about Jordan in the next day or two. "Lisette, are you coming here to talk to Trace?"

"Actually, I was going to send Jarbi. I'll have her swing up to Wellington and then over to Colorado. I have some other matters here that I need to attend to, and anyway, Jarbi is very good at what she does. If anyone can get Trace to talk, Jarbi and those gorgeous blue eyes of hers can. The men swoon when she's around. You've seen her. You can see why."

I could see why. She was downright cute. But I knew someone else that I thought could get Trace to talk, and that someone wouldn't be tied down to giving Miranda warnings and following police protocol. "Would you mind terribly if I spoke with Trace while I'm here?" I asked.

"Not at all. In fact, I'd appreciate it. If you can get him to admit to the killing and get it recorded, that certainly wouldn't hurt my feelings."

"I'll talk to him then, and I'll let you know what I learn."

We chatted for another minute, and then she said, "I've got to get back to work. I'll talk to you later, Major."

She seemed to have a hard time calling me by my first name, but I guess I didn't mind. I put my phone away and turned my attention back to the officers who were swarming all around Trace's crashed plane. I was told that our suspect and the injured trooper had both been taken back to a hospital in Grand Junction. They were waiting now for a hearse to arrive and take the body of the unfortunate Mrs. Jones away.

When I was told I was no longer needed at the accident scene, I flew to the Grand Junction Regional Airport and fueled up my Jet Ranger. Then I rented a car and drove to the hospital where they had taken Trace. He was in surgery, so the state trooper who was there to keep him under wraps told me I would need to wait, possibly until morning, but that they didn't have any objections to my talking to Trace when he was able to speak if the Grand County sheriff didn't.

I left the hospital, drove to a nearby restaurant, and ordered something to eat. While I was waiting, I got a call from Asher Grady. She was so upset that she was having a hard time speaking. But I let her work her way through her emotions until she finally had her composure under control. "I just can't believe this. Is my mother really dead, Major?"

"Yes," I responded. "I'm so sorry."

"I hope Trace is happy," she said. Her voice was so full of hatred I could almost see it curling out of my phone and swirling in the air around me. "First he kills Dad, and then he kills Mom. He'll probably kill me next."

There was no doubt he'd killed his mother, but it wasn't intentional. It was just stupid. And there was no doubt he'd be held criminally liable since he was committing a crime when they crashed. However, it was yet to be proven that he'd killed his father, although I suspected it was true. I said none of that to my client, however. I did say, "He won't hurt you, Asher. He'll be in jail when he gets out of the hospital. But just so you know, I plan to speak with Trace when the doctors let me."

That brought another angry outburst. "I hope he dies." I guess I didn't blame her for her anger. But I also didn't feel like it was doing me any good talking to her, so I told her good-bye in an attempt to get off the phone. But before I could break the connection, she said, "Major, you have been a big help. Thanks."

"You're welcome," I responded, "but I'm not through yet. I'll keep working until I can tie things up tightly."

"I know you will." She hesitated. "There's something else I need to tell you though." The sobbing had ceased, and her voice was serious now instead of frantic and hateful.

"What's that?" I prompted after a moment of silence.

Finally, she said, "I know this has nothing to do with Trace or my family, but my husband says I should warn you about the Yost brothers."

I felt a chill run up my spine. "Oh yeah? Why's that?" I asked, trying not to let her hear my discomfort.

"He and Devan Rish were talking about my dad and what happened to him. Devan remembered hearing something, and he came over to see if my husband remembered it too," she said.

"What was it?" I asked.

"Well, at the time, it didn't mean much to either one of them, but after what happened to Dad, it got to worrying Devan," she said. "With all that was going on, my husband hadn't even thought about it. Anyway, when Devan brought it up, he remembered.

"The two of them overheard Bean talking on his cell phone. He was just outside the trailer they bunk in at the rig, and they didn't think Bean knew they could hear him. Bean—that's Jordan Yost, by the way—must have been talking to his brother, Junior. Anyway, they heard him say something about the helicopter pilot. That must have meant you. They heard Bean say that you wouldn't be hauling the guys much longer. They couldn't hear everything, but they did hear him say something about your helicopter.

"They didn't think much of it at the time, but it got to bothering Devan. He said he thought you would have said something to him Monday if you planned to stop. Anyway, we all thought you should know. It's probably nothing, but who knows."

Oh boy, I thought as the freeze in my spine spread through my limbs. She was right; it might mean nothing. But after what had nearly happened to my Jet Ranger at the airport, I wasn't about to take any chances. I had to make sure I kept the expensive investment secure. And I was afraid that might not be very easy. "Do you know if they had heard anything else—either then or some other time—that I should know about?"

"No, not that they remember, but I thought you should know. You're a nice guy, Major. Please be careful," she said, with a catch in her voice. "And please make sure Trace doesn't get away with what he's done."

First Trace and now the Yost boys seemed to want to mess with my Jet Ranger. It was a worry I really didn't have time for, and it made me really angry. "Thanks for the heads up, Asher," I said. "I'll call you either tonight or in the morning, probably morning, depending on when I'm able to talk to Trace."

* * *

As it turned out, I spent the night at a hotel near the airport where I'd secured my Jet Ranger. Trace was apparently not doing so well. He had lost a lot of blood, much of it internally. I didn't feel very sorry for him, but I did hope he'd be well enough for me to talk to him in the morning.

He wasn't when I called the hospital at eight, but I was told that if I stuck around until noon, he probably would be. So I called Crystal and explained what was happening then settled in to wait.

The sheriff called me at about eleven and asked if I'd talked to Trace yet. I told her I hadn't been able to due to his condition, and she then said, "Well, if you don't mind waiting a little longer, Jarbi will soon be there. She went to Wellington last night, but Johanna Jones's sister wasn't home. So she drove on to Grand Junction and got a room early this morning."

I would have preferred to talk to Trace by myself, but there probably wasn't anything I could do about that now. "Have her call me when she's ready, and I'll meet her at the hospital. It could still be another hour or so before they let us see him."

"All right, Major, and thanks," she said.

"You really don't have to call me Major," I told her, trying to keep my voice light. "Corbin would be fine."

She chuckled, a very pleasant sound, then said, "I like the way it feels. It fits you, Major." I could sense her hesitation, and finally she spoke again. "You need to be careful. There's been more antidrilling activity in town this morning. The tension is building, and I'm worried about it. Some of the tension is over you specifically."

"What about me?" I asked when she didn't explain immediately.

"Well, it has to do with the Yost boys. Devan Rish called me. He said that he overheard—"

I broke in. "I know about that. Asher's husband was with Devan when they overheard the threat, and she called me last night to warn me."

"So what are you going to do?" she asked.

"I'm hoping to get approval from the county to let me put the Jet Ranger out at the place you told me about, the one out near your house," I said. "Crystal is working on that, and if we can get it approved, I'll go through with the rental."

"There may be one little hang-up with that," she said.

"Oh great," I moaned. "Nora Briggs already checked with the owner. They'll even give me a lease to buy agreement if I want it."

"That's not where the hang-up is, Major. It's over the approval you need from the county."

"But Crystal thought it should be pretty smooth sailing."

"Do you remember me telling you about the fellow we've used in the past when we needed a helicopter?" she asked.

"Yes," I said slowly. "Is he the problem?"

"I'm afraid so. His name is Earl Bassinger. He's a little guy, about five six, with a colossal attitude," she explained. "He's already gone to the county leaders and complained about you horning in on his business with my department."

"But I thought he turned you down the last time you called him," I said.

"He did, but he's complaining anyway."

"Okay, so he complains. What does that have to do with where I keep my chopper?"

"He was told about the inquiry your secretary made, and that apparently put him into a tizzy, so he filed a formal complaint this morning."

"On what grounds?" I asked as I felt my anger rising.

"That it would be a noise factor in the area," she said.

"If anyone is going to complain about that, it should be you. You're the closest neighbor."

"I told that to the county councilman who called me this morning. I have several good friends and strong supporters on the council."

"So will this Bassinger guy's complaint really be a problem?" I asked.

"Probably not in the long term, but it will cause a delay. I was told that a hearing would have to be scheduled so that both sides could have their say," she said. "That means you and Bassinger, I guess. There probably isn't anyone else who cares one way or the other."

"Tell me this, Lisette. Where does Bassinger keep his helicopter?" I asked.

She chuckled. "You're going to love this. He keeps it at his brother's place out of town, not anywhere near my place."

"Sounds like he's a bit of a hypocrite," I suggested angrily. "I'll bet he didn't have a hearing."

"I'm sure he didn't. And yes, he is a hypocrite. You have no need to worry though. He won't prevail in this, but like I said, it will cause a delay. But I spoke to my councilman friend about a temporary solution. He says he's sure he can get the others to go along with it until a hearing can be held. He understands that the county has some liability out at the airport and that they can't guarantee the safety of your chopper out there without a lot of additional expense."

"Yes, I can see that. So what's the temporary solution?"

"Keep it at my house," she said.

That made me laugh. "I'll bet Bassinger will like that."

"I'm sure he'll have a fit, but he's landed at my place before and even left his chopper there overnight once. Don't worry, the council is meeting tomorrow, and they'll talk about it then."

"Thanks, Sheriff. But what about the issue of which helicopter you use, mine or his?" I asked.

"That will be up to me. I have a budget, and I can use it how I see fit. The only thing he might raise an issue on with the council is who charges the least."

"That will be me," I said firmly. "Whatever he charges, I'll charge less."

"Thanks, Major. Now back to the danger you and your chopper are in," she said. "What can we do about that?"

"I'll just have to be careful. There isn't a lot more I can do. Now, what about Trace's blue Dodge pickup? Has it been searched yet?" I asked.

"Yes, and we found some interesting things. For one, he had a detailed manual on the exact model of Jet Ranger that you fly. It's a used manual, so I suppose he got it online or something."

That brought a troubling thought to my mind. At first, I tried to brush it off, but it wouldn't go. "What kind of helicopter does Earl Bassinger fly?"

Lisette didn't answer for a moment. When she finally did, she said, "It's a Jet Ranger. Are you suggesting what I'm thinking you are?"

"I'm not suggesting anything," I said. "But I would be interested in knowing the exact model . . . Where is the book now?"

"We have it," she said.

"What are the chances of having it fingerprinted?" I asked.

"One hundred percent," she responded, following my train of thought. "I would hope that Earl Bassinger wouldn't stoop so low as to help Trace, but I promise I'll find out."

Chapter Eight

I met Detective Jarbi Patterson outside the hospital at noon. She was still tired from her late-night drive, but her light-blue eyes were shining with excitement at the prospect of interviewing a murder suspect.

She was not in uniform but wore instead a pair of tight gray slacks and a black blouse. She looked really nice. She ran up to me and surprised me with a hug. "It's good to see you, Major," she said. "You look really good this morning."

I wasn't so sure about that—and the ugly scar on my face didn't help—but it didn't hurt my ego any hearing her say it. "So do you," I complimented her back.

"Thank you," she said with a grin. "Are you ready to help me with this interview?" she asked, taking me by the arm and leading me in the direction of the entrance.

"I sure am," I said. "But I have a favor to ask."

She smiled up at me sweetly, and said, "Whatever you want, Major."

"I'd like to talk to Trace alone for just a minute before you come into his room."

Her smile faded, and her eyebrows lifted. "What, you don't think I know what I'm doing?"

I flashed my best Major Daniels smile and said, "Oh, it's not that at all, Detective. Actually, I believe you're probably better than me at this kind of thing."

"You do?"

"I do. I can't dazzle anyone with the kind of smile you have," I said.

She brightened at that. "You think I'm pretty."

"That's a given," I said. "I'd have to be blind not to."

Her face turned a pretty shade of red, and she said, "Thank you, Major. But why, then, do you want to meet with him first?"

I stopped walking and gently turned her toward me. "I do have one advantage that you don't. It's a little thing called Miranda. I'm working for a client not for law enforcement. If I can get him to say something incriminating, I can use it in court. You can only do so if you Mirandize him."

She nodded. "You're a smart guy, Major. And don't sell yourself short on the looks part either. I think you're very . . . well, cute. And that scar that seems to bother you so much gives you character."

Character? I'd never been told that before. "Thanks, Detective," I said sincerely.

"I'm Jarbi to you, remember?"

"Yes, Jarbi it is," I said with another smile.

"Okay, you go in first. Don't even tell him I'm in the hall until you're ready," she said, taking me by the arm again. "This is fun, working with you. I hope we get to do a lot of this."

"I hope so too," I agreed.

Once we got to the front door of the hospital, she let go of my arm and got a very serious look on her face. "Okay, Major," she said as I held the door for her. "Let's go talk to a killer."

I left her chatting with the officer outside Trace's hospital room. He was young and wasn't wearing a wedding band. Jarbi was talking his ear off when I went in. Trace was lying on his back, eyes closed, with several tubes running from his arm to various hospital gadgets.

I stood looking down at him for a moment. His eyes opened. "Who are you?" he asked as I made sure my little digital recorder was running.

"They call me Major Daniels," I said, "but my name is actually Corbin Daniels. I've been hired to investigate your father's death. I need to talk to you for a minute about that."

"You're the guy who was chasing me yesterday, aren't you?" he said as his eyes began to smolder with anger.

"Following you would be the correct term," I said firmly. "Do you mind if I record our conversation?"

"Do whatever you want," he said. "You got nothing on me anyway."

I made no attempt to counter his assumption, but I spoke into my recorder for a moment, making a record of who I was talking to, the time, and the date. Then I said, "So Mister Jones, tell me what you know about your father's death."

"I don't know anything. If you're implying that I pushed him from my plane, that simply isn't true," he said without blinking. "I'd be lying if I told you I was broken up over it, because I'm not, but I do believe someone else killed him. And I think I know why."

"Really? Why don't you tell me?" I suggested.

"Because he was like you in a way. He thought the sun rose and set on the oil rigs and the drilling out there. Someone besides me didn't like that."

"What makes you think I'm in favor of drilling?" I asked.

That seemed to stop him for a minute, and he adjusted himself in his bed, his eyes looking away from mine. Finally he said, "You have to be. You haul those guys out to the rigs."

"I'm making a living," I said. "I haul anyone around who's willing to pay me."

"Even pigs like those guys on the rigs," he said. It was a statement, not a question, so I didn't respond. I just looked at him. He squirmed again, and then he said, "You need to quit hauling them if you don't want to give people that impression."

"What makes you think I care what people think about me?" I asked.

"You should," he said. "It could get dangerous for people who like to destroy the environment."

"Is that why you tried to sabotage my Jet Ranger?"

Again, he looked away. I waited. When he didn't speak after a couple of long minutes, I said, "I have proof that you did it, and that makes me think you also killed your father. Why else would you try to make a run for it when all I did was show up at your house?"

He looked at me again, and his eyes narrowed. "I was just taking Mom for a plane ride. She's been really upset about what happened to Dad, and she wanted to get away for a while. I didn't have anything to talk to you about, so I told her I'd take her up."

"That was nice of you," I said. I debated telling him that I knew she had left home before his father died and that she'd been at his aunt's house. I decided not to. I looked at him closely, and then I let my eyes go cold. "It was nice, that is, until you killed her."

"I didn't mean to kill her. That was an accident," he said, his eyes suddenly filled with what seemed to be genuine remorse. "I loved my mother."

"If you had nothing to fear from me or the cops, why didn't you land when you were told to?"

"Mom didn't want me to," he said.

"Oh really," I said, the doubt obvious in my voice. "Why wouldn't she want you to? Surely she didn't have anything to fear from me or the law."

Once again he turned away, but not before I saw something in his eyes that disturbed me. I fired another question at him before my last one had even gotten cold. "Did your mother have something to do with your father's death?"

"That's insane. I'm through talking to you," he said. "I got nothing more to say."

"Are you sure?" I asked. "I know about your father filing for divorce. That gives your mother a motive."

"My mom was a good person. Dad was a jerk," he said without looking back at me. "Now get out; I'm hurt and need some rest."

"Not until you answer another question," I said firmly. "Did you attempt to sabotage my helicopter?"

"No," he said rapidly. "I did not."

"But your truck was there. Someone saw it, temporary sticker and all. And you left a pry bar there with your fingerprints all over it." Actually, I was bluffing. I didn't know that the bar had his fingerprints. I didn't know if it had any fingerprints at all.

"I didn't leave anything there because I wasn't there."

I had him talking again, so I pressed on. "Then who had your truck? It was there. That can be proven."

"You can go now," he said.

"If someone else was driving your truck, I would suggest that you tell me who it was; otherwise, I'll do everything I can to see that you're charged with the burglary at the airport that day."

He said nothing, so I picked up my tape recorder and took a step back from his bed. He turned his head in my direction again. So I fired yet another question. "Why did you shoot at me outside your house if all you were doing was taking your mother out for a ride?"

For a moment, he had a blank look on his face, like he'd forgotten that little incident. "You did do that," I reminded him as I stepped back to the bed and leaned over him. "The cops here have your gun—the one you shot a Colorado officer with after your crash—and the cops in Blanding have the bullet you fired into my car. We can prove that you fired the shot by comparing the bullets. Why don't you tell me why you shot at me?"

I would swear that a tear appeared in his eyes, but he blinked it away and then said, "My mother told me to."

"Your mother again?" I said darkly. "It's easy to blame things on her now that she's dead and can't disagree with you. Frankly, I don't believe you. I believe you killed your father. And I plan to prove it."

"You can't," he said. "I didn't do it."

"If you didn't, then your mother hired someone to do it," I said.

"That is a lie," he snapped. "You don't know my mom. She was a good person." He again turned away, and I left the room.

Jarbi was still talking to the young officer outside the door. She turned to me hopefully. "Did he admit anything?"

"No, I'm afraid not," I said. "He says he shot at me in Blanding because his mother said to and that he didn't land his plane when he was ordered to because she told him not to."

"That's crazy," she said.

"Maybe," I said.

"What? Why would she do that?" she asked, her eyes suddenly wide. "You aren't saying she had her husband killed, are you?"

"No, but the thought has crossed my mind. I guess it's your turn with him. Maybe you can do better."

"Okay. Let's go back in," she said.

"No, I better let you go alone. He's mad at me, and that might make it harder for you to soften him up," I said.

She stood looking at me for a moment; then she said very astutely, "Maybe I should wait a few minutes so he won't know we came together."

"That sounds like a good idea to me," I agreed. "Would you let me buy you lunch while you wait?"

She blushed again, and once more it looked good on her. I grinned, as did the young officer standing guard. He even spoke up. "I'll take her to lunch, and you can sit outside this door and wait if you'd rather."

"That's okay, Trooper Stone," I said, glancing at his nameplate. "I don't mind at all. And I sure wouldn't want to get you in trouble by leaving a civilian with a murder suspect. Anyway, I wouldn't mind spending a leisurely lunch with such a lovely lady." That brought another blush from the deputy, and Stone and I both chuckled. I took Jarbi's arm. "Come on, Jarbi. Surely you wouldn't mind having lunch with me."

She grinned. "I'd love to," she said, and she said it in such a way that I knew she meant it. It could have made me blush, but I'm not prone to such things.

I took Jarbi to a nice restaurant, and I very much enjoyed her company. We talked at first about what Trace had told me, and I let her listen to the interview on my recorder. After that, I got to know her better. By the time we were finishing up our pie, I felt like it would be both easy and enjoyable to work with Jarbi in the future. When we got ready to leave, I picked up the check.

"Why don't you let me get that?" she said. "This is on the county."

"No, it's on me, Jarbi," I said. "I asked you to lunch, remember?"

"So is this like a date?" she asked with a twinkle in her eyes.

"If you want it to be," I said with a grin. That made her blush again, which is why I said it. I really like how she looks when she blushes. That's not to say that she didn't look good when she wasn't blushing.

When I dropped her off back at the hospital, I told her I'd probably be on my way, but she said, "Oh, please don't go yet, Major. I might need your help. And for sure, I'd like to talk over with you what he says."

"If you want me to, I'll wait," I agreed.

"I want you to," she said. Once again her cheeks got rosy. Then she entered Trace's room.

Trooper Stone grinned at me and said, "She likes you."

"She's a pretty gal and good at what she does," I said.

"No, I mean she really likes you," he said with emphasis.

Whoa. That set me back a little. So I countered with, "Is that why she was flirting with you while I was in with the suspect?"

"She wasn't," he said. "I would have enjoyed it if she was. I think she's really cute. But no, all she could talk about was you. I got the feeling that she's a little jealous because her boss has spent quite a bit of time with you. And according to Jarbi, the sheriff is attractive too." He sighed. "But if I were you, I'd strike while the iron's hot with Detective Patterson."

Okay, I'd had enough of this talk. "I'm not really looking for romance."

Trooper Stone grinned like he didn't believe me, but I let it go and changed the subject. In about ten minutes, Jarbi came out of the room. And from the look on her face, I could tell that she wasn't happy. I asked her how it went.

"Terrible," she said.

"You were in there ten minutes, Jarbi. Surely he must have told you something," I pressed.

"All he wanted to do was flirt," she said with a disgusted shake of her head. "He kept telling me I was hot and that he was single now. And he went on and on."

"Well, he's right on both counts," I said, bringing a grin to her face. "I guess we should go now."

"Just as well," she agreed. We both said good-bye to the trooper, and she again took my arm as we headed up the hallway.

When we were out of the trooper's earshot, I said, "So what did he say? Did he admit anything to you?"

She looked up at me. "Not really anything he hadn't said to you."

"Did he know that you knew I'd been there earlier?" I asked.

"No, I didn't mention it, and neither did he."

"So what did he tell you?"

"I asked him some of the same things you did, only I tried to ask differently. He agreed, by the way, to speak without an attorney. He told me that what he did, he did, and he'll have to suffer the consequences. But what it boils down to is that he adamantly denies killing his father—who he admits he hated—and he blames his actions yesterday on his mother—who he says he loved—and denies breaking into the hangar at the airport."

"Well, we'll see about that," I said, but I was beginning to wonder about whether he had killed his father. I wanted to believe that he did, but it bothered me that he'd agreed to talk to Jarbi about it without a lawyer.

My phone went off in my pocket, and I pulled it out and answered. "Hi, Major," Lisette said. "Did you and Jarbi get a confession?"

"Far from it," I answered, glancing at Jarbi. I then gave the sheriff a quick summary of what we had learned. By the time I'd finished, Jarbi and I had reached her patrol car. We stopped there, and Jarbi finally released my arm, which she had been holding pretty possessively. I concluded my report. "The only thing we learned for certain, or at least that Jarbi learned, is that he has a huge crush on your detective."

Jarbi slugged me on the arm. Lisette laughed. "I told you she had a way with guys."

"She does at that," I agreed. Jarbi playfully slugged me again, even though she was only hearing one side of the conversation. I became serious and asked the sheriff, "Were you able to learn anything about the manual you found in Trace's pickup?"

"As a matter of fact, we did get some fingerprints," she said. "And none of them were Trace's. Of course, he was probably wearing gloves."

"Maybe, but it would be hard to flip the pages with gloves on," I said. "So if his prints weren't on the manual, whose were?"

"Are you ready for this?" she asked mysteriously.

I immediately thought about mine. I kept it in my chopper, and whoever had broken into the hangar hadn't yet gotten into my aircraft. Or had he? Doubt flooded my mind. "It's not my manual, is it?" I asked.

"Oh, no, of course not. At least, I don't think so. Do you still have yours?" she asked.

That worried me. "I think so, but I won't know for sure until I get back to the airport. I keep it in my helicopter."

"I'm sure it's still there," Lisette said with a chuckle. Jarbi was standing about as close to me as she could get, trying, I could tell, to hear both sides of the conversation. She must have picked up much of what her boss was saying, if her facial expressions were any indication.

"Okay, Sheriff," I said formally. "Whose prints did you find?"

"The guy who is trying to cause you grief with your helicopter business. Earl Bassinger's prints are all over the manual."

Chapter Nine

AFTER THE PHONE CALL WITH the sheriff was finished, Jarbi and I looked at each other. I spoke first. "I have some more questions for Mr. Trace Jones."

She nodded. "Let's go back in there," she said. "Do you want to go first again?"

"Let's do this one together," I said. "But let me start the questioning, if that's okay."

"Back already?" Trooper Stone asked when we marched up to the door of Trace's room again.

"We need to talk to him again," I said. "We just learned something that we need to get his reaction to. Is it okay if we go in?"

"It's okay with me," he said, looking a little nervous. "But I don't know about the nurse. "She just told me—"

I interrupted before he could tell me what the nurse said. "I don't need to know what the nurse said; we're going in."

The trooper looked a little flustered, but I shoved the door open. We walked through, shutting the door behind us. Trace's eyes flew open in surprise when I stepped over to the bed and shook his shoulder. "You've got some explaining to do," I said before he had a chance to say a word. "What was Earl Bassinger's Jet Ranger manual doing in your truck?" I asked, gripping his shoulder. "And I want a straight answer."

"What? I don't know what you're talking—" he began.

"Don't go trying to deny it," I interrupted, my grip growing tighter. "I know it was there, and you know it was. The question is why."

"I didn't have it," he insisted.

"Wrong answer," I hissed. "Try again."

I heard Jarbi gasp beside me, but I didn't look away from Trace.

"Hey, you're hurting me," he whined.

I let up some of the pressure on his shoulder, but I leaned lower over his face and said, "What was that manual doing in your truck?"

"I . . . I . . ." he stammered.

"Tell me now," I said, once again tightening my grip.

"Okay, okay," he said. "Earl borrowed my truck. Big deal. He and I are friends. I don't know why he had the manual in there. Is that all?"

"Not yet," I said, backing off with the pressure on his arm. "When did he borrow your truck?"

He told me, and then I looked at Jarbi. She nodded. I looked back at Trace. "So you're telling me Earl Bassinger had your truck yesterday morning when someone tried to mess with my Jet Ranger?" He nodded. "Is that a yes?" I asked, conscious of the little digital recorder at work in my pocket.

"Yes," he said.

"Why?" I asked him.

"He said his truck was in the garage and that I could use his car if he could borrow my truck," he said.

"Did he say why he needed a truck? Couldn't he have just used his car?" I pressed.

"I don't know. He didn't say why. But like I told you, we are friends. So when he said he needed it, I let him take it."

"What time did you let him take it?"

"I don't know, maybe about five in the afternoon."

"When did he bring it back?"

"Yesterday morning. And that's what happened."

I shook my head and said, "Are you sure?"

"Of course I'm sure," he said.

"Where was your mother when he borrowed your truck?"

"At her house," he said.

"How did she get there?" I asked, keeping the questions coming. "She was at your aunt's house in Wellington."

"My aunt brought her down, and I stayed the night with her. We went back to my place yesterday morning."

"After you got your truck back from Bassinger?" I asked.

"Yeah, that's right."

"I don't believe you," I said. "You borrowed the Jet Ranger manual from Bassinger. You were trying to figure out the best way to mess with my helicopter."

"No, honest, I didn't do it. Earl must have gone up to the airport in my truck."

"Sure he did. He'd have a reason to mess up my chopper, but you don't," I said sarcastically.

"He doesn't like the oil rigs either," Trace shot back. "He doesn't carry guys back and forth like you do. He respects the environment."

"How does he make money with his helicopter?" I asked.

"He takes tourists out, that kind of thing."

"Why?"

"So they can see this beautiful country without having to hike all over it."

"And while he does that, he's burning fuel and polluting the air, just like you do with your plane. You're both hypocrites. Furthermore, I think you killed your dad," I added, once again applying pressure to his shoulder.

"No! No, I didn't!" he insisted. "Somebody else did that. Dad's never even been in my plane. I wouldn't have taken him for a ride if he'd asked me."

"Loved your dad, didn't you?" I rolled my eyes.

"I hated him. He was a jerk," he said. "But I didn't kill him."

"So you're suggesting somebody else killed him, someone who thinks the environment is more important than the people who live in it."

"I don't know who did it," he whined. "I just know Dad thought the drilling was the best thing to hit this county in years."

"Give me a break, Trace. What makes you think your dad was so much in favor of the oil companies?" I asked.

"I already told you," he said, his voice growing weak. "He took a job as a security officer for an oil company."

"That might be true, but did you know that he had a suitcase full of antidrilling pamphlets when he died?"

"No, he didn't," he said.

"Yes, he did," I countered. "I saw them. I think he was on your side, and you didn't even know it."

"Oh," he said weakly.

"Did your mother agree with you about the drilling?"

"Of course," he said.

I had tired him, and I knew I better quit pretty soon. But I still had one more question. "Did Earl Bassinger kill your father?" I asked.

"No, he wouldn't do that," he protested. "He's a good, honest man."

"That's all I have," I said, releasing his shoulder. "Jarbi, do you have anything to ask this weasel?"

"No, I think you've covered it pretty well," she said.

Just as we were coming up the hall, a nurse approached. She looked at us, and her eyes narrowed. She lit into the trooper about how he was not to allow visitors into the room again until she gave her the okay. I glared back at her and said, "This is a murder investigation. You better get your priorities straight. I thought it was your job to care about people. That man killed his mother." I pointed toward Trace's door. "And he probably murdered his father, as well. And he tried to kill me. He is a bad man who couldn't care less about anyone else. So don't go blaming the trooper here. It was my decision to go in there. And if I need to again, you better believe I will. Let's go, Detective."

We left the nurse stammering and Trooper Stone staring. Neither of us spoke until we were outside again. Then I said, "What do you think?"

She grinned. "I think I don't want you questioning me," she said. "But I also think we better take a closer look at Earl Bassinger. He's a jerk, just like Trace is. Will you wait while I call Lisette?" she asked.

"You and I seem to think alike," I told her, nodding. I looked to the west and groaned. There were huge, black clouds accumulating there. A cool wind gusted around Jarbi and me. Those storm clouds could delay my flight back to Moab. That didn't make me very happy as I was anxious to get home. I had to pay a visit to the guy I had yet to meet but who had already become a huge thorn in my side, Earl Bassinger. It would be a visit I didn't think he would enjoy at all.

I started back to my rental car when Jarbi held up her hand and signaled for me to wait. She had her phone to her ear. I stepped back toward her and listened to her talk for a moment. The report she was giving Sheriff Statton was right on the mark. I couldn't have been more thorough myself. The only thing she left out was the pressure my right hand had applied to Trace's left shoulder. But I wouldn't have mentioned that either.

Then after listening to Lisette for a minute, Jarbi said, "Yes, I'll do that right now." She listened again then said, "I'll ask him." She moved the phone from her ear. "Lisette wondered if you would go with me and observe as me and a couple Colorado cops search Trace's plane. They're going to take fingerprints and whatever else they think they should."

I glanced again at the rapidly approaching storm and said, "Sure. I can't leave until that storm passes anyway. It looks like it might be packing a punch."

"Okay," she said and put the phone back to her ear. "He wants to help me," was the way she put it to the sheriff.

Jarbi followed me to the airport, where Trace's wrecked plane had been impounded. A couple of officers, a state trooper and a deputy sheriff, met us at the hangar. There were also two men who were introduced as lab technicians. Jarbi introduced herself first and then me. "Major Daniels is the guy who was tailing Trace Jones in the air yesterday," she explained. "He's very interested in what we find here."

It was what they didn't find that proved to be of the most interest to me. Nowhere in the plane were there fingerprints of Trace's father. That didn't mean Trace hadn't killed him then wiped the fingerprints away, but it did give at least some credibility to what Trace had told us.

By the time the search was almost finished, the storm had blown over. For a while, I'd stood at the door of the hangar and watched the thunderstorm. It was loud, it was wet, and it produced very high winds. But not long after that storm had moved out, I was disappointed to see another one approaching. I called Crystal and told her I wasn't sure when I'd get back. I also filled her in on the day's events.

Jarbi had already reported to the sheriff when we approached the door and stepped outside a few minutes later. The wind was blowing, and it was cold. The smell of rain was rich, and the sound of thunder was loud and almost constant. I glanced at my watch. It was almost six o'clock. I was hungry again, and I suspected that Jarbi was too.

She wrapped her arms around herself and shivered. "It wasn't this cold when I left or I'd have brought a heavy coat," she said as she sidled near me. I put my arm around her and pulled her against me. "That's better," she said. Her body was shaking, and her teeth were chattering.

"When do you plan to go back to Moab?" I asked as we stood near the building, sheltered from the worst of the wind.

"Lisette just told me to wait until morning. I don't want to drive in this bad weather," she said. "Not if I don't have to. What about you?"

"There's no way I can fly until this is over. And I'm not sure it will be anytime soon. How about if we see if we can get rooms for both of us? After that, if you don't mind, I'll take you to dinner."

She grinned and snuggled closer. "Are you asking me out on another date?" she asked.

"Sure, why not? Maybe we could see a movie afterward."

Her reaction was clear. I'd just made her day. Frankly, I could use a little rest and relaxation, and she was fun to be with. I just hoped she wouldn't get her hopes up too high because I wasn't interested in a relationship. I just wanted her company tonight. At least, that's what I told myself. And I tend to believe whatever I tell me.

* * *

We ended up with adjoining rooms at a hotel near the airport. We went to dinner at a nice downtown restaurant. And we enjoyed a movie after that. We didn't get back to the hotel until nearly ten. By then I was exhausted. She gave me a peck on the cheek, hoping, I thought by the look in her eyes, for a little something more than that. She didn't get it. We went into our rooms.

The first thing I did was make a call to my client, Asher Grady. She wasn't happy with my report. I think that she had it in her head that when I talked to Trace, he would confess to everything. I tried to explain that not all the evidence pointed to him.

"But he did it," she insisted.

"Maybe, but we need proof, and so far, I haven't been able to find any," I said. "But I'll keep looking if that's what you want me to do."

"Please do," she said. "I don't want you to think I'm not happy about what you've done; I just know he was involved."

I hadn't told her what Trace had said about their mother insisting he shoot at me and keep flying in an effort to get away from the pursuit. I told her now, and it really upset her. "That lying twit!" she raged. "I can't believe he would accuse Mom of something like that. It isn't like her at all. What's worse is that Trace was always Mom's pet. It's outrageous that he would accuse her like that. But I guess at this point I shouldn't be surprised at anything he says. After all, Mom's dead because of him. He can say anything he wants, and neither she nor Dad are here to call him the liar that he is."

"It's true. They can't refute anything he says."

There was a pause. Then she said, "You know, now that I think about it, sometimes when Mom was mad at Dad, she asked Trace to do something that she knew would make Dad mad. Sometimes they were kind of mean. She and Dad were always fighting."

"Can you give me an example?" I asked.

"Well, let's see. Once they had had a big argument. It was fall, deer hunting season, and Dad wanted to go hunting. Mom had arranged to go to Salt Lake to a concert. She liked concerts; Dad didn't. Anyway, they argued about it. Finally, Dad simply told Mom she'd have to go alone, that he was going to be hunting. She asked Trace to hide Dad's hunting rifle."

"Really?" I asked. "That seems kind of strange."

"Well, that's the kind of thing she'd do. And Trace, being the mean kid he was, would always do worse than what she asked. That time, he didn't hide the gun; he pawned it. Dad was in a rage for weeks. Mom and Trace insisted they didn't know anything about it. Finally, thinking it might have been stolen, Dad checked the pawn shops and found it. He went ballistic when he found out Trace was the one who'd done it."

"Okay. And I suppose there are other things that she asked him to do," I said.

"Yes, there were," she said. "Mom and Trace were mean to Dad. I'm the only one that treated him the way he deserved."

"So, it sounds like it might be possible that she did ask him to do what he claims and, if she did, that he'd do it," I concluded.

"Only worse," Asher said. "She might have suspected that Trace had killed Dad. If so, and she told Trace to get away from you, he would take it one step further by shooting at you. That makes sense to me."

"Maybe," I said, but I wasn't convinced. I was getting a different picture in my head about Johanna Jones, and it wasn't a pretty picture.

I let the matter drop. "I'll let you go, Asher, but thanks for your time. I'll let you know when I learn more."

I spent the next thirty minutes making notes on the interviews with Trace and the search of his plane. Then I showered and went to bed, where I lay wide awake. My mind was churning, and I couldn't slow it down. Trace Jones would be going to prison. That was almost certain. But would he be going for the murder of his father? I was beginning to doubt it. Somehow, as much as I was repulsed by the man, what he told me in his hospital room had a ring of truth to it.

By the time I finally fell asleep, I hadn't drawn any certain conclusions. But I had concluded that the list of suspects, which I kept Trace on, also included his mother; the Yost brothers; and finally, my tormentor, Earl Bassinger. I especially wanted to talk to him. But that was for another day.

I awoke early the next morning, a sunny, clear day, one that would be good for flying home. And I intended to do that as soon as I had some breakfast.

Chapter Ten

JARBI WAS ALSO UP, AND she asked me if I'd go to breakfast with her at the restaurant in the hotel. She grinned when I met her outside her door. "Three dates in two days," she teased. "That's a record for me."

It was for me too. Three dates in a year was also a record. I was worried that Jarbi—sweet, pretty gal that she was—was setting herself up if she really did have a crush on me. I looked at her across the table a few minutes later and wondered why she wasn't married. Not that I had any intentions of changing that. But I had to admit she was fun to be with. We had an enjoyable breakfast, so enjoyable it made me uncomfortable in a strange sort of way.

"So are you heading back to Moab now?" she asked as we left the restaurant.

That was something I'd been thinking about since I'd woken up that morning. I had another idea. "I think I'll fly up to Denver, rent another car, and take a little drive to the University of Colorado–Denver."

"Why do you want to go there?" she asked. But before I could answer, her light blue eyes grew wide. "Oh yeah, I see. Junior Yost works there."

"Bingo," I said.

"Major, do you care if I call the sheriff and see if she minds if I fly there with you?" she asked, her face hopeful. "I've been trying to find out more about Junior myself. The sheriff just hadn't thought it was worth a trip up there yet."

Good sense would have been to tell her that I would rather go by myself. But as much as I hated to admit it, her company on the trip would be nice. And she may be able to get answers out of people up there that I might not be able to. She was watching me expectantly as I considered her request. I guess I was taking too long because she smiled at me, her perfect white teeth almost glowing, and said, "Please, Major?"

By that point, I'd made up my mind to let her come. In the interest of the case only, not for any personal reasons, I told myself—and I think I believed myself like I usually do. Anyway, I said, "Sure, that would be helpful." That was consistent with what I was trying to tell myself.

While I was getting my small bag packed, she did the same. When she came out of her room with her overnight bag a few minutes later, her face was all aglow. "Lisette thinks I should go," she said. "She wants me—or us, if it's okay with you—to talk to some of Junior's coworkers and maybe some students."

"That's exactly what I'd planned," I told her.

"That's what Lisette thought," she said. "However, she also reminded me that we may have already caught the guilty party, meaning Trace Jones, of course."

"Does she believe that?" I asked, silently offering to take her bag by reaching for it. She let me take it, and we headed for the elevator.

"I'm not so sure she does anymore," she admitted as she reached up and slipped her long, dark hair over her shoulder. "If she was sure, wouldn't she have told me to get back there as soon as possible? What about you, Major? Do you think Trace did it?"

I remembered the thoughts that had kept me from falling to sleep last night. Jarbi punched the elevator button as I slowly shook my head. "Trace is still a suspect, but there are others, and Junior Yost is right up there at the top of the list."

The elevator stopped, the door opened, and we got on. There were a couple of other people on it, so after saying good morning to them, we rode down in silence. As we walked out to the parking lot, Jarbi said, "I have Earl Bassinger on my list."

"As a matter of fact, so do I. And when I get back to Moab, I intend to see what else I can learn about the guy."

"I don't like him," she said. "I've ridden in his helicopter with him before, and it wasn't fun like riding with you. He's a rude little man, and he doesn't like women—at least not women cops. He's a lot like

Edward Jones was in that respect. He was really opposed to Lisette when she was running against Edward."

"That's what Lisette told me," I said. We reached our cars a minute later and plopped our bags in. "Let's turn my car in at the rental place and leave yours out by my chopper, if that's okay with you."

Of course it was, so that's what we did. On the short ride to the helicopter, we resumed the conversation regarding suspects.

"I know this is a stretch," Jarbi said, "but I can't keep from wondering about Johanna Jones. Could she somehow be involved in her husband's death?"

"We can't overlook that." I glanced across at her. She was looking straight ahead, and I studied her profile for a moment. It was a nice profile, but my thoughts were not so much about her physical attractiveness as about her concentration. She was in deep thought, and that, to me, was a good thing.

I kept my eyes on her a moment longer. Finally, she looked over at me and smiled, but I could tell that she'd reached some kind of conclusion. I was right, for she said, "If Johanna was involved, then someone else had to be as well. I think it was Earl Bassinger."

"I've thought about that," I agreed. "Keep talking."

"I'd like to know if Edward Jones might have left fingerprints or other evidence in Earl's helicopter," she said thoughtfully.

I really liked the way this girl was thinking. "The difficulty is going to be figuring out how to get a warrant to search it," I said. "As it stands right now, no judge in the state would give you a search warrant."

"That is a problem," she agreed as she steered into the parking area. "And that means we need to find enough evidence to convince a judge to give us a search warrant. That might be really difficult."

We both thought about that while she parked her patrol car, then we got out. I grabbed my bag, and as an afterthought, I said, "Why don't you throw your bag in the chopper, just in case."

"Just in case what?" she asked as she retrieved it from the backseat.

"That was a pretty fierce storm last night. What if there's another one? I don't anticipate that, but if it did, we'd be stuck in Denver overnight," I said.

She grinned that really nice grin of hers and said, "That's a nice thought. We could have another date." Then she laughed as I went red. "I'm just teasing, Major. I don't mean to be so, what should I say, flirty? I hope I'm not making you uncomfortable. I do enjoy working with you."

I wouldn't call Jarbi a liar, but I think she did mean to be flirty. But I wasn't minding it as much as I probably should. What I mean is, I wasn't as uncomfortable about it as I was just the day before. I chuckled along with her. "I like working with you too," I said. "I just hope we can make some headway on this case today. And I hope we can get back to Moab soon. I really am anxious to learn more about Earl Bassinger."

* * *

"I suppose we should also consider the fact that Johanna could have hired someone to bump off her husband," Jarbi said to me later, as we were nearing Denver

I looked over at her. "Are you thinking of Junior Yost?" I asked.

She adjusted her headset a little before answering. "Yes, but I'm also thinking about something else."

"Okay, and what's that, Jarbi?"

"The plane Trace has been using, the one he wrecked, it was one he rents, right?"

"That's right."

"And it didn't have any of his father's fingerprints in it."

"Right," I agreed as I suddenly had an idea where she was headed with her thoughts. And it was someplace I had neglected to go, so I listened.

"Who's to say he didn't rent a different plane to kill his father?"

"You are one smart detective," I said, and I really meant it. "Why don't you call the sheriff—" I began, but she already was removing her headset. A moment later she had retrieved her cell phone and was making the call.

When she'd finished, she put the headset back on and said, "Lisette agrees. She's going to get Ev working on that. By the way, have you met Ev?"

"Lisette has told me he's a good man and a good cop, but no, I haven't met him yet. I'd like to though."

"He's great, and he's as loyal to the sheriff as, well, as I am. And I'm pretty loyal," she said with a serious look on her face.

"I like loyalty," I said.

I was certain, as we flew without conversation for the next few minutes, that she was doing what I was doing—thinking about the case. Suddenly, I had a thought. "Jarbi, call the sheriff back and tell her I think we should check Trace's truck for Earl Bassinger's fingerprints, just in case Trace was telling us the truth about lending it to Earl."

"Yes, I was thinking the same thing." She made the call, and when she had finished and had the headset in place again, she said, "Lisette told me she's already having that done."

"Great minds think alike," I said.

Jarbi grinned. "We'll solve this thing; we will."

I hoped she was right. If we didn't, it wouldn't be because we hadn't tried.

I was glad I had a real-live police detective with me when we got to the UCD campus. My credentials failed to impress anyone when we asked for information about Junior Yost. Jarbi's, on the other hand, produced instant results.

We were lucky to find Junior on the campus. He was in his office in-between classes, but that, however, was as far as our luck went. He was surly, uncooperative, even angry. "I know who you are," he said, poking me in the chest with his finger. "That ugly scar on your face is a dead giveaway." Jarbi and I were standing in front of his desk. He did not invite us to sit down, and I suspected that he wouldn't.

"And I know who you are," I replied, making no effort to keep a frown from my scarred face.

"I'm a guy trying to make a living helping others, teaching, tutoring, and researching," he said with an angry scowl. "You, on the other hand, are making money by helping to destroy our environment."

I knew I shouldn't say what I was thinking, but I did it anyway. The guy really got under my skin in a hurry. "And you fly a plane that you have no need for. And I'll bet you drive a big SUV too," I said, staring him in the eye. "And your wife probably does too."

He blinked. Jarbi grinned, and I just continued to stare at him. He finally said, "My plane and my SUV are none of your business. And I don't have a wife anymore."

Whoever the ex-wife was, she was probably lucky to be rid of him. I shot right back, "If fossil fuels are doing as much damage to the environment as you say, then it is my business. Because of you and people like you, my air is being polluted and animals and plants that I'm fond of are being destroyed." I took a breath. "But that's not why we are here. We're here to talk to you about the death of one of the good citizens of Moab."

"I had nothing to do with what happened to Edward Jones," he said, folding his arms over his chest and looking up at me with a bit of a smirk on his face.

"Did I say something about Edward Jones?" I asked.

He gave out a depreciating laugh. "He's the only Moab person I know of who's died lately."

"Except for his wife, Johanna."

He looked taken aback by that. Apparently, he hadn't heard about her death. "I-I didn't have anything to do with her death either," he stammered. I'd rattled him with that.

"I know," I said. "Her son Trace killed her yesterday. But I'm sure you'll hear more about that from your little brother soon enough. By the way, Jordan seems willing enough to fly out and help drill for oil. I guess you and he don't see eye to eye on this fossil-fuels thing."

"You don't know that," he said. "He's just doing what he has to in order to make a living. You lay off my brother." His eyes had narrowed, and his brows lowered. "Now, you two get out of here. I have nothing more to say to you."

Jarbi didn't make any more effort to leave than I did. In fact, she acted as though she hadn't heard him. "We've known each other all our lives, Junior," she said sweetly. "Moab's not that big of a place. I'd think you'd want to help us figure out who killed Edward Jones. I'd think you'd be especially helpful, considering that he believes the same things you do."

"I don't know what you're talking about," he said sourly.

"You must. You've been very active in trying to get those oil rigs shut down, and the group you associate with is the one that printed all those pamphlets Jones has been distributing," she said innocently.

He blinked again. If he knew about Edward Jones's ties to the group, he didn't admit it. But once again, he said, "You guys need to go. I've got work to do."

We turned to leave, and Jarbi was through the office door when I turned back and said quietly, "If you or Jordan so much as lay a hand on my helicopter, I'll slowly break every finger on both your hands. You got that?"

He blinked three times. His face reddened, and I joined Jarbi in the hallway. "What did you say to him?" she asked.

"Oh, nothing much," I replied. "I just warned him to leave my Jet Ranger alone."

"What did he say to that?"

"Nothing, but it sure had him blinking rapidly. At least he knows that I know what he's been threatening. "

She smiled, shook her head, and said skeptically, "And you didn't say what would happen if he did mess with the helicopter?"

"I might have suggested something," I said and left it at that. So did Jarbi.

We spent the next two hours talking with some of Junior's fellow instructors and professors. Not surprisingly, most of them weren't impressed with him. Some agreed with his environmental concerns. Others implied he was a bit off his rocker. Some preferred not to comment, which, in and of itself, was quite telling.

As I had expected, it was Jarbi with her cute grin, expressive blue eyes, and flirty personality that got most of Junior's male colleagues to open up. She pointed out, however, that I seemed to do better with the females. "And I sure can see why. You make women's hearts flutter," she said between interviews.

I didn't really have a good response to that, so I made none, just smiled as she punched me playfully on my shoulder. It was on the last interview, one with an older professor, that we actually learned something of interest—and it was Jarbi that got the fellow to open up.

We were sitting in his office, a much bigger and much nicer one than Junior's. Jarbi told the man that we were interested in learning a little more about Leon Yost—we had gathered in our interviews that he was only known as Junior in his hometown. Here at the university he was Leon.

The professor's name was Emmett Haas. He was a genial and distinguished man, who looked to be in his midsixties. He had a white beard, which was short and neatly trimmed, and white hair that flowed neatly to his collar and covered his ears. He assessed the two of us with piercing blue eyes. I judged him to be around five ten, and he appeared trim and fit. I could see him, even at his age, running marathons.

His voice was deep and clear, a pleasant voice to listen to. Seeming satisfied with his assessment of us, he looked Jarbi in the eye and said, "You remind me of my late wife when she was about your age. She was a beautiful girl. To me she was even beautiful after the cancer ravaged her body." He nodded his head, and for a moment, he seemed to be remembering. Then he said, "Yes, you favor her a great deal."

"Thank you, professor," Jarbi said. "That's a wonderful compliment. I wish I could have known her."

Professor Haas turned slightly and pointed to a large bookshelf behind him. There was a framed picture of a smiling young couple that had previously been hidden from our view by the professor's body. I felt my jaw drop. He turned and retrieved the picture then handed it to Jarbi, who held it so we could both see it clearly. There, but for the clothing and style of dark hair, was Jarbi smiling at us beside a handsome young man with blond hair and a neat blond beard. "Beautiful, isn't she?" he said with reverence in his deep voice.

Jarbi was staring at the photo, her hand trembling slightly.

I answered for both of us. "Yes, professor, she is indeed beautiful. Very beautiful."

I glanced over at Jarbi. Her hands still trembling, a flush crept up her neck and across her face. "You're beautiful too," the professor said, reaching as she handed the picture back. "And apparently, your colleague here thinks so as well."

Her blush grew darker. The professor sat the framed picture on the desk, facing us, and then leaned forward, one hand absently stroking his beard. "That's enough of memories for the moment. What do you want to know about Mr. Yost? Why are you interested in him?"

Jarbi glanced at me, and I nodded for her to go ahead. She turned back to the professor. "There have been some crimes committed in Moab, Utah, where we both live and work. Mr. Yost's name came up in the course of our investigation. We are trying to find out more about him and to determine where he was last Sunday night and Monday morning."

Professor Hass leaned back in his chair and rubbed his eyes for a moment. "He's a deeply troubled young man—highly intelligent but very unstable."

We waited for more. When he said nothing further, seeming in deep thought, Jarbi finally said, "Troubled in what way, professor?"

He shook his head, focused his eyes on her again, and smiled. "I'm sorry. I'm having a hard time keeping my concentration. I miss my Jane so much, and you could be her, sitting there smiling at me. Please forgive me. About young Mr. Yost. His views are extreme, but extreme views are common—even expected and encouraged—on university campuses across the country. Some would probably say I have extreme views. But never in my life have I attempted to force my views on others or to resort to threats of violence to stop others from expressing their views. I think Mr. Yost is a potentially violent young man. What exactly is the crime you're investigating?"

Chapter Eleven

Silence hung thick in the air around us. Then a clap of thunder shook the building. I turned toward the professor's window. I hadn't even seen the storm approaching, but then, we had been inside for the past two hours. I looked back. Jarbi's eyes were locked with the professor's.

"Murder," she said at last.

"I feared as much," the professor said, showing no surprise on his face. "Yes, Leon Yost could do such a thing and not have so much as one second's remorse over it."

Those were pretty strong words, and I opened my mouth to voice that fact, but an even louder, more violent clap of thunder rocked us. It was followed by two more in quick succession. Then the relentless sound of pounding rain and hail made it hard to continue the conversation. My thoughts turned to my helicopter. I hoped the airport wasn't getting pounded like we were here.

Five minutes passed in which very little was said. When the storm finally relented enough to make communication possible again, Professor Haas said, "Wow, what an interruption. But frankly, that storm sort of describes the way I see Leon Yost becoming. He's a young man prone to violence." His eyes connected with Jarbi's again, and he went on. "As I was saying, murder, if not yet, certainly will be part of Mr. Yost's life sometime. He is full of anger and hatred, and I don't think he knows how to contain it. In fact, I don't think he wants to."

"Wow," Jarbi said. "He sounds like he's a scary man."

"He is at that," Professor Haas agreed.

I finally put my question to the professor. "Do you know of anyone he has personally threatened or hurt?"

"I certainly do. His ex-wife, Misty," he said without a moment's hesitation. "She's lucky she was able to get away from him before he killed her."

"Do you know what they fought about?" It was Jarbi asking the question.

"Yes, as a matter of fact, I do," he said. "She didn't agree with all his views. In fact, she hardly agreed with any of them."

"You mean like global warming?" I asked.

He tore his eyes from Jarbi and met mine. "That's one of the less controversial subjects he rants about," he said.

"So what else?" I asked in surprise.

"He's a racist," he said. "The administration hasn't heard him directly spew his views in that regard, but he certainly poured them out on poor, innocent Misty."

Jarbi pulled the professor's attention back to her. "You must have known Misty quite well."

"Yes, I know her very well. When Leon first married her, my wife and I invited them over to dinner. She and Jane hit if off quite well. When Jane was ill, Misty visited often. Leon never came with her. In fact, it was during those times that Misty would often tell Jane how she wished her husband would show love to her the way I did to Jane. Even after Jane's passing, Misty has kept in touch with me. The violence in their home was getting dangerous, life threatening, but she would never call the authorities."

"So there's not a police record of his violence in the home?" I asked.

"None, I'm sure. She was frightened of him," he said. "When she showed up at my home late one evening, bleeding, her nose broken, both eyes black, and a tooth missing, I told her it was time to report him. She told me he'd kill her if she did. I was afraid she was right, so I suggested she leave him and move away from the Denver area. We both feared for her safety and had plans in place to protect her, but he surprised us both. He simply let her go, telling her it was good riddance to bad rubbish. Her two brothers were with her, so if he had tried to do something to her then, he wouldn't have been able to. They vowed they wouldn't let him."

"Did the couple have children?" Jarbi asked.

"No, fortunately. She did get pregnant a few times, but each time she miscarried."

"Because of his beating her?" Jarbi asked suspiciously.

"I don't know. She would never tell me, but I suspect you might be right."

"Is there some way we can talk to her?" I asked.

"I'm sure there is. She lives down in Grand Junction."

Jarbi and I looked at each other, and then she said, "We were in Grand Junction this morning. My car is still there. We flew up in Major Corbin's Jet Ranger."

Professor Haas looked at me with renewed interest. "You own a helicopter?" I nodded. "Then you, my friend, might be in danger." A clap of thunder outside added a giant exclamation point to his warning. Jarbi gasped. The professor went on. "I was walking past Leon's office one day, and he was inside with the door ajar. A student was with him. He has brainwashed several students. Rumor has it there's a group forming that consider themselves neo-Nazis. All young men, all white, all some of our lesser achieving students. But it's only rumor. Nothing has been proven. Frankly, if it could be, Mr. Yost would be fired. Anyway, the two of them were talking, and I distinctly overheard Leon say, 'My brother and I are going to get that major's helicopter.'"

I shivered as I asked, "He definitely said major?"

"Oh, yes, but at the time I didn't attach any significance to what he said. He wasn't speaking in anger or in a raised voice at all. It was all very matter-of-fact. I assumed he was going to acquire a helicopter from somebody; although on his salary, I couldn't imagine how. I don't know how he paid for a plane." He looked at Jarbi again and then asked, "Does he come from a wealthy family?"

"No," she said flatly. "They do okay, but they're not wealthy by any means."

Professor Haas turned back to me. "Do you go by Major?"

"A lot of people call me that," I said.

"Are you in the military?"

"Not anymore. I was an army Black Hawk pilot."

He nodded, his face very solemn. "That scar, is that a memento of your service?"

"It is," I said.

"I'd say you got lucky."

"In a way," I said as I thought about what I had lost that day. I had been lucky, but I had also been very, very unlucky, as had my beloved Angie.

He must have sensed my feelings, for he studied me for a moment before he said, "I'm sorry that I have brought to your mind painful memories, but you must watch your back, Major Daniels—and your helicopter. Like I was saying, I thought Leon's remark was quite innocent, but now I know it was far from it. Another of the things he claims to hate is the United States military. That might seem strange, as he is a militant young man himself, but it's clearer when you know more of his background.

"Misty told me about it. As a young man in his late teens, he'd wanted to be in the Marines. He tried to enlist right out of high school, but it turned out he has a rare heart condition, and they turned him down. It made him very bitter. He claims he's as fit as the next man."

Chills ran up and down my spine, and rain was still pouring outside. Even though the lights were shining brightly in the professor's office, I felt a distinct darkness swirling about me. Unless the professor was wrong—and I had no reason to doubt him—Leon Yost had declared war on me before he even met me.

Before we left, Jarbi wrote down Misty Yost's phone number and address in Grand Junction. "I'll call her tonight and let her know you're coming," the professor said. "Do you know about when that will be?"

"Depends on the weather," I said. "I'm not flying until it clears up. So if we can't get away this evening, we'll go there tomorrow."

"I'll let her know. I think she might be able to give you even more helpful information than I have."

"Thank you," Jarbi and I said in unison.

"If you'll give me your cards," Professor Haas continued, "I'll call one or the other of you if I think of anything else. And, Major Daniels, if I hear anything at all that would be helpful in keeping you safe from Mr. Yost, I'll let you know."

I thanked him and rose from my chair. Jarbi followed suit, but before we had moved any farther, Professor Haas asked, "You say you're investigating a murder. Are you free to tell me more about it?"

"Of course," Jarbi said. She turned to me. "Why don't you tell him?"

When I'd finished he asked, "So you were shuttling workers from an oil rig when you found the body?"

"That's right."

"Was there anybody on your aircraft that day that might be acquainted with Leon Yost?"

"You're a very perceptive man, Professor Haas," I said. "He has a younger brother, Jordan, who was on that flight and has flown with me several other times."

"A brother, huh?" he said, more to himself than to us. "Is that the brother who would help Leon do something to your helicopter?"

"Yes. The sheriff already received a tip that Jordan Yost was overheard talking to someone, presumably Leon, about damaging my aircraft," I said.

"So you already knew you were in danger?" he asked.

"Well, I knew I was a target because of the oil rig controversy, but what you told us sheds a whole new light on things. You have no idea how much I appreciate it, professor. I'll be doubly careful now."

"You better be," a sober Jarbi said tenderly, touching my arm for a brief moment.

As we approached the professor's office door, he came around his desk and offered his hand to me. We shook, and then he turned to Jarbi and offered his hand to her as well. But he got more than that. She gave him a fierce and emotional hug. When I walked out the door, I saw tears in his eyes. Like me, he had suffered a terrible loss.

Over the next hour, we managed to interview a handful of students. Some liked Leon; some thought he was a terrible teacher. One young man spoke highly of him, and from a few things the student said, I concluded that he might be one of Leon's ardent followers. Two young women—a black girl and a Hispanic girl, both pretty—expressed fear. They said it was the way he looked at them.

"They have reason to fear him," Jarbi said as we walked through the rain to our rental car. "I don't know about you, but I think we need to look much closer at Leon Yost when it comes to Edward Jones's murder."

I couldn't disagree. In fact, Leon had risen to the top of my list of suspects.

* * *

I didn't dare fly my helicopter back to Grand Junction—because of the weather, not Leon Yost's threats. We had missed lunch while we were at the university, and it was after five by the time we wrapped up there. I offered to buy dinner again and broke the news to Jarbi that we would be spending the night in Denver.

She didn't make any more statements about another date when we went to dinner. She did call, and both of us spoke with, Sheriff Statton.

"Anything yet on fingerprints from Trace's truck?" I asked.

"I've tried to call you both several times, but apparently, the storm you had up there caused a disruption in cell phone coverage," Lisette said. "But yes, and Trace is telling the truth about the truck having been driven by Earl. Earl's fingerprints were all over the interior of the truck, including the steering wheel. And we found some outside on the door handle as well as on the hood and tailgate. He did drive that truck at some point, so it's likely he borrowed it. Also, I don't think I told you this yet, but there were no fingerprints on the wrecking bar that was used to force the way into the hangar. Whoever it was probably wore gloves."

"I'm sure that's right," I said.

After we told her about what we'd learned concerning Leon Yost, she agreed that we should visit his ex-wife before we came back. "And when you get here, Major, let me know. I've got the okay to let you keep your helicopter at my place until the matter of your request is acted on."

My next call was to Crystal. She was holding the fort down, but the next morning was a problem. A crew needed to be shuttled to a rig and another shuttled back. It wasn't Devan Rish's crew, but it was one I was regularly hauling. I asked her to let them know I couldn't be back in time, even if the weather cleared. She promised to take care of it.

She called back later saying they'd be transported by ground. It was a long way around, but they would do it as long as I promised not to let this happen very often. She said that the man wanted me to know that they counted on me as other pilots didn't like to fly men to the rigs.

The weather was beautiful the following morning, and we headed for Grand Junction around eight. Jarbi called Misty and made arrangements to meet her. Misty said she would be available at noon if we could meet her for lunch somewhere. She named a restaurant close to where she worked, and it was set.

As soon as I saw Misty, I could tell from her slightly disfigured face that Leon Yost had done a lot of damage to her. It angered me that he had gotten away with it. Despite the disfigurements, she was still an attractive woman with an engaging smile. She introduced herself, and then Jarbi introduced the two of us. "Do I know you?" Misty asked, looking closely at Jarbi.

Jarbi also had that look of recognition on her face. "Are you from Moab?" she asked.

"Yes, I went to high school there through my junior year; then we moved to Denver. "You were one of the most popular girls at school," Misty went on, her face brightening. "I must have been a sophomore when you were a senior. You were the homecoming queen that year, weren't you?"

"Yes, and I remember seeing you around. Is that when you met Junior?" Jarbi asked.

"No, he was already out of school by then," she said. "I actually met him in Denver, at the university. We hit it off, and even though he was a senior and I was a freshman, we dated on and off for a couple of years, while he was in graduate school. We married when I was twenty-two." She brushed at her short, brown hair with slender fingers and then added, "What a mistake that was. How about you? Did you marry someone from Moab?"

Jarbi grinned and showed Misty her ring finger. "I've never found the right guy. I hope I do before I'm too old for anyone to even look at me."

"Oh, you don't need to worry about that," Misty said. "You're gorgeous." She looked at me. "Don't you think so, Mr. Daniels?"

"Certainly, but why don't you call me Corbin?"

Jarbi grinned at me as we followed the hostess through the restaurant to a table near the back where we could have some privacy. "Call him Major," she said to Misty. "That's what most people call him."

"Major?" Misty asked, giving me a questioning look as the hostess asked us if that table would be okay. Misty said, "Yes, thank you." Jarbi and I sat side by side, and Misty sat across from us. "Were you in the military?" Misty asked. I noted her eyes lingering on my scar for a moment.

Jarbi answered for me. "He was a Black Hawk pilot."

"Oh, do you miss it?" Misty asked.

"No, I fly a Jet Ranger now, so I don't have to worry about surface-to-air missiles and such things," I said.

"Oh, my dad's cousin flies a Jet Ranger," she said brightly. "Do you know Earl Bassinger?" She didn't miss the look that passed between Jarbi and me. "I take it you do," she said, "and that it's not good."

Jarbi spoke right up. "We are here to ask you about Junior, but since you know Earl, we might have a question or two about him as well."

Misty shifted in her seat and seemed relieved when a waitress approached just then. She gave us glasses of water and menus and then left. Misty didn't say another word about Earl, although I knew it would come up again before we were through talking to her. If Jarbi didn't bring him up, I certainly would.

Misty seemed very uncomfortable, and one hand touched her nose self-consciously. It would have been a cute nose if it wasn't slightly off-kilter. I remembered Professor Haas telling us that it was a broken nose and other injures that had finally convinced Misty to leave Junior. It must have been broken badly to still be visible.

Misty finally shrugged, as if to shed herself of her discomfort, and asked, "Has Junior finally done something to someone who isn't afraid to press charges?"

"We don't know, Misty," Jarbi said softly. "We suspect him of something though. We're just trying to learn all we can about him right now. Professor Haas thought you might be able to fill in some of the gaps he couldn't."

"I guess I can, though I haven't seen Leon since our divorce, and that was almost two years ago," she said. "What's he done?"

"We don't know that he has done anything," I said.

"Actually, he has done something," Jarbi said. As I looked over at her, her face was filled with sudden anger. "He threatened to do something to Major Daniel's helicopter. Several men have heard the threat."

Misty gasped then quickly covered her mouth with her hand. "Oh no," she said. "He hates anybody that was in the military. I'm sorry.

Junior is a violent and dangerous guy—as you can see." She pointed at her damaged face.

"I'm sorry he hurt you," I said. "Rest assured I'll be taking steps to prevent him or his brother from damaging my Jet Ranger."

"So there's something else?" she asked, her eyes wide with worry.

"Yes," Jarbi said. "There is something else. It's an unsolved crime we're investigating."

Misty looked from Jarbi to me. "I thought you said you were a private investigator."

"That's right," I confirmed. "I do both that and commercial helicopter flying."

"Then why are you investigating a crime?" she asked.

Jarbi answered for me. "Major Daniels has been hired by a private citizen to look into the death of a man from Moab. Sheriff Statton and her department, of which I am a part, are looking into the same death."

Misty rubbed her crooked nose again. "So the death is a murder, and Junior Yost is a suspect."

"A person of interest," Jarbi quickly clarified.

"I hear that term all the time now," Misty said. "So how is that different from a suspect? Or is it just the politically correct way to say the same thing?"

"Let's put it this way," Jarbi said. "A man was thrown from an aircraft and killed. That's murder. Junior has an airplane. That gives him the means to have committed the murder. And the man who was killed had just gone to work for an oil company as a security officer."

Before Jarbi had finished, Misty said, "And that's motive. He's against the drilling that's being done in that part of Utah. Actually, he's against any drilling, but I would guess that he's particularly incensed by it being done near such a beautiful area. Am I right?"

"That's the way we see it," Jarbi agreed.

Misty was thoughtful for a moment. "The man who was killed. Who was he?"

"His name is Edward Jones."

"Oh my goodness!" she exclaimed. "We lived next door to him when I was growing up. He was a nice man. His family must be devastated."

"How well did you know his family?" I asked, ignoring the devastated bit.

"Very well," she said. "The son, let's see, what's his name?"

"Trace," I said.

"Yeah, Trace and my brother are the same age. They hung around together a lot," she said. "Their daughter was the oldest, probably four or five years older than me. I think her name was Ashley."

"Asher," I corrected.

"Oh yeah, that's right. She was sort of weird," Misty said.

"In what way?" I asked, even though I was pretty sure what she'd say. And I was right. Apparently, Asher had always dressed and worn her makeup and hair to the extreme—at least since she was a teenager.

"But she was nice," Misty added. "Too bad I can't say the same about Trace. He and his dad were always fighting. Mr. Jones was a deputy, but I guess you guys knew that. Anyway, Trace was always doing something that was right on the edge of getting himself arrested. My brother was always right there with him too. My parents used to tell Wyatt to quit hanging out with Trace, but he wouldn't. Anyway, the two of them caused a lot of trouble."

"I don't know your brother, but it sounds about like Trace," I said.

"What are Trace and Asher doing now?" Misty asked.

"Asher is married. Her husband works on one of the oil rigs. In fact, he's one of the men I haul in my helicopter. He seems like an okay guy," I answered.

"And Trace?" she pressed.

I looked at Jarbi, and she shook her head before saying, "Trace is in the hospital right here in Grand Junction."

"What happened to him?" she asked.

Jarbi looked at me and said, "You tell her, Major."

Misty didn't interrupt one time as I told her. When I got to the part about Johanna being dead, she got big tears in her eyes.

When I finished the story, she said, "I heard somebody talking about the plane wreck at work, but I didn't realize it was Trace Jones that was flying it. So he and my ex-husband have something in common. They both fly planes."

"And they both are opposed to the oil drilling," Jarbi added.

"Does that mean Trace is also a person of interest, as you guys say?" Misty asked.

"That's right." Jarbi nodded. "Now, would you tell us more about Junior?"

"Like what?" Misty asked.

"Anything you can think of that might help us solve this murder," Jarbi told her.

"I'm still not sure what happened to Mr. Jones," Misty said.

"He was pushed from a plane a few miles out of Moab. One of the guys I was hauling that day spotted his body below us. I landed, but of course Mr. Jones was dead. One of the other oil workers on the helicopter that day was Jordan Yost."

"He was always a nerdy sort of kid," she said. "I can't believe Junior has poisoned him with extreme views and hatred."

"Tell us more about Jordan and Junior," I said.

For the next few minutes we talked, but we didn't learn a lot more than we already knew. Finally, I said, "Now, Misty, if you don't mind. Tell us what you remember about Earl Bassinger."

She got kind of pale. "Do I have to?" she asked.

Chapter Twelve

Detective Patterson and I insisted that Misty tell us about Earl Bassinger. Misty rubbed at her crooked nose again. I couldn't help thinking that people wouldn't notice it so much if she wouldn't do that. I tried not to draw attention to my scar, but like her nose, people saw it anyway. But her thing with her nose was clearly a sign of nervousness. We waited for her nerves to calm so she could tell us about her father's cousin.

She finally shrugged, looking very unhappy, and said, "I hate to say anything bad about my relatives."

"Does that include your brother?" I asked.

She nodded, her eyes getting a little teary. She squared her shoulders, touched her nose briefly, and then folded her hands in her lap. "I guess you want to hear about both of them?"

Jarbi and I both nodded. Jarbi said, "Tell us about Earl Bassinger first."

Misty took a deep breath, then she said, "He and my dad are cousins, but they're not at all alike. My dad is a great guy. He's honest, he's fun-loving, he has a great sense of humor, and he cares about other people more than he cares about himself. He's very unselfish."

I guessed at that point that we were about to hear that Earl was the opposite of her father. That's exactly what she told us. "Earl is selfish, self-centered, and has absolutely no sense of humor. I don't think he necessarily does anything illegal, but he sure doesn't care about hurting people if he thinks it's in his own personal best interest."

It was discouraging to think that this was the guy who was fighting me over the use of my helicopter. Jarbi shook her head as our eyes met.

Then she said, "That pretty much describes him, all right. He's not a very nice man."

"Yeah, well, he and his family don't have much to do with our family. I only know about his helicopter because of a family reunion I attended a couple of years ago," she said. "Earl was telling everyone who would listen that he's the best helicopter pilot in the state of Utah. Fortunately, no one asked him if he was ranked high in any other states." She grinned slyly when she said that.

"I've ridden with both Earl and Corbin," Jarbi piped in. "I'd ride with Corbin over Earl any day."

Misty smiled. She had a pretty smile, almost perfect teeth. I suspected that it had required a lot of expensive dental work. I remembered that Professor Haas had specifically mentioned that Misty had sustained damage to her teeth from her husband's brutality. Maybe someday, she could get her nose fixed too, I thought. Then I realized that was not a nice thing to think, and I mentally scolded myself. She was pretty despite her nose and scars.

After a moment of silence, I asked, "But tell me, Misty, is it your opinion he could be a dangerous man?"

"I don't know him that well," she acknowledged, "but I do know that my dad claims Earl could never have come by his helicopter honestly. He didn't have enough money. Dad says Earl cheated a brother and two sisters out of an inheritance and that that's how he was able to afford the helicopter. None of them were at the reunion. He's not an honest man, in my opinion, and I know he isn't somebody I would like to spend time around."

She couldn't tell us more about Earl, but what she had said was interesting. Honesty was clearly not his strongest trait.

Next we encouraged Misty to tell us about her brother. Again, she was reluctant but finally said, "He spent a couple of years in prison here in Colorado."

"For what?" Jarbi asked, almost able to hide her surprise.

"He was convicted of burglary, but if what he told my dad is true, he didn't do it," she said. "I think he did. Dad did some checking and found out that he had a long criminal record. This wasn't his first burglary. He'd been on probation for felonies twice before that. I'm surprised he didn't spend more time in prison."

"Where is he now?" I asked.

"I have no idea," she said. "My folks live in Montana now, and I talk to Mom at least once a week. They haven't heard from him for a long time."

"I don't suppose you have any idea how your brother . . . what did you say his name is?" I asked.

"My maiden name is Mortell. I've thought about getting my name changed back to that, but I haven't gotten around to it," Misty said. "Anyway, his name is Wyatt Mortell."

"Do you have any idea how Wyatt feels about the oil rigs or the environment in general?" I asked.

She shook her head. "I have no idea. Frankly, I doubt if he cares about much of anything anymore. I'm sure he doesn't care about me or my parents." She brushed at an errant tear and looked down at her hands where they rested on her lap.

"When was the last time you saw him?" I asked.

"It was before he went to prison," she said. "He came to see me and Junior one day. It wasn't long after we were married."

"So did he still consider you family back then?" Jarbi asked.

"I don't think so. I think he came to see Junior," she answered glumly.

"What did he want to see Junior about?" I asked.

"I don't know. Neither one of them said. They left me sitting in our apartment. When Junior got back, I was already in bed. Wyatt didn't come back with him."

* * *

We left shortly after that. Back in Jarbi's car, I asked, "Do you mind if we go see if we can talk to Trace again?"

"I think we should," she agreed.

Trace was still in the same room. I felt sorry for Trooper Stone. He was on duty again and stood when we approached. "I bet you're glad to see us," I said.

He grinned. "Anything to brighten up my day."

Jarbi flashed him one of her stunning smiles and said with a lilt in her voice, "So are you still here, or are you just back again?"

"Back again," he said. "Just like you two. I assume you want to talk to my prisoner again."

"We do have a few more questions for him," Jarbi said. "But I promise we won't be long. Are you going to get in trouble if you let us in?"

"No, I don't think so. Anyway, I don't really care. Trace Jones is not someone I hold in high esteem," he said with a grin that was aimed at my pretty companion. "Go on in, you guys."

Trace appeared to be sleeping, but as soon as I spoke his name, his eyes opened. He squinted for a moment and then said, "Oh, it's you two again."

"Yes, sorry to be a bother," I said, not feeling sorry at all, "but there are a few things we need to clear up, if you don't mind helping us."

"I'll talk to you," he said. "I screwed up, and because of me my mother is dead. Asher called me. She really got after me." He paused, appearing thoughtful, and then he spoke again. "She was right about a lot of it, but she's wrong about one thing. She thinks I killed Dad, that I murdered him. I didn't."

"You tried to murder me," I reminded him, but I said it with a smile, hoping to keep him talking but at the same time venting some of the frustration I felt toward him.

"I'm glad I missed," he said. "Anyway, it was only your car I wanted to hit. And I guess I did, huh?"

"Yes, you did," I said with a forced grin. "You blew the battery to bits."

"Sorry about that, but like I told you before, that was Mom's thing. She was scared of you for some reason. Scared for me, I guess would be more like it."

I let that go as I turned on my little recorder. I spoke, recording that Detective Patterson and I were in the room with Trace and then asked him again if he was willing to talk with us. He said, "I already told you I would. So what do you want to know now?"

Jarbi stood on one side of his bed while I was on the other. Trace was flat on his back. I looked over at Jarbi, and she nodded, indicating for me to proceed. I looked back down at Trace. "Detective Patterson and I just came from visiting with Misty Yost."

There was a tic in one eye, indicating that he knew who I was speaking about. But I wanted to hear him say it. "You used to be her neighbor. She was Misty Mortell back then. I'm sure you remember her."

"She was a cute girl," he said. "I can't believe that idiot Junior messed up her face like he did. Why would a guy do something like that?"

"Yeah, that's really sad, but she's not looking too bad," I said. "Anyway, she said that you and her brother Wyatt were good buddies."

"Yeah, we were. Wyatt was a good guy," he said.

I looked across the bed at Jarbi. She was frowning. Apparently, she had also noticed that Trace's definition of a good guy was obviously not the same as most people's. I continued, "So, Trace, when was the last time you saw Wyatt?"

He looked me straight in the eye. "About an hour ago."

I don't think I hid my surprise very well. "He was here, in this room, visiting you?"

"Yep, he sure was. He feels real bad about what's happened," Trace said.

"To you?" I asked.

"Yeah, and to my dad and mom," he responded.

"What did you talk about?" I asked.

"He wanted to know if I knew who killed my dad," he said.

"Do you?" I asked.

"Nope, all I know is that it wasn't me—or my mother."

"When was the last time you saw Wyatt before today?" Jarbi asked.

Trace moved his eyes to her. He stared at her for a minute, but I think he was just trying to remember. "I guess three or four years," he said. "It was a while before he went to prison."

"So he asked if you knew who killed your father," I began, "and you told him you didn't. What did he say after that?"

"He asked me if the cops knew who did it," Trace said. "I told him the sheriff thinks I did."

"What was his response to that?" Jarbi asked.

"He laughed and told me that was hilarious."

"Did you laugh too?" I asked.

Trace's face grew hard. "No, I don't think it's funny, and I told him so. I asked him who he thought did it. He said he didn't know and didn't care."

"Do you believe him?" I asked.

"Did I believe if he cared?" Trace asked, looking puzzled.

"No, did you believe that he didn't know?" I clarified.

Trace's shoulders moved a little. I think he was trying to shrug. At any rate, he said, "I don't know. I'm not sure why he even came here asking. He must care some or he wouldn't have looked me up."

Trace had just said what I was thinking, so I didn't ask him more about that. "Did he say where he's living now?" I asked instead.

"Somewhere around Denver," Trace said. "But I don't have an address. I couldn't have remembered it if he'd told me. And I don't care anyway."

I could see another trip to Denver in my near future. Wyatt's trip to the pen was recent enough that I was sure he'd still be on parole. I would find him if I needed to, and I was pretty sure I'd need to. "Did he mention Junior Yost when he was here?" I asked next.

"Yeah, he did. He said he'd been to see Junior."

"When?" I asked.

"I think it was recently. Maybe yesterday or the day before."

"Did he tell you why he went to see Junior?"

Trace did what passed for a head shake. Then he said, "Is there anything else? I'm really tired."

"Yes, there is one more thing," Jarbi said. "Do you think Wyatt could have killed your father?"

The only answer we got was one we'd heard several times before. "I didn't do it," Trace said and closed his eyes.

I had a feeling that he did suspect Wyatt or at least that Wyatt was somehow involved. I looked at Jarbi, and she nodded. It looked like we agreed that we had gotten all we were going to from him, so we left.

As Jarbi and I walked toward the elevators, we had a short discussion about what Trace had told us about Wyatt. I asked, "Why is Wyatt asking the kinds of questions he is if he's not involved?"

Jarbi answered, "I don't know, but I think we need to find out."

"I'm going back to Denver," I announced. "I intend to find Wyatt Mortell and have a talk with him."

Jarbi wanted to go with me, but her boss had different ideas. Over a short phone call as we were leaving the hospital, Jarbi and Lisette discussed the idea. After the call was over, Jarbi said, "Lisette wants me to head for Moab. She says she wants me and Ev to talk to some of the people involved in the protests. Even though she feels like we have some pretty serious persons of interest, she doesn't want to ignore other possibilities."

"I agree," I told Jarbi. It was too early in the investigation and too little evidence to eliminate anyone from our growing roster of suspects, which now included Wyatt Mortell.

* * *

I was in the air and on my way to Denver an hour later when the sheriff called me on my cell phone.

"I'm sorry I pulled Jarbi away from you," she began. "But I feel like we need to spend some time with the protestors. They're getting more vocal all the time, and I want to see if we can determine if any of them are upset enough to resort to violence."

"I agree with you, Lisette," I told her. "But I very much want to have a chat with Wyatt Mortell."

"You're on the right track there, Major," she told me. "I'm getting a lot of pressure to find the killer and get him behind bars. The press, some of the public, even several members of the county council have been calling me. They all expect results sooner rather than later."

"I'm sorry about the pressure," I told her. "I'll help as much as I can."

"I know you will," she said. "You've already done a lot, and I appreciate it. You're great."

I don't know how great I was, but I had a personal stake in this investigation. At least, I assumed that I did. I couldn't imagine that the death of Edward Jones and the threats against me and my Jet Ranger were not closely related, that the same people with the same motives were involved. I couldn't rest—even if my client were to fire me—until I had some definitive answers and had extracted both myself and my helicopter from danger. "I'll let you know what I find out," I promised. "By the way, with all the fuss Earl Bassinger is making, are the county officials upset with me assisting in this investigation?"

"It's really none of their business," she said matter-of-factly. "I am the elected sheriff, and this is my job not theirs. I can use who I want in any way I want to get it done. That said, as far as I know, they haven't got wind of the fact that you're working on the case. And if they do, I'll let them know you're working for a client and I can't control what you do in that regard."

"Thank you," I told her. "I'll see you back in Moab. With a little luck I'll be there late this afternoon."

I was ready to finish the call when Lisette said, completely out of the blue, "Have you enjoyed working with Jarbi?"

"Yes," I said. "She's a sweet person. And you're right about her being smart."

"She's pretty too, and she likes you a lot," Lisette said. There was something in her voice that gave me the feeling she wasn't happy about that. Maybe she didn't want her people forming close ties with me after all.

"I hope that isn't a problem," I said. "I'm not looking for a relationship with her, if that's what you're thinking."

"Sometimes things just happen, you know," she said. "We can't always control who we're attracted to or the feelings we develop toward others."

I puzzled over her comment for a moment, and then I said, "I suppose that's a good thing in most cases."

She didn't answer directly. Instead, she said, "Well, I'm glad you enjoy her company."

That something in her voice was getting stronger. I stepped out on a limb and said, "I do find her fun to work with, but frankly, I enjoy working with you even more."

I must have said the right thing because the tone of her voice changed. "Thank you, Major. And by the way, if you get back in time tonight, I was wondering if you'd like to come to dinner later. I mean, you know, since we'll probably be neighbors and all. And, ah, maybe your associate would like to come as well. I'd like to get to know her."

I thought for a moment about the meals I'd shared with Jarbi and the date we had to the movies. I'd enjoyed the time we were together, but the prospect of spending some nonworking time with Grand

County's attractive sheriff was very appealing—even if my cousin was also there. "I'd like that," I responded. "I'll let you know when I have a better idea of when I'll be landing at the airport."

"You can put your helicopter behind my house," she reminded me.

"My truck is at Canyonlands Field, so I'll need to leave my chopper there for now. But I would like to move it to your place later."

"Just come here, park it—or whatever it is you do with helicopters," she said with a chuckle. "I'll take you back to the airport to get your truck. I'd like to talk this case over with you some more, and that would give us a few minutes alone to do that."

After the phone call was over, I examined my feelings. I was attracted to both Jarbi and Lisette, but I especially liked Lisette. But I was not looking for another relationship, I kept reminding myself. I had been in love and lost someone irreplaceable. And yet, here I was with two pretty women who both appeared to enjoy my company. I felt both a touch of excitement and a little discomfort at the same time. It was confusing. It wasn't something I was looking for when I came to Moab. I decided I should think of something besides those two women, so I thought about the murder of Edward Jones and the threats that had been made against my Jet Ranger, which were synonymous with threats against me personally.

That got my mind off the sheriff and her detective and stirred up renewed feelings of anger. I made a couple of phone calls from the air as I got close to Denver. By the time I was ready to land, I had an appointment with Wyatt's parole officer in Denver. He picked me up at the airport and took me straight to Wyatt Mortell's apartment. I was disappointed that the man wasn't at home. We then went by his place of employment even though he wasn't due there for another couple of hours. We were told by his supervisor that Wyatt had called in sick a couple hours earlier, and he wouldn't be to work that afternoon. Wyatt apparently told them he hoped he'd be better by the next day but that as rotten as he was feeling, he wasn't sure he'd be able to work then either.

I was even more disappointed because I had really wanted to sit down and have a frank discussion with the guy. Wyatt's parole officer was angry. We went back to Wyatt's apartment and knocked on the door again—very hard and very loud. When there was still no answer, the parole officer found the apartment manager and ordered him to unlock the apartment. At first the man refused, but the parole officer was able to convince him that it would be done one way or another.

The apartment was empty. And I don't mean empty in the sense that Wyatt simply wasn't at home. I mean empty in the sense that the place was cleaned out. Wyatt Mortell had moved out without advising the manager, but worse yet, without notifying his parole officer. That was a serious violation of his parole. The last thing the angry parole officer said to me when he let me off at the airport was that he'd have a warrant issued for Wyatt that very day and if and when Wyatt turned up, I would get a call.

I got back to Moab in the early afternoon. I was unhappy that I hadn't found Wyatt, but I was also looking forward to seeing the sheriff again, possibly too much. I needed to be cautious. My future did not include any kind of serious relationship with a woman. I had been hurt too badly before. I was done with that.

Chapter Thirteen

WHEN I CALLED, LISETTE TOLD me she was in her office but that she'd drive out to her house and meet me there. We set a time, and then I flew into Canyonlands Field and fueled my Jet Ranger. I liked to keep it full since I never knew when I might need it on short notice. A few minutes later, I set my helicopter down in a fenced area not more than a hundred feet from the sheriff's house.

She met me as I climbed out. She looked really good, and I got the impression that she was glad to see me. Her eyes were shining, and her face was glowing. I realized I could get to like this sheriff a lot. I tried to stuff those feelings someplace dark where they wouldn't get me in trouble.

We headed straight for the airport, discussing the case as she drove. We were about halfway to the airport when the dispatcher's voice called for Sheriff Statton over the radio. The dispatcher told Lisette she'd be receiving a phone call from a Colorado state trooper on her cell phone momentarily.

"It must be about Trace Jones," she said. "I hope he hasn't done something else stupid. Even if it turns out that he didn't kill his dad, he's in a lot of trouble. I would think he wouldn't want any more."

"I don't think he could have done much since I talked to him a few hours ago," I said. "He's pretty banged and busted up. He could hardly move his head this morning. The only part of him that is functional is his mouth."

Lisette's phone rang, and she let it sync to her car's sound system. I heard the trooper's voice as he spoke. "Sheriff, this is Trooper Gunner Balda."

"Good afternoon, Trooper Balda," Lisette said. "I suppose this is about Trace Jones."

"No, actually, it's a different matter," he said. "I'm sitting about a mile east of the Utah border on Interstate 70. One of your vehicles is parked just off the shoulder of the westbound traffic lanes. It's light blue, unmarked, and no one's in it. I just wanted to check and make sure you knew about it."

I was watching Lisette's face as the message was delivered. All the color drained from it. I had a feeling that the same was happening to mine. Jarbi Patterson's unmarked patrol car was light blue. It should not be abandoned anywhere.

The sheriff's voice was surprisingly strong, despite the shock she was clearly experiencing. "Is it a Chevy?" she asked.

We both knew it was. "Yes," was the trooper's answer. "Would you like the license plate number?"

"Please," she said as she looked at me in dismay.

The trooper read it off and then asked, "What would you like me to do with the car?"

"Can you stay with it until I get there?" Lisette asked as she turned her car around on the narrow highway and headed south again at an extremely accelerated rate. She even activated her siren and turned on the blue-and-red flashing lights.

"If you want me to, I can. How long will it take you to get here?" he asked.

She glanced briefly at me. I nodded at her implied question and answered, "Not much more than an hour if we fly."

"Did you hear that?" Lisette asked. "That was Major Corbin Daniels. He's going to bring me in his helicopter."

"Great, I'll be waiting. Is there anything else you need me to do?"

"I'll get back with you. I need to try to call the officer that was driving that car."

As I feared, Jarbi did not answer her cell phone or her handheld radio. Lisette called the trooper back. "I can't raise my officer. Will you put an attempt out to locate her?"

He agreed, and Lisette gave him Jarbi's full name and a detailed description. When she finished, she said, "Trooper Balda, Detective

Patterson is working on a homicide case. There have been some threats in relation to the case. Her leaving her car like that makes no sense at all. Needless to say, I'm very worried."

After they disconnected, Lisette called her office and told them to have an officer meet her at her house with the spare set of keys to Jarbi's car just in case. She asked if Jarbi had called in. She hadn't. The sheriff instructed her secretary to keep their conversation to herself for now. Then she used the radio and called Chief Deputy Evan Belgar. "Where are you?" she asked.

"I just stopped to get gas," he said. "Then I was going to—"

"Meet me at my house," she ordered, cutting him off midsentence. "We have a change of plans. I'll explain when I see you."

I was worried sick, and I could tell that Lisette was too, but she was very much in control as well. Lisette kept off of the radio after that for the sake of security—too many people listened to the police frequency on scanners, and she didn't want to start any rumors. Instead, she used the cell phone to give orders to her department. "I wish I hadn't talked to Ev on the radio," she told me between calls. "I don't know what I was thinking."

"You were very careful with what you said to him," I assured her. "There was nothing to cause alarm or make anyone think anything out of the ordinary was going on."

She nodded an acknowledgment. "Did you tell Crystal about dinner tonight?" she asked as we approached her house.

"Not yet," I said.

"Good because it looks like that's not going to happen. Sorry. I'll make it up to you another time."

We turned into her driveway, and we both jumped out. I headed around back to start the helicopter while Lisette met Ev, who was just driving up. Apparently Ev was up-to-date by the time he and the sheriff joined me in the aircraft. Lisette was on her cell phone. She finished the call just as I began to increase power in preparation for taking off. She quickly introduced Ev and me to each other, and everyone took their seats.

Once we were underway and all three of us had our headsets on, Lisette said, "I was talking to Trooper Balda. He's going to see if he can get someone to bring a tracking dog out there. We need to see if Jarbi left her car on foot."

I looked over at her, and she shrugged. "I know that's a long shot, but we need to be sure," she said. "Maybe she broke down and caught a ride with someone."

"She'd have let somebody know," Ev said from the backseat. "I don't think she broke down."

He had just hinted at what all of us feared. But we had to hold out hope that Jarbi hadn't been forcibly taken from the car. Lisette thought aloud, "Why would she have stopped out there? That's pretty desolate country at the state border."

She was trying to be upbeat and positive. I was trying to get to the border as fast as I could. When we arrived, I set the Jet Ranger down in some short brush a safe distance from the freeway, and Lisette and her chief deputy jumped out and ran up to Jarbi's abandoned vehicle, where there were now several state and county patrol cars parked.

I shut my aircraft down and then got out and walked over to join the others. By that time, Lisette had succeeded in ruling out car trouble as the reason for Jarbi's stop. There was nothing wrong with the blue Chevrolet. "Her cell phone is busted," Ev told me as he pointed to where the remains of it were badly smashed on the pavement beside her car. "Someone made sure it was beyond fixing," the chief deputy added, his eyes full of anger.

A few minutes later, as the car was being processed for fingerprints, an officer arrived with a large German shepherd. It didn't take long to determine that Jarbi hadn't stepped more than a few feet off the shoulder of the road. The dog pulled the handler west for a hundred feet or so then stopped. If the dog was right—and his handler assured us that it was—Jarbi had been taken toward Utah.

"They might have continued in that direction," Ev pointed out, "or they might have turned somewhere and headed back to the east."

"Jarbi's been abducted. It's time to get a search going all through Utah and Colorado," Lisette said. "In fact, we better include the surrounding states as well." While she and one of the troopers put that into motion, I wandered around the car, peeking inside without touching anything.

Then I had a thought, and I stepped back by my helicopter and made a call on my cell phone. What I learned made my stomach twist uncomfortably. That call was followed by another. When I had finished the second call, I walked back to Jarbi's car.

"Where is her handheld radio, Sheriff?" I asked when she rejoined me beside the Chevy.

"It's not here," Lisette said with an angry shake of her head. "That means that whoever took Jarbi can listen in on our radio conversations. I don't like that at all. We'll have to be especially careful what we say."

Ev nodded in agreement and then stooped down beside the trashed cell phone. "Sheriff," he said. "Come look at this."

She knelt beside him and studied the shattered pieces of plastic. "This isn't an iPhone," she said.

Trooper Balda joined them as Lisette held out several fragments for him to examine. "It's a Blackberry," he said.

"It must have belonged to whoever took her," Ev suggested. "But that makes no sense. Who would destroy their own Blackberry?"

Nobody attempted to answer, but I could see that Lisette was deep in thought.

"What is it, Sheriff?" her chief deputy finally asked.

"Before the county bought iPhones for everyone in the department, we each had whatever we'd purchased for ourselves. I'm pretty sure Jarbi had a Blackberry. I remember her making a comparison one day between it and her new iPhone."

"Jarbi's a smart girl," Ev said. "I wonder if she somehow fooled them into thinking this was the one she used. Maybe she has her iPhone with her."

"We can only pray that she does and that she'll get a chance to use it," the sheriff said. She called for all of the officers to gather around for a moment. When she had everyone's attention, she said, "We have no idea who abducted Detective Patterson, but someone did. Any leads any of you can get would be appreciated."

I cleared my throat. I was the outsider in this little group. To the Colorado officers, I was just the pilot. They more or less ignored me, but Lisette and Ev didn't. Lisette said, "You have something on your mind, Major?"

I nodded, and she told the group of officers, "Major Corbin Daniels is not just a helicopter pilot. He is also a private investigator, and a very good one, I dare say."

The officers didn't seem to be impressed, but Lisette wasn't deterred. "He's also working for a client on the murder case that you all know about, the murder of a former deputy, Edward Jones. He and I have been sharing what we've learned. In fact, he and Detective Patterson spent the last two days in Denver and Grand Junction. So, Major—" she began.

Trooper Gunner Balda cut her off. "What's the Major about?"

Lisette smiled. "Oh, sorry. Everybody calls him that. He was a major in the military, a Black Hawk pilot, actually."

"I take it you saw action?" the trooper asked me.

"Way too much," I said, and I gave them a brief rundown of my experience. After that, everyone seemed to want to include me. I guess I had some credibility now. So I went on. "I just made a couple of phone calls," I said. "One was to a parole officer in Denver, and one was to a professor at a university there."

"Was the parole officer the one assigned to Wyatt Mortell?" Lisette asked. Then before I answered, she explained to everyone else who Wyatt was.

"I did speak with Mortell's parole officer," I said when she was finished. "He and I were at both Mortell's apartment and work earlier today. Mortell had called in sick to his employer and had moved out of his apartment."

One of the deputies asked why that would be significant to Jarbi's abduction. "He had been at the hospital and talked with Trace Jones just a short while before Detective Patterson and I got there this morning to see Trace. The two men were old buddies," I explained.

They all nodded knowingly; they had made the connection. "So are you saying Mortell could be involved in what happened to Jarbi?" Ev asked.

"He's certainly one I think we need to look for. And there's another guy we need to be looking for as well. He teaches at the university with a Professor Haas. I talked to Haas on the phone a few minutes ago as well. Haas told me that Leon Yost has someone covering his classes today. In fact, for the whole week," I explained. "Yost and Mortell are also old buddies."

It seemed that every officer there understood the significance of what I'd learned.

"Do you have a description of what those men might be driving?" Lisette asked.

My stomach took another painful tumble, and my spine turned to ice. "Yes, but, Sheriff, the first thing we need to do is find out where Junior's plane is."

The color drained from Lisette's face. "They plan to do to her what they did to Edward Jones," she said in a choked voice.

I didn't disagree; neither did Ev. That was a distinct possibility. There was a lot of action for the next few minutes. I gave the officers a description of the cars the two men drove while a state patrol sergeant called the airport where Junior Yost kept his plane. There was no good news out of that call. Both of the men's cars were at the airport, and the plane was gone.

Lisette had regained her composure, and she turned to me. "Let's get in the air, Major. We're going to Denver and then to Grand Junction."

"Grand Junction is closer," I reminded her. "Why don't we go talk to Trace first? Then we can go to Denver."

The state sergeant offered to clear us to land at the hospital. Lisette threw the spare set of keys to Ev and said, "You take Jarbi's car back to Moab. Lock it in the impound yard. Then call me, and I'll let you know what I need you to do next."

He nodded grimly. Then Lisette and I headed for my Jet Ranger.

* * *

Good to his word, the sergeant had cleared us to land at the helicopter pad at the hospital. Soon, we were running down the hallway to Trace Jones's room. There were two officers on duty. They grimly waved us into the room without a word, and one of them followed us in.

Trace looked at me, his eyes wide with surprise. "Why are you here again?" he demanded. "And why is Sheriff Statton with you this time?"

Before I could answer, Lisette said, in a voice that meant business, "We need some information, and we need it now."

I produced my small recorder, and Lisette went through the ritual of making sure his rights weren't violated. He seemed to have no qualms about talking to us.

I began the questioning and got right to the point. "Detective Patterson has been abducted," I said. "We think it was your friends who took her. Where were Junior and Wyatt going to take her?"

I was watching his face very closely for his reaction. He seemed genuinely shocked. "Why would they do that?" he asked in a weak voice.

"Trace," I said, leaning close to his bandaged face. "If you know anything about those two, you better tell us now. If they harm her and you know about it, you will be charged right along with them."

"My mom's death is my fault," he said as tears formed in his eyes. "And shooting at you was my fault. But I swear I don't know anything about what happened to my dad or to Detective Patterson. I swear."

Now Lisette leaned down low. "Trace, please, if you have *any* idea, even any guesses, please tell us. We've got to find her before she gets hurt."

"Sheriff, I know you're a good cop. I know my dad was a jerk. And I know that Detective Jarbi is a good cop too. I swear if I knew anything, anything at all, I'd tell you. You've got to believe me."

"Please, Trace," I said. "We need help."

"She's in love with you, isn't she?" he said out of the blue. "And I don't blame you if you love her. She's a good gal and as pretty as they come. And you've been fair to me. I swear that I don't know what those guys are up to. If I could help you get her back, I would."

I straightened up. "Trace, I'm not in love with Detective Patterson, but she is a very good friend, and I'll move heaven and earth to find her. And if anyone hurts her, they'll have me to answer to."

"And me," Lisette said darkly. She laid a card on the small table by Trace's bed. "If you hear anything at all, you call me."

"I will, Sheriff. I promise."

Back in the hallway a minute later, the officers and I talked. Lisette asked that everything Trace said to anyone, on the phone or in person, be monitored. The two officers agreed readily and promised that until Jarbi was found, there would not only be an officer outside the door but one in the room as well. She thanked them, and we headed up the hallway.

"I don't know what else to do," Lisette said as we walked toward the elevators. "So help me, if anything happens to that girl . . ." Her voice trailed off, but I could feel her pain. I felt my own. I wasn't in love with Jarbi, but I was very fond of her. We had developed a strong bond in the short time we'd spent together.

"Let's get up to Denver," I said. "I think I know what we'll find, but at least then we'll know more about what we're up against."

Chapter Fourteen

LISETTE AND I HAD JUST walked onto the helicopter pad when my cell phone began to ring. It was Crystal. "Corbin, where are you?" she asked. "I've had people calling."

"I'm sorry, Crystal, but I'm in Colorado again."

"I didn't know you'd ever come home," she said.

"I need to start my chopper. I'm going to hand my phone to Sheriff Statton, and she can fill you in on what's happening," I said. "But before I do, you need to know that you and I are both in danger. Keep that little gun with you at all times. And use it if you have to." Then, before she could reply, I handed the phone to Lisette.

I was ready to take off by the time Lisette had joined me in the helicopter. She handed my cell phone back to me. We were airborne with our headsets on before either of us spoke. I said, "I'm sorry I dumped that on you. But we don't have time to waste."

"That's okay, Major," she said. "You certainly did frighten her."

"I meant to. Crystal is great, but she doesn't always take dangerous situations as seriously as I'd like her to," I said.

"She's taking this seriously," Lisette said. "She promised to lock her doors and keep her gun with her even in the shower."

I looked over at the sheriff. "She actually said that?"

"She sure did, and she also said that she'd take care of the hearing tomorrow on your request to keep your helicopter at the rental property," Lisette said. "And when she tells the councilmen what's going on, I'm sure they'll grant your request."

"Will Earl be there?" I asked.

"He's the one who demanded the hearing, so I'm sure he will. But that cousin of yours will pin his ears back or I miss my guess."

"Lisette, speaking of Earl, I can't help but think he's somehow involved in this whole mess."

She looked at me with wide eyes. "Do you really think so?"

"I do," I said and left it at that. I had a lot more thinking to do about Earl Bassinger before I said more.

We flew right to the hangar where Junior Yost kept his plane and talked to everyone we could find in the area. Most of the people knew Junior and his plane, but that was about it. One after the other, they told us that they knew he'd taken it out and was flying somewhere. They knew his car was parked there, but they hadn't actually seen his plane take off. But then finally we hit pay dirt. We found a witness who saw Junior, another man who fit the general description of Wyatt Mortell, and a woman get in the plane just before it taxied onto the runway.

The woman had been wearing baggy clothes and a baseball cap pulled down over her eyes. She'd never gotten so much as an inch away from the man we were pretty sure was Wyatt Mortell. Sick at heart, we put the word out, and every airport in Colorado and the surrounding states were alerted to be on the lookout for the plane and its three occupants. Law enforcement was alerted as well. Everything that could be done had been done before Lisette and I headed once more for Moab.

It was late in the evening when we got back. I dropped Lisette off at her house and told her I'd leave the Jet Ranger at the airport for now since she had so much to worry about. She didn't argue. So I flew back to Canyonlands Field and filled the chopper with fuel, something I was doing a lot of the past few days. I couldn't wait to get the bill on that! I took the time to put my helicopter in the hangar, one with a new lock on the door, and then I drove my truck home. But I was only at my apartment long enough to pick up a surveillance camera, checking to make sure the battery was good. I drove all the way back to the airport, positioned the camera so it covered my helicopter, and then drove home. If anyone stepped close to my Jet Ranger, an alarm would go off beside my bed, and I'd be able to look at my monitor and determine what was happening. For now, that was the best I could do. At midnight, I went to bed.

At two o'clock my phone roused me from a deep sleep. I answered it, my heart hammering in my chest. Nobody calls at two in the morning to just chat or even to deliver good news. "Hello. Hello. Is anybody there?" All I could hear was what sounded like whimpering.

Finally I heard a weak, muffled voice say, "Major, it's Jarbi." There was a long pause, then, "Junior and Wyatt kidnapped me." Then it was silent again, and all I could hear was someone breathing and a few more whimpers. Finally, Jarbi spoke again, her voice so soft I had to strain to make out what she was saying. "I don't know where I am, but I have my cell phone." Another break. "They don't know I have it. Can you find me by its GPS signal if I keep it on but have it on silent mode?"

"I'll do my best," I promised.

Heavy breathing was again all I heard for a moment, and then she said, "Gotta go. I hear them coming." Then there was nothing.

I sprang into action. I wasn't sure why she'd called me instead of Lisette, but I rectified that by calling the sheriff myself. The phone rang and rang, and when she finally answered, her voice was slurred with sleep. "Sorry to wake you," I said. "It's Corbin."

"What . . . what's going on? I think I barely fell asleep. Are you okay?" she asked.

I cut right to the chase. "Jarbi called me. She wants us to track her by her cell phone GPS."

"Jarbi? She called you?" she asked. I could hear her coming fully awake as she spoke. "I wonder why she called you instead of me." She was silent for a moment, and then she said, "I guess she tried. I have a missed call from her phone. I must have been so sound asleep that I didn't hear it."

"It took a bit for me to wake you," I agreed.

"I'm glad you did," she said, sounding very much awake now. "Meet me at my office."

Then she was off the phone. I scrambled into my clothes and beat Lisette to her office by about three minutes. I waited for her by my truck, working on my phone, activating the app that I was praying would lead us to Jarbi. As soon as the sheriff arrived, we rushed inside together.

Just as Lisette was saying, "I'll call AT&T right now," my phone found Jarbi's.

"I already have her located," I said. She looked stunned. I held the phone out and showed her. "She's quite a few miles from here in a rural area in the southern part of Wyoming. Let's head to the airport."

"I wish your chopper was here," she said, working her phone for a moment. Then she said, "Ev, get dressed. I'll pick you up in a couple of minutes. We know where Jarbi is."

As soon as Ev climbed in the backseat of Lisette's car, we headed toward the airport at breakneck speed. Ev got on his phone, and with Lisette shouting instructions, he made several calls. One was to the FBI, another to the local sheriff of the Wyoming county where we believed Jarbi was being held. And another was to AT&T. In case my phone lost the signal, we wanted others to be honing in on Jarbi's location as well.

During our swift flight north, we did, from time to time, lose cell phone signal. But I had our destination set on my helicopter GPS, so we didn't worry about not being sure where we were going. Lisette and Ev made arrangements to meet FBI agents and local cops at a large parking lot just a few miles from where the GPS told us Jarbi was being held.

By the time I put my chopper down, dawn was breaking. It looked like a small army had assembled in the parking lot. There was a SWAT team as well as a couple dozen other officers. The FBI had already taken charge since the kidnapping involved the crossing of state lines, and they already had a plan drawn up. The location had been pinpointed to a lonely farmhouse, away from any other buildings but with a dirt road leading past it. We agreed that it was likely the plane had landed on that road. Maps had been distributed, and we were almost ready to move out when my cell phone rang. "It could be her," I said and then I answered.

The voice was muffled, but it wasn't Jarbi. "Major Daniels," the caller began. "I have your girlfriend. If you don't do exactly what I say, she will die. That's a promise."

"I'm listening," I said as others hovered around.

"Okay, here's the deal," the abductor said. "All four rigs down in the Moab area are to be immediately shut down and disassembled."

"Good grief, man," I said, shocked at the request. "That'll take time."

"It better not take too much because your girl's life is in the balance. We'll kill her if you don't do as you're told. Get those rigs pulled off the sites. And that's not all. You're also to tell the sheriff to close the case on Edward Jones. It was an accident. That's all she needs to say to anyone—he accidentally died—and then close the case. It's simple."

"Let me talk to Jarbi," I said when the caller paused. I picked up on the fact that the caller used *we* instead of *I* a couple of times. That just confirmed what I was already sure was the case. There were at least two abductors. "You're asking for a lot," I continued. "I want to know she's okay before I start trying to meet your demands."

"She's okay," the muffled voice said.

"I need to hear her tell me that," I insisted.

"You're just going to have to take my word on it. So get to work." The call was terminated.

"I suppose you have all figured it out," I said to the assembled officers as I tried to control my breathing and heartbeat. "That was one of the abductors."

"What are their demands?" Lisette asked.

I told them, and there was a lot of surprise in the group. The lead FBI agent, Special Agent Denzel Warner, said, "That can wait. First we see if we can rescue her. You have your assignments. Let's move out."

Lisette, Ev, and Special Agent Warner piled into my Jet Ranger. I fired it up and lifted off. I made a beeline for the location where a signal was still coming from Jarbi's phone, and I circled around the area. Warner was using binoculars, trying to get a visual on the house and the plane. It was light enough now that he was able to do that. "There are no vehicles near the house," he reported. "And I can't see the plane."

"Junior may have landed on the road, dropped Jarbi and Wyatt off, and then left," Ev suggested.

I knew that was possible, but I was thinking we'd be lucky if that was what had actually happened. I wasn't getting a good feeling about this, but I kept my thoughts to myself. I flew a little closer now. If they heard me and tried to leave on foot, there was really no place except open fields and acres of brush to flee to.

Police vehicles were approaching below us. Warner barked orders into his radio. Within minutes, the house was surrounded. I put my helicopter down a couple hundred yards north of the house, and all four of us got out.

Within minutes, the SWAT team entered the house. No shots were fired. We waited. Then one of the SWAT officers appeared at the door and signaled that all was clear.

My heart sank as I heard Special Agent Warner's radio come to life with a report that the house was deserted. We all went in, but we found only some empty fast-food wrappers and Jarbi's cell phone. The phone was on the kitchen table, and beside it was a handwritten note that read: *Sorry we missed your little party. You know what to do if you want to see Detective Patterson alive.*

"I wonder how long they've been gone," Ev said to no one in particular.

"Who knows," I began. "They might have discovered her phone right after she called me. They could have left then. We were stupid. We should have had someone out here before we flew in."

"I agree. The cell phone thing threw us off. They could be anywhere by now," Special Agent Denzel Warner said. "It looks like we're back to square one. And now we have no cell phone GPS to guide us."

"I wonder who this old farm belongs to," Lisette said. "Maybe we should try to find out, in case there's a connection to either of the kidnappers."

Denzel agreed, and some phone calls were made. The farm, it turned out, was listed for a tax sale, and anyone could have found that information. Another dead end, it seemed. They could be anyplace, and I didn't have a clue where to start to figure it out. It seemed that no one else did either.

After a quick breakfast with Denzel and a couple of his men, the sheriff, Ev, and I flew back to Moab. I only ate because I needed nourishment. I hadn't tasted anything. We made some plans. Meeting part of the abductor's demands would be easy. A press release by the sheriff could easily state that the death of Edward Jones had been determined to be an accident and that the case was closed. Of course, that didn't mean the case really would be closed; it wouldn't be, though outward signs of an ongoing investigation would be as invisible as the sheriff's department and the FBI could make them.

The other demand was a different matter entirely, but we felt like we had no choice except to attempt to get the rigs shut down. No one expected that the oil company, with all it had invested, would comply. But the FBI, having the most influence, offered to try, but we all feared it wasn't going to happen. All we could do was wait and hope and pray that we would get a miracle and that Jarbi would eventually be released alive.

I dropped Lisette and Ev at Canyonlands Field to pick up her SUV, then I flew down and landed behind her house. They picked me up and drove me back to the office, where my truck was parked. We were all so tired and discouraged that it was hard to function. We did manage to write a press release, and Ev faxed it to the local paper and radio stations. "It'll get disseminated quickly from those locations," he assured us.

"And we'll start getting phone calls," I said. I could already imagine Asher Grady contacting me and demanding to know what was going on, but I had an answer for her. I would say what had to be said.

Lisette finally said, "We aren't getting anywhere. We all need to go home, get three or four hours of sleep, then come back to work. By then, maybe we'll hear something from Denzel Warner."

I didn't go straight home. Instead, I went to my office. Crystal was working at her desk and looked up with a big smile when I walked in. But her smile faded when she looked at me. "Corbin, you look like you've been run over by a truck. What's happening?"

I told her, and with a forlorn look in her eyes, she said, "How could it get any worse?"

"I don't know," I said. "I just pray it doesn't. Now, give me your good news. You were smiling when I came in."

"It doesn't even seem important now," she said, "but the council approved your request. You can park the Jet Ranger on the property beginning now."

"I don't imagine Earl was too happy," I said.

"I don't know. He didn't show up." She shrugged. "They tried to call him, but he didn't answer any of his phones. They even sent someone by his house, but he wasn't home."

"What about his Jet Ranger?" I asked.

"Apparently, he's gone somewhere in it," she said, and chills passed through me. "Corbin, you need to go home and get some sleep, unless you want to call Nora first and tell her we'll take the house. She was at the hearing, but I told her I'd have you call her to let her know officially."

"You call her, Crystal. Tell her we'll move in as soon as we have time. See if you can get the keys, and tell her I'll swing by to sign the lease after I get some rest."

"Consider it done," Crystal said with a forced smile.

I fell asleep fully clothed. I just plopped down on my bed, and that was the last thing I remembered until my phone woke me up. I looked at the time and saw it was after four in the afternoon. I'd slept for almost three hours.

I answered the phone, bracing myself.

Asher Grady was angry. "How can the case be closed?" she demanded without even identifying herself. Not that she needed to. "My dad's death wasn't an accident. Trace is going to get away with this, and you and the sheriff could care less."

I let her rant for a minute or two, then I broke in. "I don't work for Sheriff Statton," I reminded her. "We have been working in cooperation with each other, but she has decided, for whatever reason, to close the case. That doesn't mean I have to do the same, and unless you tell me that you want me to quit, I'll keep working for you."

I heard her give a big sigh, and then she said, "I'm sorry. I just thought . . . Oh, never mind. I was wrong. Thanks for not giving up. I want you to keep working."

"Then that's what I'll do," I said.

"Have you talked to Trace since the last time I talked to you?" she asked.

"I spoke with him yesterday at the hospital. I'm afraid I'm not making much headway with him."

"He still claims he had nothing to do with Dad's murder?" she asked.

"That's what he says, but he did admit that he was guilty of causing your mother's death and of shooting at me," I told her. "He even seemed to indicate that shooting me was his idea, not hers. At any rate, he seems willing to take whatever punishment he's given."

"Well, that's something, anyway," she said, sounding like herself again. The anger seemed to have dissipated. "I'm sorry I shouted at you, Major. I'm just so upset. First Dad and then Mom. It's awful. I've never felt so miserable." I agreed that it was a terrible thing that had happened to her family, but I finally managed to end the conversation without divulging anything the sheriff wanted kept quiet.

I thought about trying to rest for another hour or so but decided I was okay. So I took a shower instead. In clean clothes and feeling much better, I drove back to my office. Crystal had left me a note saying she was at the new house and if I could, she'd like me to come out there. She had written that she had the lease papers; all I had to do was sign them, and she'd get them back to Nora Briggs.

I decided to go to the house and get the lease signed. I was almost there, just passing the sheriff's house, when my phone rang. It was Lisette. "Are you through sleeping too?" I asked.

"Yes, so I didn't wake you? I'm sorry if I did."

"No, Asher Grady took care of that. I'm just heading to my new house. Crystal got everything worked out. All I have to do is sign the lease. I'm actually passing your place right now."

"Can you stop?" she asked. "There has been a development."

"Of course. I'll be right in." I could tell from the tone of her voice that all was not well.

Chapter Fifteen

SHERIFF STATTON MET ME ON her front porch. "Junior Yost is in custody," she said.

I raised an eyebrow. "Just Junior? Not Wyatt?"

"Yes, I guess the FBI got a call that he'd landed at a small airport to get fuel, and they were able to snag him," she explained. "I'm glad for that, at least."

We stepped off her porch as I asked, "Where is he?"

"In Great Falls, Montana," she said. She stopped walking and looked at me, her face lined with worry and grief.

"I don't suppose he told them where Jarbi is?" I asked.

She shook her head and blinked back tears. She was a strong woman, but I wasn't sure how much more she could take. She turned away, rubbing her eyes as she said, "Junior says he doesn't know anything about her or Wyatt. It was Special Agent Warner that called. He said the FBI has impounded the plane and is getting a search warrant."

"They'll find something, enough to hold Junior on," I told her. "Did Warner say anything about the oil company?"

"Yes," she said. "Why don't I ride with you to your new place so you can sign your lease?"

"Thanks," I said.

As soon as I had the engine started, she said, "Warner talked to several people at the oil company, and they just kept referring him higher up the ladder. He finally talked to the president of the company in Austin, Texas.

"I suppose I can guess at the response he got," I said.

"If you were going to guess that the guy told him the drilling would go on no matter what, then you were right," she said. "I asked him what we could do now. He didn't know what he could do, maybe a court order to stop the drilling, but he admitted that didn't seem likely. He said it would be like giving in to the demands of terrorists, and that's not likely to happen."

"In that case, I guess it all comes down to putting more pressure on Junior Yost," I said.

"Yeah, like what? Waterboard him?" she scoffed.

"No, Lisette, there are other ways." I had just pulled into my new driveway and parked beside Crystal's car. "Come on in," I said, even as I was thinking of the other ways that came to mind. Other ways that, for the most part, the police couldn't use, but I could, and I would if I felt it necessary.

The house was almost fully furnished, upstairs and down—one of the things that had been appealing to both me and my cousin. The furniture wasn't new, and it had taken a hit from the former renters, but it was still good stuff and all that we needed for now. Furthermore, in addition to the stairs inside, there was a separate outside entrance to the basement. Crystal was excited about that.

After I had signed the lease, Crystal announced that, unless I had any objections, as soon as she'd taken it back to Nora, she would move her stuff into the basement. I envied her, but I had other things I needed to do, so I might not get to move in for a while.

Lisette and I talked about Jarbi, wondering what she was going through and how she might be handling it. We were on our way back to Lisette's house. As I parked, the sheriff said, "Jarbi's tough. To look at her, you'd never guess it. She's so pretty, the kind of pretty that isn't usually associated with toughness—except in the movies. But she's made of stern stuff, Major."

We sat in my truck, neither of us making a move to get out yet. "Everyone, I suppose, has a breaking point though."

"Yes, I suppose that's true," she replied. "That's why we've got to find her before she reaches hers. Will you meet Ev and me back at the office in a few minutes?"

"Sure," I said.

"No, wait, I have a better idea," she said. "Ev can come here. I'm sure you're hungry, and I know I am. I'll whip up something quick, and we can eat while we talk. If you don't mind, that is."

"That would be great," I said. We both got out of the truck and walked up to her front door.

"I'll call Ev and tell him to come about six thirty. We should be done by then. Unless he wants to eat with us, but he'd probably rather eat at home first," Lisette said.

There was a knock on the door a few minutes later. It was Crystal. "I saw your truck here," she said. "I thought I'd stop instead of calling you. I just got a call from a prospective client. I tried to put her off, but she insisted she had to see you."

"Do you have her number?" I asked.

"I do," she said, handing me a slip of paper with a number and a name written on it.

Lisette came in from the kitchen. "Hi, Crystal," she said. "I was just going to fix a little something to eat. Would you like to join us?"

"Are you sure?" Crystal asked. "I don't want to put you out."

"Of course I'm sure. Anyway, I had planned to invite you and Corbin over for dinner soon. I've really been looking forward to getting to know you."

"Will you let me help fix it?" Crystal asked.

"If you don't mind, that would be great," Lisette said. She turned to me. "So do you need to make a call to a prospective client?" she asked.

"I guess so," I answered.

Lisette was giving both of us a puzzled look. Then she asked, "Crystal, how did you get a call from someone looking for Major Daniels when you weren't even in your office?"

I answered for her. "The office phone is set to automatically ring to Crystal's cell phone when she's out of the office. She can shut that feature off when she needs to, but it's been very handy, especially since she helps me with some of the investigations we do."

"That's convenient for potential customers, but it can't be much fun for you, Crystal," Lisette said.

"Oh, it's not a problem. I can change it anytime I want when I get ready to leave the office, but I usually don't. I like the work we do, and this gives us—or me, at least—a lot more flexibility. If I get a call I don't want to answer, I ignore it. Corbin's fine with that."

"Where did you find this girl?" Lisette asked, with the first grin I'd seen on her face in a while.

"I guess I just got lucky," I said. "You know how the saying goes— you can choose your friends but not your relatives. Well, in this case, though we were born related, she is also a very good friend."

The two ladies went into the kitchen, and I made my phone call. "Dayna Simonson, please," I said when the phone was answered.

"I'm Mrs. Simonson," the woman on the other end answered.

"My name is Corbin Daniels," I began.

"Oh, Mr. Daniels, thank you so much for calling me back. I need some help, and I think you can give it to me."

"I do private investigating," I told her. "Is that what you're looking for?"

"Oh, yes, sir, it is. Are you in your office now? This is very important," she said.

Anytime a person got desperate enough to call somebody of my profession, their problem was very important, at least to them. I also knew that sometimes that simply wasn't the case. There was only one way for me to find out, and that was to talk with the individual. So I said, "I'm tied up for a while. Can this wait a day or two?"

"Oh, no, please, Mr. Daniels, can I come talk to you now?" she asked, her voice suddenly filled with emotion.

"Hold on a second," I said and put my hand over my phone. I stepped to the kitchen and said, "Lisette, do I have time to meet with this woman before dinner? I could just run up the road to my new place."

"Of course," she said. "We'll be thirty or forty minutes."

"I'll go then, but I'll be back in time for dinner," I promised and headed for the door as I again spoke into my phone. I gave Dayna my address and asked her how soon she could be there.

"Ten minutes," she said.

"Okay, and that will give us twenty minutes to talk," I said, laying out the parameters since I had no intention of missing dinner. I was starved.

I welcomed Mrs. Simonson into the house, and we both sat down. She was a short, heavy woman, and I guessed she was in her midsixties. "I have another appointment in twenty minutes," I reminded her. "So let's get right into it. What are you asking me to do for you?"

"I seem to have gotten myself in a spot of trouble," she began. I said nothing, just nodded and waited for her to explain further. After a few seconds of hesitation, she said, "I know you're new to the area, Mr. Daniels, but you've probably heard about the controversy going on over the oil drilling in the county."

"Yes, I'm very much aware of it. So how are you involved in it?"

"Well, a man asked me to help him distribute some literature. He didn't say what the literature was except that it was supposed to be something informative to the public. I wouldn't have even considered it if I'd had any idea what it was, but I didn't, and the pay he offered was very good. I'm a widow, and I live on a fixed income, part of my husband's retirement and some social security. So I accepted without checking what it was about. He'd said it was something that would help the public."

"I'm assuming it's something to do with the controversy," I said. I wasn't sure this was something I needed to be involved in. I didn't say that, however. I just watched her as she fussed with her frizzy, short gray hair.

"Yes, it is, but I didn't know that until today. He paid me two thousand dollars and gave me two boxes of pamphlets to distribute to businesses in town and the surrounding area. That was on Tuesday afternoon, but I told him I couldn't do it until today. Anyway, when I opened one of the boxes this afternoon, I realized that the pamphlets were very inflammatory and that they did not agree with my own views."

"So what is it you're asking me to do?"

"It's like this. I called the guy today on his cell phone and told him I didn't agree with the literature and could not in good conscience distribute it, that I would bring them back to him and give him back his money," she said. I waited, and I was sure I saw fear cloud her hazel eyes. She finally went on. "He said I had to do it. I told him I didn't want to, but he wouldn't tell me where he was, just that I was obligated now."

"What's his name?" I asked.

"I don't know," she said, coloring in embarrassment. "I'm such an old fool. I have his cell phone number but that's all. That's why I need your help. I want you to see if you can find out who he is and get him to take the money and pamphlets back."

"Did he threaten you?" I said.

"He certainly did. He said it could be harmful to my health if I didn't distribute them the way I had agreed. He also said that another man was going to do it but that the guy had died unexpectedly."

I had about made up my mind to tell her I didn't have time to help her and that she probably couldn't afford my fee anyway. But first I asked if she had one of the pamphlets with her. I was curious and wanted to see exactly how inflammatory they were. She pulled one from her purse and held it out to me.

I took one look at it and felt that far too familiar ice begin to creep through my veins. I knew what I had to do. "I think I can help you, Mrs. Simonson. But there's someone else you need to talk to as well."

"Who's that?" she asked. "I can pay you, but I can't afford to pay two people."

"Don't worry about paying the other person," I said as I looked at my watch. "I'm having dinner with my neighbor, Sheriff Statton. In fact, I probably need to be on my way over there. Why don't you follow me? The sheriff will be very interested in what you have here." I waved the pamphlet. "This thing spells trouble, huge trouble."

* * *

Mrs. Simonson was very nervous when I walked her up the sidewalk to Lisette's door. I knocked, and Lisette answered. "You're just in time," she said then took note of Mrs. Simonson. "Why, Mrs. Simonson," Lisette said. "How nice to see you. Won't you come in?"

"I plan to help this good lady with a little problem," I said. "But her problem will be of interest to you too."

Crystal came out of the kitchen. "We're almost ready, boss. Oh, you have someone with you."

"Yes, this is Dayna Simonson. You talked to her on the phone earlier. Mrs. Simonson, this is my associate, Crystal Burke," I said.

"I don't want your dinner to get cold," Dayna said. "So I won't take long."

"That's okay, Dayna. It isn't quite ready yet anyway," Lisette replied.

I turned to Crystal. "I know you sometimes have copies of our contract in your car. You wouldn't happen to now, would you?"

"As a matter of fact, I do," she said. "I'll get one."

As she headed out the door, Lisette said, "Mrs. Simonson, Crystal and I just mixed up a salad, and I've got a large casserole and some rolls. We have lots, so why don't you join us? Then while we eat, we can talk at our leisure. I know it's important or Corbin wouldn't have brought you here."

"Oh, Sheriff Statton, I don't mean to impose," Dayna said, fussing with her frizzy hair.

"It's not an imposition," Lisette said. "Major, why don't you and Dayna have a seat. I'll go back in the kitchen and set another place."

When Crystal returned, our new client was sitting on Lisette's sofa, clutching her purse like a security blanket. I got the impression she was more frightened than she had at first admitted. I said, "Crystal, Lisette is setting another plate so that Mrs. Simonson can join us. Why don't we take care of this contract now, and then we can all eat and discuss the problem she's facing?"

We went over the details of the contract and discussed my rates. Finally, we both signed, and she pulled a checkbook from her purse.

Just then Lisette came back in. "Anytime you're ready, we can eat."

Once again Mrs. Simonson said, "I really don't mean to be a bother, Sheriff. But Mr. Daniels felt like you should look at one of the pamphlets I was asked to distribute. They're just awful, and I won't do it, even though I had said I would."

I pulled the pamphlet she'd given me from my pocket. "Sheriff," I said. "This is what we need to talk about."

Lisette took it from me; her eyes widened ever so slightly, and she seemed to hold her breath for a moment. Then she said, "Oh my. Isn't this interesting? Yes, I certainly needed to see this. This is most inflammatory indeed." Her eyes caught mine.

"When Mrs. Simonson opened one of the boxes of pamphlets she'd been asked to distribute, she decided she simply couldn't do it.

When she tried to return them and the money she'd been paid, the man demanded that she do what she'd been told to do."

Lisette then asked the same question I had. "Did that person threaten you?"

"Yes," she said with a quiver in her voice.

"We'll fill the sheriff in while we have dinner."

"Very good," Lisette said. "Let's eat."

We moved into the kitchen, and Lisette showed us to our places. "It's nice to have company for dinner," Lisette said. "It can get lonely here."

Crystal and I knew that feeling, but I told myself I was content with it. Crystal, on the other hand, was not. Mrs. Simonson said, "Yes, I know what you mean. My old house is awfully quiet since my husband passed on."

At Lisette's request, I offered a prayer, and then we began to fill our plates.

"Dayna, who hired you to distribute the pamphlets?" Lisette asked.

"I don't know his name, but I can describe him. And I know he was driving a white car. I first talked to him on the phone, and then he came to my house and gave me the boxes. I saw his car from my living room window. I'm not good with makes of cars, so I don't know what kind it was. He never told me his name, he paid me in cash, and the only contact information I have is a cell phone number. That's why I hired Mr. Daniels. He is going to try to find the man so I can give back the money and the pamphlets. I just don't want any trouble."

The casserole was delicious. So was the salad. I could see that the sheriff had other talents outside of her career. For a while we all simply enjoyed our dinner, but finally, Lisette asked, "How long have you had these pamphlets, Dayna?"

"Since Tuesday afternoon," she answered.

"The guy told Dayna that he'd hired someone else to distribute them but that the man had died, so that was why he needed her help," I explained.

Lisette and Crystal both looked at me with concern. Then Lisette asked, "Did he say who the other man was?" she asked.

"No." Mrs. Simonson shook her head.

"Did he say when the other guy died?"

"No. Well, actually, I think he said something about it being recently."

"Did he know how the guy died?"

"Not exactly. He just said there had been an accident."

"I'm assuming you never saw the man before he came to your house. Is that right?" I asked.

"That's right."

"You said you could describe him," Lisette said. "Will you do that now?"

Dayna did, and I couldn't suppress a shiver of concern. I didn't tell my client, but I was almost positive I knew the man the pamphlets had come from. I also knew he would be very hard to locate.

Chapter Sixteen

WE URGED MRS. SIMONSON TO keep her doors locked and to be very watchful when she had to go outside. "Specifically," I said, "if you see him or his car, you call my cell phone."

She agreed.

"If for some reason you can't reach Major Daniels, you can call me," Lisette said, handing the older woman a business card.

"And if you can't reach either of them," Crystal said, "then please call me."

Lisette and I looked at each other. She looked as worried as I was. "Do you have a gun in your house, Mrs. Simonson?" I asked.

"Not anymore. After my husband passed on, I gave his guns to my sons," she said.

"Where do your sons live?" Lisette asked.

"One is in Salt Lake, one is in Las Vegas, and my daughter is in Grand Junction."

"So you have three children in all?" I asked.

"Yes, and they're all married."

"Mrs. Simonson," I said, "while I am working on your case, I think it would be best if you stayed with one of your children."

She looked at me, fear in her eyes. "You're worried, aren't you?"

"Very," I said. "We all are. You see, there are some things happening in our community that have the sheriff and her deputies very concerned."

"Like the death of Edward Jones?" she asked perceptively.

"Yes, like that."

"I could stay at my daughter's house in Grand Junction," she said.

Grand Junction didn't sound like the best place for her. Lisette echoed my thoughts when she said, "Maybe it would be better if you stayed with one of your sons."

Mrs. Simonson lifted one hand to her gray hair and began to brush at it. Her hand was shaking. Her eyes were fixed on the plate of cooling food. The rest of us took a bite of casserole before she spoke again. "Is there a reason I shouldn't go to my daughter's house?" she asked.

I let Lisette handle that question. "In investigating the death of Mr. Jones, we've had to spend some time in Grand Junction. There may be people there who are connected to the man who threatened you."

Dayna shifted her eyes from her plate to look at Lisette. "Then I'll go to Salt Lake. I'll leave tonight. I could stay in a motel in Price if I get tired."

"Let's finish our dinner, and then you can call your son," I suggested.

It appeared that our discussion had not helped Dayna Simonson's appetite. She just sat and stared at her food while the rest of us finished up. Later, after she had gone home to pack and Crystal had gone to her apartment, I helped Lisette clean the kitchen.

I'm not normally a fan of cleaning up after meals, as a view in my apartment would sometimes attest, but as I helped Lisette, I found it quite enjoyable—even despite the heavy worries we each carried. Good company has a way of making boring jobs fun. We didn't discuss our worries or Dayna's case. I enjoyed being with Lisette, and unless I was badly mistaken, she seemed to enjoy being with me.

We had barely finished when Ev rang the doorbell. "I guess we have some things to talk about," he said as he walked in.

"I'm afraid so," Lisette responded; the light mood the two of us had enjoyed the past few minutes faded away. We all sat down in the living room, and then Lisette turned to me. "Major, I noticed your reaction when Dayna described the man who had threatened her."

"Who? What?" Ev asked.

"Sorry, we had a dinner guest," the sheriff said and went on to explain about Mrs. Simonson. "Now, Major, do you know who she was describing?"

"She said he was probably in his late twenties, small with green eyes and long brown hair," I said for Ev's benefit. "Dayna didn't know him, even though I think he lived in Moab several years ago—as a teenager. Does that give either of you an idea?"

They shook their heads. "Is it someone we're already concerned with?"

I didn't mean to be making this into a quiz, I had just hoped that one or both of them could confirm my strong suspicions, but since they were unable to, I said, "I haven't seen the guy myself, but I think it could be Wyatt Mortell. The description matches what his sister, Misty, gave me as well as the picture his parole officer showed me."

I waited while the officers let my conclusion sink in. Finally, Lisette said, "If it is Wyatt and Junior Yost was alone when he was arrested in Montana, then he probably isn't a threat to Mrs. Simonson at the moment. Unless he and Junior already did something to—"

I cut her off sharply. "Let's not think the worst. We've got to be positive about Jarbi. Wyatt is probably with her right now. I intend to go to Montana and spend some time with Junior. But as for any danger to Dayna, I think you're right that Wyatt isn't a direct threat to her right now. But someone working with him could be."

"Not Junior," Ev pointed out. "And not Trace either. Do you have someone specific in mind, or are you just suggesting that it could be someone we haven't thought about yet?"

"Wyatt's father and Earl Bassinger are cousins," I said.

I waited for a reaction. Finally, Ev said, "Earl is a jerk, but I can't imagine him being involved in all of this."

"Could you have imagined Edward Jones being shoved from a plane?" I asked.

"Well, no," he said.

"For that matter, could you have imagined Trace Jones taking a shot at me?"

"No, again."

"Have you ever, in your career, had to arrest people that you honestly didn't think capable of what you arrested them for?" I pressed.

Slowly, he nodded his head. "I get your point, Major."

"Add the blood relationship to the fact that Earl, who was stirring up all kinds of trouble over my helicopter, didn't show for a hearing he requested this morning, and what do we get?" I asked.

"He didn't show?" Ev asked. "Yeah, that is suspicious."

"I suppose we should try to find him," Lisette said. "We could make a few phone calls."

"Lisette," I said, suddenly thinking of something else, "you haven't said anything about getting blood results back on Edward Jones."

"Nothing yet," she confirmed. "I don't know why it takes so long. I'll make a call in the morning to see if I can hurry things up."

I stood up. "I think I'll take a little trip up to Montana," I said. "Our top priority is Jarbi. We have to find her, and we've got to do it soon."

"I take it you think you can get Junior to tell you something," Lisette said. "How do you plan to get him to do that?"

"Let me worry about that," I said.

Her eyes narrowed. "Major, you won't do—" she began.

I cut her off, "We want to get your detective back, right?"

"Of course, why do you—"

I interrupted again. "I may not succeed, but please, I've got to try, and I've got to do it my way."

"Okay," she said. "Good luck. Ev and I will see what we can learn from some of Earl's family and friends."

I could feel tension in the air. It was clear that the sheriff didn't approve of whatever it was she thought I was planning to do to get Junior to talk. I didn't like leaving with those negative feelings. I stopped at the door and turned toward her. "Thanks for dinner. It was really good. And so was your company."

"You're welcome," she said, the slightest blush appearing on her cheeks.

"Maybe when things get back to normal, you would agree to go out to dinner with me," I suggested.

That brought a small smile to her face and deepened the blush. "Actually, Major, I'd like that very much."

* * *

Not long after leaving Lisette's, I was flying my Jet Ranger north. I hadn't had much sleep, but it had been enough. I was wide awake and alert. Now that I was on my way, I couldn't wait to get a chance to extract information from Junior Yost.

I took a break at the airport in Lander, Wyoming. The first thing I did there was use my laptop and iPhone to lay some groundwork for my interview with Junior Yost. What I was doing might not be strictly honest or legal, but it was, in my opinion, necessary if I was to make any headway with Junior. My goal was to save the life of a sweet and wonderful woman, so I couldn't let that worry me.

When I was satisfied, I found a private corner and took a quick nap. When I woke up, I ate some snacks from a vending machine and took off. Around ten, I was met at the Great Falls airport by Special Agent Denzel Warner, who had come to Great Falls for the same purpose I had. I had contacted him, not knowing he'd be there, and his presence was less than ideal. All I could do now was try to convince him that if he would allow me to have a little time alone with Junior, I might be able to get the suspect to talk. He invited me to ride with him.

On our way to the jail where Junior was being held, I asked Denzel if a search of Junior's airplane had been conducted yet. He said, "Yes. We found a long, dark hair that we're having tested for DNA. They found a similar one in Detective Patterson's patrol car and are running a test on it. If they match, we'll have proof that Jarbi was in that plane. When we get that, I'll have another go at Mr. Yost."

"Would you mind if I talk to him alone?" I asked.

I got the same kind of look from Warner as I'd received from the sheriff. He said, "Are you sure you don't want me there too?"

"It might work best one-on-one," I said stubbornly. "I won't break any laws, if that's what you're worried about." I said nothing about ones I might already have fudged the line on.

He slowly nodded. "I know your background."

"I figured you did," I told him.

"You have a spotless record."

"And I intend to keep it that way."

We rode in silence for a few minutes. Then I told him about Mrs. Simonson and my suspicions regarding Wyatt and Earl Bassinger.

"Do you know if Bassinger has returned to Moab yet?" he asked.

"I checked with Sheriff Statton while I was waiting for you at the airport," I said. "Earl isn't home, and none of his friends or relatives seem to have any idea where he is. At least if they do, they're not admitting it."

"That's not good," Denzel said.

My phone rang. I was surprised when I heard Trace's voice over the phone. "Trace, what's going on?" I asked.

The agent looked sharply at me, and I mouthed, "Trace Jones." He nodded and looked puzzled. He wasn't any more puzzled than I was.

Trace sounded like he was feeling better than when I'd seen him the last time. "I need to talk to you," he said.

"Sure," I said. "What did you need to talk about?"

"In person," he said. "Can you come to the hospital?"

I hesitated then said, "Yes, but it will take me a while to get there. Can't you tell me what it's about?"

He was the one who hesitated now. "It needs to be in private," he said after a few seconds.

"Is there an officer in the room with you right now?" I asked.

"Always," was his less-than-happy response.

"Does he know who you called just now?"

"Yes, but not why."

It was clear that Trace had something he would only say to me, and I very much wanted to hear it. "Trace, if he stepped into the hallway with the other officer, would you tell me what you have on your mind?" I asked.

"That won't happen," he said.

"Let me talk to him. Maybe I can make it happen. Hand him the phone."

Special Agent Warner kept looking over at me as he drove. I nodded at him, but that was all. A different man came on the phone and identified himself as an FBI agent. I told him what I wanted, and he told me he didn't think he should do that. I told him to hold on for a moment.

I told Special Agent Warren what I wanted and why, and he reached for my phone. "I'll take care of that." He spoke to the other agent for a moment, concluding with, "Step into the hallway. I want the detective to hear what Jones has to say."

He handed me the phone back. It was Trace again. He said, "Okay, he's gone for now. Major, I've been thinking. Wyatt told me something when he was here. You know, I told you about how he asked if I knew who killed my dad."

"Yes, I remember," I said.

"Well, I didn't tell you everything. But I've been thinking about it, and maybe I should," he said.

"Yes, you should," I said, angry but not wanting to say anything that might cause him to clam up. "Does he know who killed your dad?" I asked.

"I don't know. He might."

I felt my pulse quicken. "Tell me about it, Trace."

"Wyatt told me he'd talked to my father a couple of days before he was killed," Trace said. "He said Dad was going to work for the oil company that's doing the drilling in Grand County."

"You already knew that, didn't you?" I asked.

"You know I did, and it made me mad. It still does," he said.

"Tell me more about what Wyatt said," I pressed.

"Well, anyway, I told Wyatt I already knew that. Then Wyatt told me that my dad agreed to quit the job and help us, you know, those of us who want the drilling to stop. That was news to me, and I had a hard time believing him. I asked Wyatt what Dad was going to do to help the cause."

Trace hesitated, so I tried to prod him along. "Okay, Trace, so what did he tell you?"

"He said Dad promised to help distribute pamphlets around Moab and the other areas like Monticello, Blanding, and Green River," he said. "But then, after he got some pamphlets, he changed his mind."

"Why?" I asked.

"I don't know, but Wyatt said he told my dad he shouldn't have done that. I guess my dad really hadn't had a change of heart after all. He was still going to work for the oil company, the jerk."

"What else did Wyatt say?" I asked.

"He said my dad had made a big mistake. And he said it made him and his friends really mad."

"Did Wyatt help kill your dad?" I asked.

"I hated my dad, but Wyatt didn't have the right to kill him. If Dad hadn't been killed, Mom would still be alive and I wouldn't be here," he said.

His reasoning was self-serving, even twisted. I said, "Trace, Wyatt doesn't have a pilot's license, does he?"

"No, but Junior does."

"So you think Junior and Wyatt killed your father?" I asked.

"They might have," he said.

"Is there anyone else who might have helped them?"

"Maybe, but I don't really know. That's all I've got to say."

"Do you think they also abducted Detective Patterson?" I asked.

"That could be," he said. "But that's all I've got to say. I hope you find her, Major Daniels. And that's the truth. She's a nice lady. I'm sorry they did this to her . . . and to you."

"So am I," I said. "Trace, tell me one more thing. What do you know about Earl Bassinger?"

"Not much," he said. "He's on our side on the drilling thing. He told Wyatt he thought it would hurt his helicopter business. You know, by messing up the scenery. He figured not as many tourists would want him to fly them around."

"When did Wyatt tell you that?"

"When do you think?" he asked.

"When he was there with you," I responded.

"I gotta go now," he said.

I tried to revive the conversation, but Trace had said what he had to say. The call ended, and I said to Warner, "You can call the agent and tell him we're off the phone now."

After he had done that, I told him what I'd learned. He agreed that it was looking more and more like Wyatt, Junior, and possibly even Earl Bassinger were involved in both the murder of Edward Jones and the abduction of Detective Jarbi Patterson. I was more anxious than ever to interview Junior Yost.

Chapter Seventeen

BEFORE WE GOT TO THE jail parking lot, Sheriff Statton called me. "I have the results of the blood work on Edward Jones," she said. "I forget what the name of the drug is, but he had been heavily sedated. That explains how he could have been loaded into the airplane and forced out. One person could have done it. The next thing we need to do is find out who might have access to the drug in question."

After discussing that for a minute, I told Lisette about my phone call from Trace Jones.

"It looks like we're headed in the right direction," she said. "But I'm wondering about Earl Bassinger. For him to just disappear like he has, helicopter and all, is incriminatory in my mind."

"What about the hair samples?" I asked. I knew she would understand what I meant.

"We should know something in the next few hours," she said. "Call me when you finish with Junior. I hope you can get him to tell you where Jarbi is. I've never been so worried about anything in my life. She's like a sister to me."

"I'll do my best," I promised.

"I know you will. And Major, I'm sorry for the way I acted. I don't care what you have to do to get Junior to open up. All I care about are the results," she said.

"Thanks," I said and ended the call. Special Agent Warner had just parked at the jail.

I wasn't 100 percent sure he was actually going to let me talk to Junior by myself. When I told the officer inside that I was here to interview Junior Yost, he hesitated. I knew I had the support of the agent when he showed the officer his credentials and said, "He's assisting me. Give him as much as a half hour if he needs it."

The man nodded, and I thanked Special Agent Warner. Five minutes later, Junior Yost was ushered into the small interview room. His eyes narrowed, and his face darkened when he recognized me. "You!" he said with as much disgust as he could muster.

I hadn't expected him to be happy to see me. I was sure that news of my questions at the university, particularly with some of his students, had gotten back to him. I wasn't bothered in the least. "Sit down, Junior. You and I have some things to talk about."

"We have nothing to talk about," he said. "I'm finished here."

"All right, stand if you want to, but you will listen to me and then I believe you will tell me what I want to know," I said.

He smirked at me, and I stepped close to him. I had eight inches and a whole lot of muscle on the guy. Not that I intended to hurt him physically. No, that was not my intent at all. But I did hope to intimidate him a little bit. He stepped back and glowered up at me.

"Is your plane paid for?" I asked.

"What's it to you?" he demanded.

"Oh, I just wondered. What happens if it happens to catch fire or something?" I asked.

"That won't happen," he said. "No one would touch my plane." His arrogance was enough to make me want to punch him.

"You don't know that. You're in here, and it's out there." I swung my arm in a short arc to illustrate where out there was.

"I won't be in here long," he said. "Nobody has anything on me."

I crowded him a little closer, and he backed up until he bumped against the wall of the small room. "That's where you're wrong," I said. "It would be in your best interest to cooperate. If you tell me where Wyatt is keeping Detective Patterson, it may go a long way in making your stay a little shorter."

"I don't know anything about her. And nobody can prove different."

I stepped away from him. "This would be easier if you sat down."

"I got nothing more to say to you."

"Junior, maybe you need to sit down and listen. Then you won't fall."

"You can't touch me. If you lay a finger on me, it'll be you sitting in here. And besides that, I'll sue you as soon as they release me," he threatened, holding his nose higher than was necessary to look up at me.

"Let's talk about your plane. It could be destroyed while you're sitting in here," I said.

"Not likely. But if it did, I got insurance," he said. "I'd just get me a new one."

"Actually, Junior, you don't have insurance. You cancelled it, or don't you remember that?" I goaded.

"I did no such thing and you know it," he said.

I was getting real tired of the smirk. It was time to get rid of it. I pulled out my iPhone, accessed the Internet, and then did some typing and punching of keys. Finally I said, "You might want to look at his." I held the phone where he could see it. At first he just looked away, but finally, curiosity got the best of him.

"This is about your insurance," I said. "It's cancelled. Read closely."

I held it steady while he read. The smirk faded. "I didn't do that," he said after he realized I wasn't bluffing.

"You must have. Anyway, I think you can safely assume that your plane is history. There are people that will make sure of that, unless I can convince them that you've decided to help the FBI and me and the local cops from several jurisdictions," I said darkly.

"Nobody would do that. I have lots of friends," he bragged, trying to get the smirk back in place.

He almost succeeded. But I spoke quickly again. "I have friends too," I said. "And a lot of them are angry that you would threaten to do damage to my Jet Ranger. Lots of guys depend on me to get them to the rigs and back each week."

"I didn't—" he began.

I shut him right down when I broke in. "Save your breath, Junior. I have witnesses. You and Jordan are in a world of hurt over that. But let's talk about another thing. You say you'll be getting out of here soon. I know better, but just for the sake of argument, let's assume for a moment that you do. You'll need a place to live."

"I have a place," he said.

"Then you shouldn't have canceled your lease," I said.

"I didn't," he countered. But then he got a sick look on his face.

Again I began to work with the iPhone. "Would you like to see proof?" I asked.

He shook his head. I think he knew now that I wasn't bluffing. "Sit down," I said. This time, he complied. I sat opposite of him. "Okay, let's talk about your job. I mean, let's talk about the job you used to have. Do you need to see proof that you have been terminated?"

He shook his head. That was good because that was a bluff, although I knew he would lose his job soon. There was no way they could let him keep teaching after all he'd done.

"Oh, and you might be interested to know that a strand of long black hair was found in your plane. DNA proves it's Detective Patterson's."

He actually began to lose color in his face. That was my second bluff, though I was even more certain that the results of the DNA testing would prove that a reality. But I wasn't through with him yet. "I know you think you're awfully smart, but you really shouldn't have written that e-mail to the fellow running the campaign to shut down the rigs. That really wasn't smart," I said.

"I didn't send any e-mails—" He stopped and asked, "Did I?"

"Would you like to read it?" I asked.

He shook his head, but I opened the e-mail I had written from his account that morning from the airport in Lander. I was not a dummy with computers. This was far from the first time I had hacked an account in the course of my work. I showed him the e-mail. He read it and then dropped his head into his hands. "They'll kill me," he said. "Why did you do that?"

"Cheer up, Junior. There is a way out of this," I said. "You didn't actually send it yet. And maybe you won't if you simply tell me what I need to know."

"Wyatt will kill me," he whined.

"Or Wyatt will go to prison, and you can get a break . . . maybe," I said. "As you can see, it's all stacked against you. Why don't you just tell me where Detective Patterson is, and I'll make things better for you." I pulled out my digital recorder then. "Let's get this all recorded, shall we?"

When I rejoined Special Agent Warren ten minutes later, he said, "Did you get anything?"

I told him where Jarbi was being held. "You're sure?" he asked.

"Pretty much," I said, pulling out my little recorder. "Would you like to hear it?"

He smiled. "Later. Right now we have an officer to rescue."

"Yes, we do," I agreed. "And I think it might also be a good idea to arrange extra protection for Mr. Yost. What he's done will tick off a lot of dangerous people."

"When we have your friend back safe and sound, I'll worry about the safety of Mr. Yost," he said.

We stood in the parking lot while he used his phone to coordinate Jarbi's rescue. While he was doing that, I called Lisette. She cried when I told her we were going after Jarbi as soon as we could set it up. Then she asked, "How did you get him to tell you?"

"I used a five-letter word," I said.

"What word is that?" she asked.

"Bluff," I said. What I didn't say was that I did more than bluff.

"Oh," she said. "Well, I'm glad you are a good bluffer. I wish I was there."

"So do I," I said. Despite my best intentions, that woman was growing on me.

For the second time, a large contingent of law officers were gathered, and thanks to Special Agent Denzel Warner, I was not excluded. The location was a deserted warehouse right there in Great Falls. Once the SWAT team was in position, the building was breached. Denzel and I observed from the command center. The first report that came over the radio was that there were no vehicles inside the warehouse. "That's not good," Denzel said to me. "I would have expected Wyatt to have a vehicle of some kind in there. I'll be sick if we've missed her again, but I suppose it's possible."

That thought was also on my mind. But I didn't doubt the information I'd received, and I had this feeling deep in my gut that Jarbi was in there. "She's in there," I said. "Who's to say Junior didn't leave them there while he went to refuel his plane? He might have been planning to pick them up later and go elsewhere."

He nodded and relayed my feelings to the incident commander. We turned our attention back to the warehouse, watching with nerves on edge.

Communication from inside was regular now as one area after another was checked and cleared. Then a frantic call came to the command post. The team had spotted a suspicious package in front of a closed door on the second floor of the building—likely the office area. The search inside was frozen while a bomb-sniffing dog was brought in. That took an extra thirty minutes. But in the end, the dog did its job well. The handler reported that there was definitely a bomb in the package.

Another hour was spent in tense anticipation as a bomb squad successfully removed the package and dismantled a small but deadly bomb, one that could easily have killed anyone within a hundred feet of it. And that's not including the damage and injury that might have occurred had the upper floor given way in the explosion, which it probably would have.

The search now proceeded more slowly. The bomb-sniffing dog led the way inside. All the officers were alert for not only another bomb but an ambush by Wyatt and whoever else might be in there. The office area by where the bomb had been proved to be the main door to a labyrinth of smaller offices inside. A constant stream of whispered radio communications came through to those of us in the command post. A second bomb was discovered in front of another door, one that looked like it might lead to a small room of some kind. Another agonizing hour went by while that bomb was removed.

I was in almost constant contact with Lisette, for she called every few minutes to see what was going on. She was frantic with worry, and I didn't blame her. I wasn't exactly experiencing feelings of peace and goodwill myself.

Finally, Denzel and I got the call to come inside. We weren't told why, and my gut was churning. I whispered a frantic prayer, just another of many, as we entered the warehouse and were escorted across the building to the stairway leading to the upper floor. "What have you found?" Agent Warner asked a member of the SWAT team.

An answer was not forthcoming, but the look we got from the SWAT officer was not a good one. We hurried up the stairs. When we reached the door where the latest bomb had been, we were ushered inside. There on the floor behind a desk was the body of a woman with dark hair. I fought the urge to throw up as I knelt beside the body and gently turned the head so that I could see the face, what was left of it, which wasn't much.

When I finally stood up and moved back, every officer in the room was staring at me. "As you can see, her face is pretty well gone," I said. "But it is not Detective Patterson."

Denzel was the first to speak. "How do you know that?" he asked.

"Jarbi didn't have any earrings the day she was abducted. I was with her earlier that day. This girl does have earrings," I said, pointing. "There are three in each ear."

"Maybe Jarbi put them in later," Denzel said.

"No, that makes no sense," I said. "And even if she did, she would only put in one set, not three."

"Still, can you really be sure? The hair is the right color, isn't it?"

"Yes, and the right length, but there's also the way this girl is dressed," I said.

"That could have been changed," Denzel argued. "The witness at the airport in Denver said that the girl was dressed in something baggy. This girl isn't, but that could have been removed."

"Jarbi had on a blue blouse and black slacks that morning," I said. "And her shoes were black with flat heels."

Denzel bent down and observed the shoes. "High heels," he said.

I studied the body again. I stepped across it and looked closely. The girl's navel was showing, and there was a jeweled ring in it. I pointed it out. "Jarbi Patterson wouldn't have had her navel pierced. And there's one more thing. Look at her hands." Those hands were tied behind her back. "She has several rings. Jarbi had only one, and I can tell you exactly what it was. It was on her right hand, the ring finger, and it's what's called a CTR ring. This isn't her," I said firmly. I knew I was right about that.

"Then who is she?" Denzel asked.

I shook my head. "I have no idea," I said. "But it is not Jarbi. So now I wonder where she is. I still think she has to be here somewhere." I didn't say it, but my hope of finding her alive was very dim after what we'd just discovered.

We all stood quietly for a moment, looking at someone's daughter, someone's friend, someone who somebody would shed bitter tears over. I heard something just then. "There's a door there," I said, pointing to the back of the little office. "Has anyone checked that?"

I stepped quickly to that door and pulled it open. Another body rolled out of the small closet. It was a woman with black hair and no earrings. There was a CTR ring on the right hand that was bound tightly behind her back. It was Jarbi Patterson.

Chapter Eighteen

MY PRAYERS HAD BEEN ANSWERED. Jarbi was alive. She was also tightly bound and gagged with a dirty rag. I pulled the rag from her mouth and then gently cut the ropes that bound her hands. An officer gave her a bottle of water. She took a sip, cleared her throat, and said with a struggle, "I knew you'd find me, Major." Then tears coursed down her cheeks.

I sat beside her on the floor, holding her while I dialed Lisette. "We found her, and she's going to be fine," I said. Jarbi reached for the phone and spoke a few hoarse words while I helped steady her hand. Then I took the phone back. "An ambulance will be here in a little bit," I said. "But I think as soon as she gets her strength back, she'll be okay."

"Thank you, Major. You'll never know how much I appreciate what you've done," Lisette said, choking up. "What about Wyatt?" she asked.

"No sign of him yet. I'll call again when I know more."

The SWAT officers searched the rest of the building, but Wyatt wasn't there. While we were waiting for the ambulance, I helped Jarbi outside. She said she was fine, but I told her I thought it would be best if she went to a hospital to be checked out. As I was watching Jarbi be loaded into the ambulance, she spoke, her voice stronger now. "That other woman. The one Wyatt killed. He knew her. I think she was his girlfriend or something. She tried to help me, but it made him angry."

"We'll talk about it later," I said.

Denzel stepped beside me as they were preparing to close the ambulance door. "Why don't you go with her," he suggested. "There's nothing you can do here. A lab crew is coming to process the area. I'll wait with them for a while, and then I'll meet you at the hospital."

Jarbi called my name and pled, "Come with me, please."

I looked at one of the paramedics. He nodded, and I climbed in beside Jarbi. They began an IV on her since she appeared to be badly dehydrated. We rode in silence, but she reached for my hand and held it until we reached the emergency room. Then I stepped out and waited while they wheeled her inside. She was thoroughly checked over and given some food.

We talked about the dead girl. Jarbi told me that she hadn't seen Wyatt shoot the girl. Wyatt told the girl to help set the bombs they had made, but she said they were for blowing up things not people. The girl said that if she'd known what he was going to use them for, she wouldn't have helped make them. Jarbi had tears in her eyes. "They argued, and suddenly I heard him kick her. I heard bones crack. I don't know which ones. She cried out, and he told her to shut up. She didn't, and I think he kicked her again. There was still rope left from what he'd used on me. I could hear them struggling. She was protesting, calling him names, and telling him he'd regret tying her up.

"Finally, he must have had her bound like I was because he told her he was going to set the bombs and that when he got them set, he'd be leaving. He said that both of us, meaning her and me, would be blown up if and when anyone tried to get into the room." Jarbi stopped and took a breath.

"I'm sorry you went through all that," I said.

"I thought I was going to die. Wyatt is a coldblooded killer, nothing less," she said. "Anyway, when he told the girl he was leaving her there, she just started to scream and curse at him. Then I heard the gunshot. Wyatt grabbed me, and I thought he was going to shoot me too, but he said something about needing me alive for the plan to work.

"He shoved me in the closet, but while he was dragging me over there, I saw her. Her face was gone. It was horrible," she said. For a moment Jarbi was silent, staring off toward the far corner of the room. Finally, she turned back to me. "You know, Wyatt never did say her name. He just called her Babe. And he killed her. What an awful man."

Jarbi was pronounced fit and ready to be released a couple hours later. Denzel Warner gave us a ride to a hotel, where I got Jarbi a room. A female officer from the Great Falls Police Department met us there and offered to get Jarbi some clothes. I left Jarbi there so she could shower and rest. Denzel and I went back to the jail, where we paid a visit to Junior Yost.

This time we went together. We were shown to the same small interrogation room I had occupied earlier, and they brought Junior in. I said, "Junior, this is Special Agent Denzel Warner of the FBI. He's in charge of the investigation into the abduction of Deputy Patterson. We found her, and she'll be okay. He knows we wouldn't have found her had it not been for your cooperation."

He sat, and then Denzel sat across from him. I leaned against the nearby wall. Denzel advised him of his rights, got permission to record the conversation, and made sure Junior was waiving his right to an attorney during questioning. Despite us not telling him anything other than the fact that we had rescued Jarbi, he was subdued and ready to talk.

Special Agent Warner proceeded to ask a long series of questions, taking his time and making sure Junior understood what he was asking. Junior answered each question, and we learned how they had tricked Jarbi into stopping to help them on the freeway. They had passed her car earlier and then faked a breakdown, flagging her down to help them. Junior told us how they'd overpowered her and gave a fairly detailed account right up until he left Wyatt and Jarbi at the warehouse.

"Did Wyatt have a car?" Denzel asked him.

"No, you didn't find one there when you arrested him, did you?" he asked, causing the FBI agent and me to look at each other. "You did arrest him, didn't you?" he asked when he noted our reaction.

Special Agent Warner said, "Wyatt wasn't there."

"He was going to wait for me to come back," he said, seeming genuinely puzzled.

"Why did you come to Great Falls in the first place?" I asked as a suspicion entered my mind.

"Wyatt wanted to," Junior said. "He was familiar with this city. He told me he even had an old girlfriend here."

"Did you know the girlfriend?" Denzel asked.

"No, I never met her," he said.

"Could she have picked Wyatt up at the warehouse?" I asked.

Junior thought about my question for a moment. "Yeah, I suppose she could have. I never thought about that. Did he leave Deputy Patterson tied up or what?"

"He did," Denzel said. "And he left his girlfriend dead."

Junior's mouth dropped, and his eyes popped wide open. He stammered for a minute, but no coherent words came out.

According to Jarbi, Wyatt's girlfriend had been murdered several hours after Junior had left, but Denzel still asked, "Were you there when Wyatt shot his girlfriend?"

"No. I swear, I wasn't. I don't know anything about that. You've got to believe me," he shouted. Then his face dropped, and his eyes looked down at the table, where his hands lay folded. "I can't believe he would do that. Why would he do that?"

I knew he was talking to himself, but I was ready to spring another question. "You say you're not a murderer. Then why did you take Wyatt up in your airplane and let him push Edward Jones out?"

He slowly lifted his eyes toward me. I was now standing beside where Denzel was seated. I waited until his eyes met mine. Then he said, "You think I had something to do with killing Mr. Jones?"

"That's exactly what I think," I said evenly, even though I suddenly had some doubts.

"Mr. Daniels, you've got to believe me. I don't know anything about that. I didn't help anyone kill Edward Jones. He's never even been in my plane. I swear," he said, his voice desperate and pleading.

"You know, of course, that Special Agent Warner obtained a search warrant and searched your plane thoroughly. He and his team found one of Jarbi's hairs there. They still have more stuff that they're going through that was vacuumed from inside your plane. If there is so much as a hair or a fiber of clothing left by Edward Jones, they will find it. They also lifted a bunch of fingerprints. If Jones left any, they will find those too. And when they find any of those things, you will be charged with his murder," I said, my voice cold and calculated.

Junior said, "Some of the fingerprints are Detective Patterson's, but not Edward Jones's; he hasn't been in my airplane. I swear that I had nothing to do with him being killed."

The final thing that Denzel questioned Junior about was the bombs. Junior adamantly denied any knowledge of them. I had expected that, as Jarbi had already told us that the bombs had been brought to the warehouse by Wyatt's girlfriend.

I was surprised when a correctional officer poked his head into the room and said, "There are a couple more officers who would like to join you. Do you mind?"

"No, let them come in," Denzel said. "We're about through for now anyway."

I was surprised when Jarbi followed a couple Great Falls detectives in. The look on Junior Yost's face was one of first shock and then misery. He looked down at his hands again and didn't look up when Jarbi said, "Hi, Junior, how are you doing?"

It was pretty obvious how he was doing—not well at all. But he exhibited courage when he mumbled, still without looking up, "I'm sorry. I'm glad you're okay."

Jarbi said nothing more at that point, but Denzel spoke into his little recorder, stating we had more officers. He spoke Jarbi's name and then had the other two each introduce themselves. Then he said, "If you have questions for Mr. Yost, I would suggest you advise him of his rights again."

"I'll talk to them without an attorney," Junior said, looking directly at Denzel. "I suppose it's about Wyatt's girlfriend, and as you know, I didn't even know she'd been at the warehouse."

Jarbi spoke up. "They know that, Junior, but they still need to talk to you."

Other than walking a little stiffly, Jarbi seemed to be feeling pretty good as we left the jail a few minutes later. "I checked out of the hotel, Major. All I want to do is go back to Moab. Is there any chance I could hitch a ride with you?

"Of course," I said. "But Denzel may need to interview you first. Your kidnapping is his case."

"I'm hungry," Denzel said. "If you two don't mind, perhaps we could find a quiet table in a restaurant near here, and I could talk to you about your kidnapping then."

Jarbi said, "I think I could eat more now. My stomach is growling. I couldn't eat much at the hospital."

We ate first, and then Denzel did a formal interview of Jarbi. While they were doing that, I slipped to an empty table with my laptop and undid some of the damage I'd done to Junior by getting his insurance on the plane reinstated and his lease reestablished. I couldn't do anything about his job. That, I'm sure he was going to lose. He was facing some pretty heavy jail time, his cooperation notwithstanding.

Two hours later, we headed south in my Jet Ranger. Despite the speed of the Ranger, it was not going to be possible to reach Moab without stopping somewhere to sleep. Not that the helicopter couldn't make it; it was my body that made the stop necessary. I was exhausted, and there was no way I was going to take the chance of falling asleep while I was flying. We decided to spend the night in Rock Springs, Wyoming.

We checked into a hotel there, and after Jarbi and I had had dinner and she had gone to her room to sleep, I decided to call Crystal. I knew she had moved into the basement of the new house. I also knew that she had some flights set up for me in a couple of days to shuttle men to and from the rigs. Finally, I knew she had talked to Mrs. Simonson, our newest client, who was safely stowed away in her son's home in Salt Lake. But when I tried to reach Crystal, I got only voice mail on her phone.

I kept trying for an hour with the same result. I tried texting her. That didn't work either. I even called my office. Once again, I had no results. I began to worry in earnest, so I called Lisette and explained my concern. After what had happened to Jarbi and knowing that Wyatt was a coldblooded killer on the lam, neither of us were willing to just wait and see if Crystal eventually answered her phone.

Lisette offered to go to my house and check on her. She called me from the house and said that Crystal didn't answer either the door upstairs or the one at the outside entrance to the basement. "But her car's here," she said. That really got my stomach doing flips.

"Please call Nora," I told Lisette. "She has spare keys. Let yourself in. I've got to know she's okay. It's not like her to let her phone go to voice mail."

Twenty minutes later, Lisette called me back. "Crystal's not in the house, and her phone is on the dresser in her bedroom."

Lisette said she'd look around town and have her deputies do the same. "I'd head down there right now," I told her, "but I'm just too sleep deprived to fly."

"You go to bed," Lisette said. "I'll call you if I hear anything at all."

I tossed and turned, worried sick about Crystal. I must have finally fallen asleep because my phone woke me up around midnight. "Corbin, I'm so sorry I worried you," Crystal said. "I was on a date and forgot my phone. I feel just terrible for worrying you!"

I was so relieved I wanted to cry. "I'm glad you're okay. Just please be careful. Who knows where Wyatt is or what he's up to now."

"I had my gun with me," she said. "It was just my phone that I forgot."

"By the way, who was the lucky guy?" I asked. "I didn't know you knew any guys that well yet."

She cleared her throat. "I hope this doesn't make you mad. He's a really nice guy. And we had a great time."

"I'm glad you had a great time, but who was it?" I asked again.

"You know that guy Nora hired us to investigate, Jarrett Bloom?" she said.

"You had a date with Jarrett Bloom?" I asked, surprised.

"You don't like him, do you?" she said.

"I'm not your father, Crystal, just your cousin—and your boss," I said. "You can date who you want—within reason of course." Then I chuckled. "Hey, Jarrett's a nice guy. He just got some bad advice. And if you decide to go out with him again, you have my blessing. Not that you need it, of course, but you have it anyway."

I was able to sleep soundly after that. Jarbi and I had a leisurely breakfast the next morning. After that we checked out of our hotel rooms and headed for the airport in a rental car. My phone, which seemed to be ringing an awful lot lately, rang before we got there. When I put the cell to my ear, I heard the voice of Trace Jones.

"Major Daniels," he said, sounding scared out of his wits, "I think I'm going to die. You've got to help me. Please, help me."

"Trace," I said, "calm down and tell me exactly what's going on." I pulled over to the side of the road to concentrate on the phone call.

"There's a fire in the hospital. The officer that was in my room ran out into the hallway. Fire alarms are going off all over the place."

"They won't let you burn to death. Have you tried your call button?"

"Of course," he said, "but nobody's come except a guy in a doctor's mask and clothes."

"Then you're okay," I said. "Just calm down."

"I can't," he shouted, sheer panic in his voice. "The guy gave me a shot."

"It was probably to calm you down," I suggested.

"No, you don't get it, Major. I was calm until this guy came in. He wasn't a doctor. I don't know who he was, but he wasn't a doctor," Trace ranted. "You've got to help me."

"Did the guy say anything to you?"

"Yeah, that's how I know he wasn't a doctor. He said that I knew who killed my dad and that I wasn't going to tell anybody. That was right after he gave me the shot."

Now I was worried. "Can you get out of bed?"

"No, I can hardly move at all. I'm feeling numb. I think I'm going to drop the phone. Call somebody to help me." He was pleading now, and his voice had grown weak.

"Hang on to the phone if you can. Jarbi is with me, and she's calling down there to get you help." I nodded to Jarbi, and she began to do just that with her iPhone, the one we'd recovered from the house in Wyoming, where she had first been held.

She began to dial, and I tried to keep Trace talking. But his voice was fading; he was crying. "Trace, do you know who killed your dad?"

"No," he said. "But this guy . . . he . . . says . . . I . . . do."

"Do you have any idea who he was? Did you recognize his voice?" I asked.

For a moment, I thought he'd dropped the phone, but finally he said. "I'm . . . trying to . . . think . . ." His voice faded. I waited. Then he came back on. "Yes . . . it . . . was . . ." He faded away again.

"Who was it?" I practically shouted. No response.

"Help is on the way, and the cops are calling the agents and the troopers at his door," Jarbi said. "Tell him."

"Trace, help is on the way. Hang in there. Can you hear me?" I asked.

Nothing. "I think he passed out," I said to Jarbi as I started the car again. "We're going to Grand Junction."

Chapter Nineteen

I OBTAINED CLEARANCE TO ONCE again land on the helipad at the hospital in Grand Junction. Jarbi and I ran quickly inside. There were a bunch of officers outside of Trace's room. The hallway smelled of smoke, evidence that there had been a fire, just like Trace had claimed. "How bad was the fire?" I asked the first officer that I recognized.

Trooper Stone, who was stone-faced, said, "Bad enough, but they didn't have to evacuate any patients."

"That's good," I said. "What's happening with Trace? He called and sounded like he was scared to death."

"I guess he had reason to be. They tried to save him after you guys made the call, but they couldn't. Trace has been dead for over an hour now."

"I think he figured out who the man was that came in pretending to be a doctor," I said, saddened to hear that he had died. That was not the future I had envisioned for Trace, as bad a guy as he was. "Was he able to say anything to anyone before he died?"

Stone shook his head. "As far as I know, whatever he said to you were the last words he spoke."

"I was afraid of that," I said.

Trooper Stone looked at Jarbi and finally cracked a little smile. "You look good," he said. "I'm glad they found you."

"So am I," she said. Then she grabbed my arm and slipped closer to me. "It was because of him that I was found. The major saved my life."

"So I heard," he said.

"Do you know exactly what happened here, Trooper Stone?" I asked.

"Pretty much. I hope I don't lose my job over it. I was on duty outside the door, like before," he said, pointing to the chair he'd been sitting in. "I hope it wasn't my fault. I was sitting here when the fire alarms started going off. From what I've been able to learn, fires were started on two floors, this one and the one below. The worst one was down past the nurses' station there." He pointed in the direction he meant.

"The fire alarms went off, and the nurses started screaming for help. Smoke was starting to fill the hallway. The officer inside Trace's room ran out and left me here while he went to help. The guy who must have killed Trace came running up right then and told me he needed to check on Trace. The guy said that an alarm at the nurses' station had indicated that Trace's heart wasn't beating right."

"And he looked like a doctor?" I asked.

"Oh yeah," Stone said. "He was wearing scrubs, and he had a stethoscope around his neck. He was also wearing a mask, but I thought it was because of the smoke. Some of the nurses were wearing them too. The guy wasn't in Trace's room long, and when he came out, he told me that Trace was okay, that it was an equipment problem probably caused by the fire, and that he'd just had to reset a monitor. Then he took off running toward the nurses' station, where the fire was burning. If he had just done something wrong, you wouldn't have thought he'd head right toward where the most hospital personnel were. But that's what he did. I thought he was just going to help someone else."

"So no one had a clue anything was wrong with Trace until Jarbi called?" I asked.

"That's right," he agreed. "I went into the room as soon as I got the call on my radio. Trace was unconscious but alive. I stepped into the hallway and shouted for help. People, including the other officer, came running. They did what they could, but like I told you, they couldn't revive him."

"I guess we'll find out in due time what was in the needle that killed him," I said. "You don't happen to know if that syringe was left in the room, do you?"

"No, I didn't see one in there, but an officer did find one in the stairwell between this floor and the next one down. We don't know yet if it was the one used on Jones or not, but it will be checked for fingerprints, I guess. Not that it will help. The guy was wearing surgical gloves." Stone shook his head. "I sure wish I hadn't let that guy in the room."

"Hey, Trooper," Jarbi said. "It's not your fault. I'll bet you were told to let medical personnel in, weren't you?"

"Yeah, they were the only ones we could let in besides cops," he said.

"See, you did what you were supposed to. So quit worrying about it." She smiled at him, and he seemed to relax a little bit.

Jarbi and I were allowed in the room when the officer in charge found out who we were, but I didn't learn any more than what Trooper Stone had already told us.

We were only in the hospital for an hour. I'd given a statement as to my phone conversation with Trace, and Jarbi had given one about what she'd heard when I was talking to Trace and about what she'd done afterward.

Jarbi and I didn't get in my helicopter right away but stood beside it talking. "I guess what we need to do now is fly back to Moab. A description of the killer, with what little good that will do, has been broadcast."

"Yeah, it's too bad Trace couldn't get just a few more words out before he lost consciousness," she said.

"Well, there is one good thing," I said.

She looked at me with doubt written on her face. "There is? I can't think of anything."

I smiled at her. "I'm looking at it," I said. "You are alive, Jarbi. What could be better than that?"

"You're right, Major. And I am so grateful," she said as her eyes filled with tears. "I thought I was going to die. I thought those bombs were going to go off and that would be the end. I prayed a lot, but I was losing faith. I just kept thinking about all the things I should have done in my life and hadn't. I think I've done a lot of good things. I've always been active in the Church, but I could have done more in my callings. And I kept thinking about what I should be doing for neighbors and friends that I haven't been."

"You still must have had some faith, Jarbi, because we found you," I said. "The Lord heard your prayers."

"I know," she said with a smile. "But tell me, Major, how did you convince Junior Yost to tell you where I was?" she asked.

I didn't answer her because just then I had a phone call, not that I would have been specific with her anyway. Some things are just better kept private.

It was Special Agent Denzel Warner on the phone. "Hi, Major. We finished working with the fingerprints taken in Junior's plane, but none of them belong to your murder victim. We won't have the results back from the lab for the stuff we vacuumed, but frankly, I don't think we'll find anything proving Jones was in that plane. We did identify prints that matched Jarbi and Wyatt and Junior. There were others too. Junior's little brother, Jordan, has been in the plane, probably recently."

"He's been on his days off, but I suppose there's no way to determine if they're that recent," I said.

"That's right," he agreed. "After learning about the bombs, we had a bomb dog check the plane out. It didn't pick up anything. Its handler said if there had been bombs or bomb-making material in the plane recently, that the dog would have indicated that fact. So we can be certain the bombs were not flown into Great Falls on that plane."

"What have you learned about the dead girl?" I asked.

"She was positively identified," Denzel answered. "Like Detective Patterson told us, she was Wyatt Mortell's girlfriend. She had an extensive record. Yet unlike Mortell, she still had a little good in her, a conscience of sorts. She died because she didn't want Jarbi to get blown up."

Following the conversation with Agent Warner, Jarbi and I got in my Jet Ranger and flew over to the airport for fuel, and then we made a beeline for Moab. Sheriff Statton met us when we landed behind my new house. As soon as Jarbi was out of the chopper and on the ground, the two women ran into each other's arms and hugged for at least a couple of minutes.

They were both tough, no-nonsense cops, but they were also real women—caring and emotional. I felt a strong affection for both of them. I counted myself lucky to know them.

When they finally broke apart, I was out of my chopper and on the ground. Lisette walked over to me, shaking her head tearfully. The next thing I knew, her arms were around me, and my shoulder was getting soaked with her tears. While her head was still on my shoulder, she said softly, "Thank you, Major, for bringing Jarbi back alive. I don't know how you got Junior to tell you where she was, and if I never know, that's okay. I'm just grateful you did."

I didn't get held as long as she'd held Jarbi, but when she pulled away from me, I had the urge to pull her right back. I just couldn't help having the desire, but I didn't do it. As determined as I was not to let it happen, I was developing strong feelings for this woman.

We walked back around the house and through the gate to where Lisette's SUV was parked. Lisette looked at me, thanked me again, and then gave me another hug. Jarbi also hugged me, and when she did, she whispered in my ear, "Don't let her get away, Major. I like you a lot, but I think my boss is falling in love."

Then she broke the embrace, winked at me, ran around the car, and climbed in. I was still staring when they disappeared from view. I finally walked inside and looked around. Checking my watch, I decided that the best use I could make of the rest of the day would be to move out of my cramped apartment and into the spacious house.

Other than keeping in touch with Lisette about any developments in the case, I didn't get myself involved again that week. I did check in with my latest client, Dayna Simonson, assuring her that I knew the identity of the man who had given her the pamphlets. I'm afraid I couldn't reassure her much concerning her personal safety since Wyatt Mortell was a killer and on the lam. I did assure her that he was wanted by the law, but that didn't help her feel any better. She agreed to stay with her son in Salt Lake until further notice.

In addition to the time I spent moving my belongings from the apartment to the house, I took another hour or so to place some digital security cameras around the yard, covering all four sides of the house. My system was state of the art, and I could monitor it from my computer, laptop, iPad, and even my iPhone. I made sure my chopper was totally covered by the cameras as well. In addition to the cameras, I installed a warning system that would alert me if anyone got within fifty feet of my Jet Ranger.

Out of an abundance of caution, I also installed a couple of cameras at my office—one inside and one outside, focused at an angle on the front door so that it also covered some of the area in front of the office.

In the meantime, I was aware of but did not participate in a thorough search of Edward Jones's home. Lisette came to my house Saturday evening and reported the results. Asher was with them for the search, which was conducted with her express written permission as well as a search warrant just to make sure that there would be no problems if evidence was found.

"Did you find anything?" I asked the sheriff.

She looked weary. "Yes, we found an ampule of the drug that was in Edward's system. What that means, I don't know. It may mean that Trace was lying about being involved in his father's death, or it may mean nothing. We'll have to wait and see what else turns up as we continue to investigate."

"Was that all you found?" I asked. The look in her eye told me there was more.

"We also found a letter. It was typewritten, had no signature, and simply stated that Edward was committed," she said.

"Committed to what?" I asked.

"To distributing the pamphlets he had been given. I expect that if we could find Wyatt Mortell's computer and printer, we could prove the letter was written by him. At any rate, I think it's pretty compelling," Lisette told me.

"What else did it say?" I asked.

"It ended with a threat of sorts. It said that if Jones didn't get those pamphlets out there soon, he'd be punished. That was the word it used, *punished*," she said. "We've got to find Wyatt. I think we're building a pretty good case against him."

* * *

On Sunday, Crystal and I attended our new ward with Lisette. She even sat with us in sacrament meeting. And she invited us to dinner that afternoon. "This time, it won't be thrown together in haste," she promised with a smile. "I already have a roast in the oven, hoping you two would come and help me eat it after church."

I readily accepted, but Crystal, her face slightly red, said, "I'm sorry, Sheriff, but I already have plans."

I said, "Oh really," with a knowing smile that made Crystal's blush deepen. "And who would you be having dinner with, if I might ask?"

"I guess you can ask, and maybe since I like you so much, I'll tell you," she said, unable to suppress a grin. "Jarrett Bloom is coming for dinner." She faced me. "I would have invited you, but since you have a better offer, I guess it'll just be me and Jarrett."

"Jarrett's a good man," Lisette said. She didn't know about the innocent mistake, prompted by Trace Jones, that could have gotten him into trouble, and as far as I was concerned, she didn't need to know. Once Jarrett realized that what he was doing was wrong, he had rectified things. That gave him stature in my eyes.

For a few hours, the sheriff and I both put the troubles we'd been dealing with on the back burner. As hard as it was for me to admit, I hadn't enjoyed being with anyone this much since before the bloody fight in Afghanistan that took my precious Angie from me. For the first time in all the years since that devastating event, I found that it might be possible to love someone again. Not that I was actually at that point, but being with Lisette made me realize it was both possible and desirable. I went home around eight, feeling almost dizzy with delight. It had been a great evening.

* * *

Monday morning found me shuttling crews out to a rig again. The same three men I had brought from the rig just a week ago were headed back to work that morning. This was the first of two groups I'd be taking to the rig that morning. I picked them up at the drilling company's yard south of town at six o'clock. I stored their suitcases in the storage area of my chopper and then waited while the three men climbed aboard. Jordan Yost was the last one in, and he had a small satchel with him.

"I didn't eat this morning," he said without meeting my eyes. "So I brought some breakfast for before we go on the rig." His explanation made perfect sense, but I still felt a little uneasy. After what I'd gone through with his brother, I didn't trust the guy at all.

When we arrived at the rig site, the men climbed down from my chopper. First came Devan Rish, who had been seated beside me. He was followed by Asher Grady's husband, Bill, and then Jordan. Devan lingered for a minute while I waited for the men I was going to take back to Moab. "I wasn't sure Bill Grady would make it," he said. "I would have thought that there would be a couple of funerals for his in-laws."

"They buried them both on Saturday," I said. "And Asher told me Trace wasn't going to be buried until next week. I'm not even sure she and her husband plan to be there, though she is the only surviving member of the family."

"I can't say as I blame them," he said. He looked toward the double-wide where my new passengers were now approaching us from. "Major," he said, "I think you should check your helicopter before those guys get on it."

"Check it for what?" I asked, suddenly nervous.

"You know the bag that Jordan said had his breakfast in it?" he asked.

"Yeah."

"I was just thinking you might want to check and make sure he didn't leave anything behind."

Devan didn't need to spell it out for me. I knew exactly what he was thinking. "Keep those guys back for a minute," I said, pointing to the three tired derrick hands who were trudging toward me. "I'll take a look."

As I feared, a small brown package was jammed beneath the seat that Jordan had sat on. I tried to tell myself it could be a part of Jordan's lunch, but there was no way I was going to take a chance. I knew that if I called Lisette, it would take her hours to get a bomb squad out here. I climbed back out of my chopper, thinking.

Suddenly, I knew what I had to do. I walked over to where Devan and the other men were standing. I said, "Devan, you were right. I'd like the four of you to go inside, get Jordan, and bring him back out here. And make sure he brings that satchel he had with him."

"What if he doesn't want to come?" Devan asked.

"I think the three of you can manage to convince him."

The grins that crossed all four faces told me that Jordan Yost was not one of their favorite people. Only Devan knew what I was worried about, but the other men must have read the anger on my face.

Jordan hadn't wanted to come back out, but he came, kicking and protesting as the other men dragged him toward me. Asher's husband was also with them. "Here he is, Major," Devan said. "And here's the bag he was carrying."

"Thanks," I said. Then I turned to Jordan, who looked like he wanted to run. Two of the biggest men were holding him tightly, and all he could do was struggle. "What did you say you had in the bag?" I asked.

Jordan glowered at me. "I told you. My breakfast."

I shook the bag. "It feels empty to me."

"Yeah, I already ate it," he said with a smirk.

"You lying twit," Bill Grady said as he stepped forward. "I was in the trailer with you. You didn't even open your bag."

"Did you leave what was in it in my helicopter?" I asked.

Jordan's eyes grew wide, and suddenly he looked desperate. He said nothing, just kicked at his captors, who stopped that rather harshly. One of them threatened to break his arm if he kicked again. While he struggled, I opened the satchel. It was indeed empty. "There's nothing in here," I said. "And since Bill knows you didn't eat it in the trailer, then I guess it must still be on board my chopper. And that being the case, I'll just have you go in and get it."

Jordan seemed to have lost his ability to speak. I continued, "Bill, would you go tell whoever is in charge here that Jordan and I are going for a ride, just the two of us. And tell him that I might not be bringing Jordan back."

That helped Jordan find his voice again. "You can't do that," he said. "I have to go on the rig in a little while."

"I don't think so," I said. "I think you are going to go with me, even if we have to tie you up and throw you in the luggage area."

He began to struggle again, more violently this time. Bill started off, but he hadn't got more than a few feet away when Jordan said, "Okay, I'll get it out of there," he said.

"Fine, you do that," I said. "Wait just a minute, Bill. Let's see if he means it."

The men carried him to the door of the chopper and boosted him in. A moment later he came out clutching the package I'd seen under the seat. He started to dash away, but the other hands stopped him. "Jordan, I think it is time for you to eat your breakfast," I said coldly. "The rest of us will watch."

"You can't make me," he wailed. "I'll eat it when I get ready to."

The rig hands dragged Jordan back to me, and I put my face within six inches of him. "Open the package," I said.

"And if I don't?"

"Then these men are going to tie you up, set that thing in your lap, and wait and see what happens."

Jordan's face paled. Bill, his fists bunched and his face turning purple with rage, said, "Listen to me, Bean. I happen to know that you threatened to do something to that Jet Ranger. We aren't going to let it happen. For all I know, it was you and that worthless brother of yours that killed my wife's dad. Open the package and eat!"

"I can't," he protested as he began to sob.

"Why not?" Bill demanded. "Are you lying about what's in it?"

"No," he wailed. "I'm just not hungry."

"Then just take it out," Bill said, so angry he was shaking with rage. "And if you don't, so help me, we'll do like Major Daniels said and tie you up, but you won't be getting back in the helicopter. No, I think we'll just let you sit there with that package on your lap until something happens."

Jordan finally began to bawl, and he dropped the package. We all stepped back. "Men," I said, "take Jordan over to the bunkhouse. I'm going to move my helicopter so that, just in case there happens to be a bomb in there, it won't do the chopper any damage. Leave that thing right where it is. I don't want anyone else to touch it."

After I'd moved my Jet Ranger a safe distance away, I joined the men. By then, others had gathered around. None of them looked very happy with Jordan Yost. I approached him. He was sitting on the ground now, and the men who had been holding him stood around him, their faces filled with anger. I could imagine how they must have felt, since I felt the same way. If that was a bomb, it probably would have killed the three of them as well as me.

I knelt down in front of Jordan. "What's in the package, Bean?"

He refused to look me in the eye.

"Is it a bomb?" I pressed. He still said nothing.

Bill Grady and a couple of the other guys hunched down beside me. Jordan focused on the ground between his feet.

Bill said, "You will either answer the major's question, or I will personally shove that package down your throat." The other men indicated they would be glad to help. "So, Bean, you look up at the major and tell him what's in the package you hid on his Jet Ranger."

He still said nothing. "Give us a minute," Bill said to me, and he and three men stepped out of earshot. When they came back a couple of minutes later, Bill spoke again. "Major," he said. "We really need to get to work. Why don't you take the guys we're relieving back to town. Jordan is going to work on the rig. If he has an accident and gets all busted up, I guess that'll just be too bad. If you want, you can bring the sheriff back. This is a dangerous job, and I just have a feeling there could be an accident this morning." The other men chimed their agreement.

"All right," I said. "I guess I'll be going then. But don't anyone touch that package. And I'll need Devan to keep an eye on it from back here while I get the sheriff."

I got to my feet and started away. "Wait, don't go," Jordan said, his voice squeaking.

"I've got to," I said. "I need to get the rest of the crew here." I started to walk again.

"Wait, I'll tell you," he cried, his voice breaking as he sobbed.

I turned back. "Then tell me, and do it right now."

Chapter Twenty

"It's a bomb," Jordan said.

I thought the other men were going to beat him to a pulp right then and there. Bill Grady, who is a very big man, grabbed Jordan by the shirt and jerked his skinny body off the ground. "Don't hit him, Bill," I said. "The law will deal with him. I'll see to it."

It took a tense minute or two before Bill finally let him go. "So help me, Bean," he said, eyes blazing, "if I find out that you helped kill my father-in-law, there's no place on earth you can hide that I won't find you." Then he turned and walked toward the trailer.

"Jordan, when is that thing set to go off?" I asked. But I guessed he was through talking. He wouldn't say a word. He just sat there, hunched over on the ground again, staring at the dirt between his knees. More and more men were gathering around, including the men's boss.

I made a phone call. Lisette answered. "Hi, Sheriff," I said. "Sorry to bother you, but we have a little problem out here at one of the oil rigs."

"Oh, Major, don't tell me. Did someone do something to one of the rigs?" she asked.

"No, no, the rig is fine, but I think I was meant to be dead—me and my chopper and a crew of three men from the rig."

She gasped. "What happened?"

I told her and then said, "I don't know when the bomb's set to go off, and I'm not about to touch it. I'm guessing it was set to blow up when I was on my way back to Moab with the returning crew, but I don't know for sure, and Jordan refuses to say."

"Okay, I guess I need to find someone who can help us and get them out there to you," she said.

"I need to get these men home and the rest of the relief crew back here."

"No, you don't, Major," she said. "I'm shutting the rig down until further notice. Is the person in charge there with you?"

"He's right here," I said.

"Good, put him on the phone," she ordered.

I followed her order and stood back while she gave her instructions. Then the phone was handed back to me. "Okay, it's all set," she said. "The rig is going to be idle. Nobody is to leave the scene. He'll also keep everyone back from the bomb. And he'll keep Jordan Yost tied up so he can't get away. You can come get me and one of my deputies, if you don't mind."

I was still feeling warm inside from the hours we'd spent together on Sunday. "Where would you like to meet me?" I asked.

"Why don't you pick us up at my house," she suggested. "By the time you get there, I should have someone rounded up who can disable the bomb."

As it turned out, no one was needed for that. I got a call from Devan Rish about five minutes into my flight back to Moab. He was talking thirty miles a minute, but I was finally able to get him to slow down so I could understand him.

"Okay, sorry," he said. "It was scary. The bomb went off and blew dirt and rocks all over the place. If it had gone off in your helicopter, there wouldn't have been anything left of any of you. The guys here want to string Jordan up. But don't worry, we won't touch him—well, not too badly anyway."

I looked at my watch. It had been about seven minutes since I left the rig. I shivered. Jordan had fully intended to kill me and whoever was with me. I wouldn't have minded stringing him up myself. Thank goodness we are a civilized society and I am a law-abiding citizen. I just hoped those hands at the rig would stay law-abiding as well. What we didn't need right now was vigilante justice.

I passed the information on to Lisette.

"I was afraid of that," she said. "Thank goodness you're okay."

She sounded so genuine that it made me feel warm all over. I said as flippantly as I could manage, "Yeah, I'm kind of glad about it myself. I kind of like this chopper of mine."

"So do I," she said. "But I like you a lot more."

Lisette Statton was a great girl. I felt my heart quicken when I landed behind her house and accepted a hug, a long one this time. It rivaled the one she'd given her detective not so long ago. I also got a hug, not so long but very tender, from Jarbi.

The sheriff and the detective got in my Jet Ranger for the trip back to the oil rig. After we all had our headsets on, Lisette said, "Ev and a couple of the other deputies have Jordan's home under surveillance while they get a search warrant. They should have the search completed by the time we get through at the oil rig. Jordan intended to kill you and three of his coworkers today." There was bitterness in her voice. "I want to put him away for a long, long time. We already have plenty of witnesses who saw the bomb detonate. I'm thinking we'll find supplies for building bombs on the property." Once we arrived at the oil rig, the two officers went right to work. The homemade bomb had left a large crater in the ground when it detonated. The officers took pictures, samples of the soil from the crater, and statements from all the witnesses. The first workers they interviewed were the ones who were going off shift. When they finished with the three of them, I flew them back to Moab.

After getting fuel at Canyonlands Field, I started back to the oil rig. En route I got a call from FBI Special Agent Denzel Warner. He said, "I talked to Sheriff Statton. She called to let me know about the bomb that almost got you, Major. She didn't know if my agency would be interested or not, but we certainly are. I am making arrangements to come to the site today. I'm in Grand Junction, so I'll be there along with another agent as soon as we get a helicopter lined up."

"Then I guess I'll see you there," I said. "I'm the sheriff's transportation today. I'm on my way back there now."

"I could tell," Denzel said with a chuckle. "I can hear the noise of your helicopter. I'll talk to you when I get there."

It was late in the afternoon by the time the officers were finished at the oil rig. By mutual agreement between Agent Warner and Sheriff

Statton, the oil rig was allowed to go back to drilling. Jordan Yost, who was under arrest for a multitude of both state and federal crimes, was just being walked out to my helicopter when Chief Deputy Evan Belgar called the sheriff to report on the results of the search at the Yost residence.

Both of Jordan's parents had been arrested when they attempted to destroy evidence. They were unsuccessful, but Ev reported that they appeared to be complicit in their sons' illegal and dangerous activities. After she'd finished the call, Lisette left Detective Patterson with the prisoner and walked with the FBI agents and me a short distance away to report what had been found. It included a lot of bomb-making materials as well as detailed instructions. There was also some antidrilling literature, and some inflammatory antigovernment books and pamphlets. Some of the materials were found in the house, some in outbuildings. Besides the literature, they'd also found an illegal, fully automatic rifle in the Yosts' Dodge Ram. In addition to the charges related to the illegal items seized, the elder Yosts were both charged with making terroristic threats.

"Specifically," Lisette said as she caught my eye, "they said that since Jordan had failed to get rid of you, they'd find some other way. Both parents made direct threats against you—and against me, for that matter. I'll talk to the prosecutor and see if he'll file charges for conspiracy to commit murder."

"I suppose they're angry because of what happened with Junior," I said.

"That's right. According to the parents, they blame you for most of Junior's problems." She then turned to Special Agent Warner. "Somehow they must have communicated with Junior since Jarbi was located. They specifically threatened you as well."

Denzel smiled. "They must have wanted federal charges as well. We can accommodate them in that regard. I guess I'll be flying to Moab too."

On the way back, I called Crystal to see if there was anything I needed to know about investigations or flying. She didn't answer the phone, and my gut began to churn. "She's probably with Jarrett Bloom again," I said after telling Lisette that Crystal wasn't answering her phone.

"She doesn't strike me as someone who would make the same mistake twice," Lisette said doubtfully. "I'll call Ev and have him check by your house."

"I would appreciate that, but it is possible that she's with Jarrett. Unless I'm reading the signs wrong, I think those two are pretty interested in one another." I knew she was enamored with Jarrett, but I honestly feared she wasn't with him now, and that had me very, very worried.

When Ev called back a few minutes later, he reported that her car was not at my house. She didn't answer the door, and the house was locked up tight. I listened as Lisette said, "See if you can locate Jarrett Bloom. Maybe he knows where she is. She could even be at his house."

Ev found Jarrett at his home. He said he'd had lunch with Crystal and that she was going back to the office to work until five. It was after five now. "I'm setting this helicopter down," I said. "If I can find a place where I'll have a good signal, I can pull up my security cameras on my iPad."

"Do you have cameras at your office?" Jarbi asked from her position behind me.

"Yes, I have one that covers the door and front of the office and another one inside the reception area where Crystal's desk is located."

I landed on a high plateau where I was getting a clear signal. While Jarbi kept an eye on Jordan, Lisette and I got out of the chopper, me carrying my iPad, and then we both began to look at what my cameras had recorded.

It seemed that the office had been pretty quiet until just before five. Then the inside camera showed a man with a blue baseball cap over long, dark hair; a scraggly black beard; some baggy gray clothes; and large sunglasses entering the office. He spent a moment talking to Crystal. She said something and smiled at him. Then she reached down and opened a drawer of her desk. At that moment, the guy pulled a small pistol out of the pocket of his pants and pointed it at her. "Here we go again." I closed my eyes against the sudden dread that washed through me.

The camera showed Crystal looking at him with shock, but she appeared very cool and collected just moments later. She stood up and walked around her desk to the door. The outside camera had captured them walking out of the office, the perpetrator directly behind Crystal. The way I had installed the camera, it shot a wide angle that included the front door and part of the sidewalk and road as well.

At one point, the man turned just right so that the camera got a picture of the pistol that he had pulled on her. It was poking against Crystal's back. We watched as it showed the abductor forcing Crystal into a small white car with California plates, but the angle was such that we couldn't quite read the plate number. I was still examining the video when Lisette contacted her chief deputy.

"Go to the major's office," she told him. "Someone abducted Crystal Burke from there about thirty minutes ago."

As she finished her call, I was already clambering back into my chopper, my heart in my throat and a prayer in my mind. Lisette received a call from Special Agent Warner moments after we took off again. I heard her explain why we'd landed and what was happening. When the call was finished, she put her headphones back on and said, "Denzel will meet us at my house. His pilot will land there."

* * *

Both choppers had unloaded when Lisette got a call from her chief deputy. She talked to him as we rushed for her car, leaving Jarbi to take Jordan to the jail in her blue Chevy. The FBI agents joined us in the sheriff's car, and we sped toward my office. "The door to your office was unlocked when Ev arrived there," she said. "There was no sign of a struggle."

"What about her purse and phone?" I asked. "I didn't see them on the video."

"Her purse is beside her desk, and her phone is in it," she said.

"Was her gun in her purse?" I asked.

"He didn't say anything about a gun."

That gave me some hope. Crystal carried it in her purse sometimes, but other times she also carried it on a concealed belt holster. I didn't mention the gun, but I prayed that Crystal could use it if the opportunity presented itself.

I did a more thorough check of the office when we got there. Her gun, which I knew she'd been faithfully carrying since Jarbi's abduction, was nowhere to be found. I could only hope the guy who forced her out of the office didn't find it and take it away from her.

Lisette had Ev and another deputy do a fingerprint check of the office surrounding her work area, on the door handles, and so forth. Finally, we locked up and went to the jail, where the FBI agents could conduct interviews with the Yosts—all three of them, Jordan and his parents.

Lisette took me back to my chopper, and I moved it to my house, and then, after she'd gone back to her office, I carefully checked the house—both the main floor and the basement—but didn't see anything amiss.

I felt like I was unraveling, not sure what to do next. That was not a feeling I liked, but here it was. I prayed for calm and direction. I read my scriptures for a while. The calm came. The direction didn't. But the calm helped me to be patient, to know that I would soon understand what I needed to do.

I pulled a pizza from my freezer, cooked and ate it, then sat down and began to review everything I could think of about the troubles that had been swirling around this normally peaceful town over the past few days. To help myself think, I made notes.

By ten o'clock that night, I was finally getting sleepy. I decided the best thing I could do was to get some rest. I had only just entered my bedroom when my phone began to ring in my pocket. I whipped it out and looked at the number. I didn't recognize it, but I recognized the voice that spoke to me, and my heart jumped in my chest.

"Corbin, I'm okay." It was Crystal.

"Crystal, where are you?" I asked.

She told me she was somewhere along the Colorado River, past the Red Cliffs Lodge. "I don't know who this guy is, but he wasn't very smart. He didn't bother to check me for a gun."

"Did you shoot him?" I asked.

"Yes," she said in a subdued tone, "but I didn't kill him. He needs an ambulance. I'm using his phone to call you. And don't worry, he can't hurt me now."

"Are you in a building?" I asked.

"No. We're off the road to the south of the river a few miles and quite a ways from the lodge. I can't tell you exactly where, but if you

184   Clair M. Poulson

can bring the Jet Ranger out here, I can signal by flashing the car's lights. I'm sure you won't have any trouble spotting me."

"Okay, I'm on my way," I said, relieved.

I called Lisette as I ran from the house to my helicopter. I explained what was happening, and she said, "Pick me up behind my house."

Within minutes we were streaking through the dark night sky. Lisette called her dispatcher from her cell phone. She told him to have an ambulance head out of town on State Highway 128, which leads from Moab to I-70. She also told him to call Ev and Jarbi and to alert the FBI agents who were staying in a local motel.

After that, we concentrated on finding my cousin. I was flying high enough that we could see a long ways in all directions while staying close to where Highway 128 was strung out below us. Crystal made it easy for us to find her. She flashed the lights of her abductor's car when we got over the general area. When we spotted the lights, I veered to the south and dropped rapidly. She was a good three miles from the highway on a dirt road. I set the chopper down close to her.

We saved the hugs and tears for later. Right now, we needed to attend to the injured man, although Crystal had patched him up fairly well after tying his hands with his own belt. She'd managed to pull her pistol from her waistband and shoot him in the shoulder while he was driving. He had been momentarily distracted by a deer that ran across the road, narrowly missing them.

"I'm proud of you, Crystal," I told her after an ambulance had arrived and the injured man was loaded into it.

"I can't believe I let him take me in the first place," she said. "When he came in, I got a bad feeling. But when he said that he needed a private investigator, I decided the feeling was only because of the way he looked—he is really a creepy-looking guy. I was pulling a contract out of a drawer when he pulled the gun on me."

"Yeah, that was all captured on our new camera system," I said.

Jarbi, who'd arrived with Ev not far behind the ambulance, walked over to us. "We found the guy's wallet in his car. So at least we know who he is."

"Is he a local guy?" I asked.

"No, but I've seen him at some of the protests the antidrilling people have held," she said. "Which reminds me, there's going to be a big protest right in front of the courthouse tomorrow at noon. They think they can get the county council to listen to them and somehow shut down the drilling. Lisette wants me to be there."

"I think I'd like to be there as well," I said. I wasn't sure why, but I had an uneasy feeling I needed to attend.

Chapter Twenty-One

THE MAN WHO HAD TAKEN Crystal at gunpoint was identified as Lonnie Summers from San Francisco. His long hair was greasy and his eyes glazed. He was in his midtwenties and had a record of petty offenses, most of them in and around San Francisco. He had a bit of an attitude, I was told later, and didn't seem to have a job. I heard later that when the officers spoke to him, he mostly spouted about the drilling and other causes of controversial nature.

He was patched up at the hospital and then booked into the jail. "Your jail is getting kind of full," I said to Lisette the next morning when I met her there—at her request.

She smiled when I walked in. "We're thinning out the pool of potential suspects," she said. "But we still don't have whoever killed Edward Jones. At least I don't think so—I guess I can't rule out Junior Yost, even though they didn't find Edward's fingerprints in his airplane."

"Have you learned anything new from any of the Yosts or from Lonnie Summers?" I asked.

She shook her head. "No, they've all demanded lawyers but Summers; he simply refuses to talk to anyone—me, Ev, or the FBI."

It was my turn to smile. I had a feeling I knew why she had invited me to meet her here. "What did you need me for?"

"Well . . ." she began hesitantly. "Summers did commit a crime against your cousin, and that means he committed a crime against you." She paused, looking me right in the eye. There was a bit of a twinkle there. "I thought you might like to visit with him."

"I would like that," I said, pleased that I'd correctly divined her intention.

"If you happen to learn anything of value to my investigation, you will share it with me, won't you?" she asked.

"It's a big if, but yes, if I figure out a way to get him to talk, I'll let you know what he says," I said with a grin.

"I'm guessing you might be able to do that," she replied.

"I'll need a private room." I didn't want anyone observing my sometimes slightly questionable methods of extracting information.

She gave me a knowing look. "That can be arranged."

"By the way," I asked her, "have you seen or heard anything from Earl Bassinger?"

"He's back in town," she said with a frown. "He's already lodged a complaint with the county council about you parking your helicopter behind your house. One of the council members called me this morning."

"I hope they aren't considering rescinding my permit."

She shook her head. "No, and that made Earl angry. He apparently claims he got called out of town on urgent business, and he told whoever he talked to that they shouldn't have proceeded with the hearing without him. He also demanded that they order me to use his helicopter instead of yours for sheriff department business."

"And are they going to so order?" I asked, trying to appear worried.

"No," she said. "They set my budget, but they don't tell me how to use it. I am an elected official who has the authority to run my department as I see fit. The council members know that, and they respect it."

A few minutes later, I found myself alone with Lonnie Summers in a plain, windowless room inside the jail. He was frowning and looking at the table where he was seated. I sat across from him and said, "I guess you know who I am."

He said, "A cop, and I've got nothing to say to you. I already told those other cops that."

"No, I'm not a cop," I said, catching his eye and seeing surprise there. "I'm your worst nightmare."

"I don't know you, and I got nothing to say to you." He scowled. "So you don't scare me none."

"Not yet anyway," I said. Then I suddenly hammered my hand down on the table so hard that it made both Lonnie and the table jump.

"You will talk to me before either one of us leaves this room. Believe me, you will."

He leaned back as far as he could in his chair. "I want an attorney," he said.

"I told you, I'm not a cop. You don't get an attorney to talk to me."

"Then who are you?" he asked.

"You came into my office yesterday and told my associate that you needed a private investigator. Well, here I am," I said as I sat back in my chair. "What was it you needed me to investigate?"

His glassy eyes opened wide, and his chin dropped. After the surprise had had a moment to work on his feeble brain, he finally spoke. "I don't know what you're talking about."

"Don't give me that," I said. "I have you on video. You were recorded coming into my office. I saw you talking to Miss Burke. I saw you pull a gun on her. I saw you take her out to your car. And I saw you, in person, lying on the ground beside that same car with a bullet wound in your skinny shoulder. You're in more trouble than you can even imagine."

He blinked, but his eyes stayed glassy. I supposed he'd just done so many drugs in his life that his eyes decided it would be easier just to stay glassy. "You're lucky you didn't die out there last night," I said. "Miss Burke is a crack shot. She could have killed you if she'd wanted to, especially sitting so close to you. She must have only wanted to knick you, to scare you. You're obviously not a very bright man, but I'm here to see just how stupid you really are."

"I'm not stupid, and I got nothing to say to you," he protested, though his protest seemed a little weak.

"Listen, Mr. Summers, and listen carefully. I have a client—a real, paying client—not a fake sack of garbage like you. Her father was murdered. I am going to find out who murdered him. And right now, I'm thinking it was you."

"I didn't kill nobody," he said, suddenly visibly shaking. "You can't pin nothing like that on me."

"You don't think I can?" I challenged, crossing my arms. "You'll either talk to me, tell me what I want to know, or you'll see exactly what I can do."

"I didn't hurt your secretary," he said. "And I didn't kill nobody."

"Then I guess it's too bad for you because I don't believe you," I said. "You didn't hurt Miss Burke because she hurt you first. I think you intended to kill her. And if you don't want to go down for killing my client's father, then you better tell me why you kidnapped Miss Burke and what you planned to do with her."

I shut my mouth and waited, hoping he'd say something. He rubbed his glassy eyes, ran a hand through that horribly greasy hair, and wiped some spittle that was drooling from his mouth. He looked at me like I was a monster or something. I'd scared him, there was no doubt about that. But had I frightened him enough to make him talk? I could only hope. I had more scare up my sleeve, but I didn't want to use it if I didn't have to. "Talk to me, Mr. Summers," I said. "Why did you take Miss Burke at gunpoint? Why did you force her to go with you?"

He opened his mouth, wiping more spit away, and finally said, "I had to."

"Who said you had to?" I asked, my eyes boring into his.

He trembled. "I can't tell you."

"You just did. The only person I can think of that could scare you bad enough is Wyatt Mortell," I said.

He didn't need to say a word to let me know I had hit the mark.

"How much did he pay you?" I asked.

He kept running his hand through his greasy hair and blinking those horribly glassy eyes. "Not enough," he said after a long pause. That was all the admission I needed. But I was patient, and it paid off. "He said he'd kill me if I didn't bring your secretary to him."

"Yes, he would do that. He's leaving a trail of bodies behind him. Where did you see him?"

"I didn't see him. He called me," Lonnie said.

"Where was he when he called you?" I asked.

"I don't know," he whined. "He didn't tell me."

I believed him. "Where and when were you going to meet him?"

"Last night. At the end of the road where she shot me," he admitted.

"How much farther?"

"I'm not sure. Five or six miles, I think."

"So he knows now that you didn't do as he'd ordered you to," I said darkly.

"He'll kill me." He blinked more rapidly.

"Not if I get to him first," I said. "Why did he want you to take my associate to him?"

"So he could get you to meet him. He told me that you had caused him all the trouble you were going to and that he was going to get rid of you since some guy called Bean didn't."

So Wyatt was tied to Jordan's failed attempt to kill me. I might just have to speak with Jordan again. "Do you know where this Bean fellow is now?" I asked.

Summers shook his head.

"Well, it just so happens he's in here, in this jail. And as you can see, I'm alive and well. And I intend to stay that way. I'm afraid the same can't be said of your friend, Wyatt," I said. "By the way, how did you come to know Wyatt?"

"We met in New York," he said.

It looked like I had him on a roll now, so I kept asking questions before he decided to close down again. "What was he doing there?"

"Oh, it was at Occupy Wall Street," he said. "There were a lot of us there trying to get the greedy rich people to quit hoarding all the money."

That told me a lot about the guy. He was one of those who weren't interested in a job or legitimate work. He—along with a growing minority in America—believed that everyone else owed them a living. The rich, or even just the average hardworking person, owed people like him a living. I shuddered at the thought of all the dolts out there. I'm sure a lot of those lazy people aren't violent, but a lot of them are. They're just looking for an excuse to hurt someone.

I had another question for the dolt sitting across from me, one who was clearly not averse to violence. "What brought you, and for that matter, what brought Wyatt to Moab?"

I knew the answer, but I wanted proof on the little recorder stashed in my pocket. He said, "The drilling, what else? Wyatt is from here originally. He loves this area, and he hates seeing selfish, greedy people destroying it."

"What is it about the drilling that disturbs you?" I asked.

"You don't know?" he asked like I was some kind of dummy. "It pollutes the air, it ruins the scenery, it gets roads carved all over the place. It just ain't right, man. It takes people like me and Wyatt to keep things in balance."

The hypocrisy of it all was appalling. It made me angry. "You drive a car," I reminded him. "Don't you realize that your car burns the stuff you claim is polluting the earth?"

"My car doesn't contribute much," he said in the pat answer I'd expected. "Anyway, we don't need to drill for oil here. There's more than we need in other countries."

I knew I was beating a dead horse, but I was so peeved I could hardly contain myself. "So it's okay to ruin other countries' environments, just not ours?" I asked.

"Yeah, I guess so," he said with a puzzled look on his face.

Frankly, I didn't think Lonnie Summers was able to think for himself. Shrewder and, frankly, eviler people like Wyatt Mortell planted the seeds of anger and hatred into weaker, dependent people like Lonnie. I finally forced myself to get back to the matter at hand.

"What time was Wyatt supposed to meet you last night?" I asked.

"He said about seven, but he was running late. I called him, and he told me that he'd had an emergency and that it would be closer to ten," he said. "So I just kind of hung around out there, driving back and forth on dirt roads, trying to keep your secretary from driving me crazy. She has a big mouth. I didn't think she'd ever shut up."

I had to smile at that. I could picture Crystal trying to talk him to distraction. Being frightened probably made it worse. I suspect she did have him going crazy. Maybe it was more than the near collision with the deer that finally gave her the chance to get her gun out.

"What's so funny?" he asked.

"Oh, I was just thinking that Miss Burke must have succeeded. She must have driven you to distraction. That way she was able to shoot you."

"It wasn't her. It was a deer that ran in front of my car," he protested.

"Whatever. Do you have Wyatt's phone number?"

"It's in my phone. If you get my phone, I'll get it for you."

"No, that's okay," I said. The sheriff had confiscated his phone, and she was getting a search warrant so she could go through it. I let that matter drop. I popped another question at him, hoping to catch him off guard. "Did Wyatt kill a man by the name of Edward Jones?"

"You mean the man who fell out of the sky?" he asked.

"Yeah, that's the guy."

"I don't know. I do know that Jones made Wyatt mad. He told me that. Jones was supposed to help the cause but went to work for the oil company instead," he said. "Jones was a traitor."

"How well did you know his son, Trace Jones?" I asked.

"Hey, Trace was okay. I didn't know him very well, but Wyatt liked him a lot. He wasn't at all like his dad. He used to fly Wyatt around in his plane. I even got to go with them once," he said.

"If they were such good friends, why did Wyatt kill Trace?" I asked, once again hoping to catch him off guard.

"Huh?" he asked with a stupid look on his face. "Trace ain't dead."

"That's where you're wrong. I saw his dead body. Wyatt killed him. I was just wondering if he said anything to you about it."

Summers was shaking his head vigorously. "I don't know nothing about that. I don't know nothing about anybody killing anybody."

I had a feeling he really didn't. "Did you know Junior or Jordan Yost?" I asked.

"I met Junior once. He's a pretty cool guy. He's doing a lot of good for our cause," he said, and I think he actually believed that.

"And Jordan?" I asked. "What about him?"

"I knew him too, but he was working undercover for us." The guy actually smiled when he said that. "He really has them fooled."

"Which is why he's in jail, right?"

Once again my question stunned Lonnie Summers. He knew that whatever Jordan was supposed to do to me hadn't worked, yet he hadn't known the guy was in jail until I told him. Wyatt had found himself a real stooge in this guy.

"Why's he in jail?" Lonnie asked, his face white.

"Because he's not so good at undercover work. Let's just say he blew it big time," I said and left it at that.

"Wyatt will kill him," he said.

"That seems to be all Wyatt thinks about, Lonnie. And I'm sure you're on his list now too."

I left Lonnie Summers trembling with fear. I'm sure he'd had no idea how much trouble he was getting himself into when he hooked up with Wyatt Mortell.

Chapter Twenty-Two

THE MAIN REASON I'D WANTED to show up at the protesters' rally was to see who was there. The matters that were of interest to me all seemed to involve a small, although growing, group of people. I knew there could be more, and I wanted to know who they were. I was hoping that at the rally I could observe people and try to pick out the more radical ones. Those are the ones whose faces I would try to memorize and watch for later. Lonnie Summers had been a complete surprise. I didn't want to be blindsided again.

Jarbi was standing with a couple of uniformed officers at the main entrance to the courthouse. There were fewer than a hundred people when I arrived, but it didn't take long for the crowd to double. They began to chant and shout, calling for members of the county council to come out and listen to their demands.

No one came out, and anger began to build among the protesters. Jarbi had spotted me, and when two more uniformed officers, city police this time, showed up, she moved slowly around the crowd until she reached me. I was standing on the fringes near the back, not really close to anyone.

She stood beside me for a minute, not saying a thing. Finally, she slipped close enough to make herself heard over the din. "I don't like the feel of this crowd," she said.

"Yeah, they seem a little explosive," I agreed. "Do they have a leader?"

She shrugged but then said, "See that short guy with the longish brown hair and green-and-white baseball cap?" she said, nodding toward the left side of the crowd.

"Yeah."

"That's Earl Bassinger," she said. "I wonder what he's doing here."

"That's Earl, huh?" She had me thinking. A moment later, a bald, heavyset man wearing a sort of derby hat approached the crowd from the same side that Earl was standing on. He looked like he was maybe forty years old. I didn't see where he'd come from, but I watched as he neared Earl. He nodded his head at Earl, and Earl nodded back.

Jarbi poked me. "Did you see that?" she asked.

"I did. Apparently, those two know each other. Who is the new guy?"

"I have no idea, but it looks like he's a friend of Earl's, and what's more, I think he's going to address the crowd."

Sure enough, he worked himself around the edge of the protesters, climbed onto the steps, glared at the four officers there, and then turned to face the crowd. He had a deep, loud voice that carried easily in the open air. When he began to speak, the noise of the crowd subsided. He appeared calm at first, but within a minute or two, the anger he harbored appeared, and soon he was speaking of either getting the council to take an action to stop the drilling or taking matters into their own hands.

"Jarbi," I said, leaning close so I could speak without being overheard. "Do you know many of these people? Are they locals?"

"I know very few of them," she answered. "I think most of the troublemakers are from out of the area and have inserted themselves into our business here."

"Perhaps it's a few local people that started it though; could that be right?" I asked.

"It could be. People like Trace and the Yosts and even Wyatt, although he hasn't been around here for a long time."

"And maybe Earl Bassinger?"

"Maybe, although that would surprise me," she said. "But I guess you never know for sure about people."

The speaker was getting the crowd worked up. "We demand that the county council come out and meet with us," he shouted. "Are they such cowards they can't even talk to us?"

That brought an angry roar from the crowd, and many of them began to shout for the county leaders to come out. One of the deputies began speaking into his radio mike. All of the officers had concerned looks on their faces. Jarbi turned to me and spoke loudly into my ear so I could hear her above the ever-increasing roar of the crowd. "I think we're about to have a riot," she said.

"I hope not," I shouted back, but I feared she might be right.

I was watching Earl, especially interested to see what he might do. So far, I didn't think he'd participated in the shouting. When the crowd suddenly stilled, I looked back at the speaker. He was raising and lowering his hands, apparently attempting to quiet the crowd. A particularly boisterous woman near me was having a hard time complying. When she finally did, I slipped close to her and tapped her shoulder to get her attention. "I'm new here," I said. "That guy's pretty impressive. Who is he?"

"That's Louie Fagan. Isn't he great?" she said. Before I could reply, she turned her full attention to him.

I stepped back beside Jarbi and said, "His name is Louie Fagan. You might want to see if you can find anything out about him."

"I'll do that right now," she said and slipped away, heading for her patrol car, which was parked across the street about a hundred yards away.

She wasn't the only one slipping away. Earl Bassinger had worked his way to the back of the crowd, and then he simply turned and walked away. I turned my attention to what Mr. Louie Fagan was saying. It was inflammatory, derogatory, and filled with language like I hadn't heard since I got out of the military.

The crowd was surging forward as he spoke. Some began to chant again, but once more he stilled them. So they began to silently pump their fists in the air. Louie said, "It looks like the cowards aren't going to come out. Who would like to follow me inside? We'll make them listen."

When he turned and marched toward the four officers at the door, the crowd surged after him. The poor officers did the only thing they could and moved aside; otherwise, they would have been crushed. A small handful of the crowd followed the lead of Earl Bassinger and slinked away. The rest soon disappeared inside the building.

The officers followed them in. A moment later, I could hear sirens. More cops—deputies, city police, and a couple of Utah Highway Patrol troopers—showed up. Then the sheriff and the police chief pulled in. Jarbi trotted back as those two stopped next to me.

"What's going on, Major?" Sheriff Statton asked.

I explained and then said, "I hope they don't do more than just try to be heard in there."

Lisette turned to the chief. "I guess maybe you and I better go inside. The same goes for the rest of these officers too."

"Before we go in," Jarbi said, "you need to know who's leading them today. He's a guy by the name of Louie Fagan."

"I've heard that name," Lisette said. "Johanna Jones's maiden name is Fagan . . . Isn't he her brother? They aren't originally from around here."

The police chief confirmed that Louie was Johanna's younger brother.

Jarbi said, "And he has a record of assaults, theft, trespassing, and other crimes. I was just checking."

"That's good to know," Lisette said. Here was someone else we might want to take a closer look at. Perhaps he and his brother-in-law hadn't been on good terms since Edward Jones had been a lawman. Lisette turned to the officers assembled all around us and said, "Let's go inside."

I hadn't been invited, but curiosity got the better of me, and I trailed behind them. The courthouse was loud with shouting and stomping of feet. I wasn't sure of the exact number of officers, but I think there were now close to fifteen in the building. Ev Belgar came running in a couple minutes later. Even with him, law enforcement was outnumbered ten or twelve to one.

Not good odds. All of the officers carried pistols; some probably had Tasers or carried mace. I hoped they wouldn't have to use anything though. The crowd in the hallway finally settled down, and some of them disappeared into what I thought must be the council chambers.

They were in there for quite a while. Probably fifty people drifted to the door and went back outside. Some stood around out there; others left. The odds were getting better, but they still weren't good. I thought about leaving, but chauvinist that I am, I wasn't about to leave as long as Lisette was in here. The very thought of her getting hurt made me tremble.

Five more minutes passed, then ten. Lisette was asked to go into the room with the council and the protesters. Another ten minutes passed, and then Lisette came out, followed by Louie Fagan. As they passed me, I heard her say, "Louie, you've got to understand that the county council doesn't have the authority to do what you're asking."

"If they don't get those rigs out of here, we will," he threatened.

She escorted him to the door, and the rest of the protesters followed. Everyone, including the officers, exited the building. I was the last one out, and I stayed by the door watching to see what would happen next. The officers fanned out around the group, but before long the protestors began to disperse. Louie kept telling small groups of them that he'd be in touch to let them know what came next. Finally, even Louie left.

The officers talked in small groups for a few minutes. They seemed to be winding down after all the tension. The chief and his officers soon left, followed by the highway patrol and all the deputies but Ev and Jarbi. I talked to Lisette, Jarbi, and Ev for a few minutes, filling them in on my earlier interview at the jail with Lonnie Summers. Then I said, "Sheriff, if you don't mind, I'd like to go talk to Mr. Summers again. Maybe he can tell me more about Louie Fagan."

Lonnie didn't seem happy to see me again, but when I mentioned Louie Fagan, he went absolutely pale. He didn't tell me much other than the fact that Louie and Wyatt were close friends. That was what I had expected, but just as I was ready to leave, I thought of something else. "Lonnie," I said, leaning across the table toward him, "tell me about Wyatt and Earl Bassinger."

He didn't say anything for a moment, but I could tell he was thinking. Finally, he said, "Wyatt sometimes goes flying in Mr. Bassinger's helicopter."

"Are they good friends?" I asked.

He shrugged his shoulders, wincing as he felt the pain in the one Crystal had shot. "I don't know," he said.

"Lonnie, you've been a big help," I said, "but can you tell me this? Is Louie Fagan the leader, the person behind even Wyatt?"

To my surprise, he slowly shook his head. "No," he said. "I think it's a woman. But I don't know who she is."

That stunned me. Who in the world could that be? I thought about the crowd of people at the courthouse. I tried to picture the faces of the women there. One stood out, and I mentally kicked myself for not getting her name. The woman I had spoken with had said nothing but good about Louie. Somehow, we had to find that woman again. Of all the people I had seen at the gathering, she seemed like one who could be behind it all. Her almost fanatical worship of Louie could have really been pride for the way he followed her every order. I had to know.

I spent a couple more minutes with him and then gave up. It looked like I had learned about all I could from Lonnie Summer.

Next I went to the office and caught up on some paperwork. Crystal wanted to know everything I'd learned about Lonnie and Wyatt. She deserved to know. After all, she could have lost her life at the hands of those two.

An hour later, Lisette came in. She spoke to Crystal for a moment and then stepped into my office, where she sat down wearily. "Hi, Major. Sorry to bother you."

"What can I do for you?" I asked.

"Nothing. I just needed to see you." She smiled.

Wow! That was not what I had expected, but it was most welcome. In fact, it made my spine tingle. It was easy to smile back at her. "I'm sorry you had to deal with all those protestors this afternoon," I said. "I'm afraid I wasn't much help."

She favored me with another smile, a brighter one this time. "Just knowing you were there gave me a huge boost of confidence. Thanks for staying."

"I was glad to," I said. "And since you're here, let me tell you what I learned from Lonnie Summers on this latest trip to your jail."

After I'd recounted my interview, she said, "What a tangled web we have here. I wish I knew how it all fit together. We've got the Yosts—all four of them—Wyatt Mortell, Lonnie Summers, Louie Fagan, and I guess I should include Earl Bassinger. Then there are the three dead Joneses. And finally, there's some mysterious woman who Lonnie says is the real leader. How were they all connected, and why did one or more of them kill Edward Jones? And I am convinced that's what happened."

"I wish I knew." I shook my head as I thought about all of the people she'd mentioned. Then I added, "Maybe I need to talk to my client again. Perhaps Asher can shed some light on it, especially considering that the latest arrival on your list of people of interest is her uncle."

"Do you think she'd mind if I went with you?" she asked. "For that matter, do you mind?"

"Let's just do it," I said and got up from behind my desk.

I told Crystal where we were going, and then we left, both of us riding in Lisette's Ford Expedition. We found Asher at home. She invited us in, glanced warily at the sheriff, and then invited us to sit down.

"Major," she said, "I'm sorry I got you into this mess. My husband called me last night from the rig. He told me all about what Bean did. You don't have to keep working for me. It's too dangerous. Trace is gone, and he's the reason I asked for your help in the first place."

"I have another client now," I said as I thought of Dayna Simonson. "I haven't been putting any hours on your account since Trace was killed."

"Get me a bill, and I'll pay it," she said. "I'm still not sure Trace didn't kill Dad or at least have something to do with it. Are you?"

"I'm pretty sure Trace isn't the guilty party," I said. "We—the sheriff and I—have some other suspects that are pretty high on the list now. My new client was threatened by one of them. She's in hiding until we catch the guy."

"Can you tell me who you're after?" she asked. "Is it Wyatt Mortell?"

"He's one of them. But there are others. The reason Sheriff Patterson and I are here now is to talk to you about a man who just came to our attention today. His name is Louie Fagan."

Asher's eyes narrowed. "Dear Uncle Louie, Mom's baby brother," she said scornfully. "He's as bad as Trace." She shook her head. "I didn't know he was around. If anyone was helping Trace, it would have been Louie."

I shifted in my chair and then looked Asher square in the eye. "What kind of relationship did Louie have with your mother?" I asked.

She shook her head, ran a hand through her short, spiky hair, and then said, "She thought the sun rose and set in Louie. He couldn't do anything wrong. I was glad he didn't come around much because he wasn't good for Mom."

"Why would your mother keep a strong injectable sedative in her house?" I asked, changing the subject.

She looked surprised. "I can't imagine. Did you find something in the search?"

"Yes," I responded.

"I have no idea." She paused and looked thoughtful for a moment. "I wonder if Louie's been around lately," she said. "He would stay with Dad and Mom on the rare occasions that he came to see them."

"I suppose that could be," I agreed.

Asher suddenly lifted her index finger and then shook it toward me. "Wait a minute, Major. Are you telling me that Louie's been around lately?"

I chuckled. "I was about to, yes."

"What's he doing here?" she demanded.

"He seems to be one of the instigators behind the protests over the oil rigs."

"That creep," she said fiercely. "He doesn't even live here. What does he care?"

"He cares enough that he's threatened to get the rigs shut down. He led a group of protesters at the courthouse today, demanding that the county council shut them down. He almost started a riot." I stopped and looked at her for a moment, watching the anger on her face. Then I added, "I heard that he and Wyatt Mortell are pretty thick."

"That figures," she said.

"Another name I was wondering about is a guy by the name of Lonnie Summers," I said.

"Never heard of him," she responded. "Is he a friend of my uncle's too?"

"They're acquainted." I turned to Lisette. "Sheriff, do you mind if I tell her about what happened with Crystal last night?"

"Of course not," Lisette said.

As I rehearsed the events of the kidnapping, Asher's face grew scornful. "I still bet that Trace put this all in motion," she said when I had finished.

"I don't think so," I said. "This Lonnie guy I just told you about says there's a woman behind this all. Until then I'd thought it was Louie. Louie seems to have a very strong personality. The out-of-towners here in Moab almost seem to worship him. But there was one woman there who seemed especially fond of Louie who could be pulling his strings."

Can you think of anyone, any woman who might have that kind of influence over your uncle?"

She thought for a long time but finally said, "I can't think of anyone. Of course, I don't know his friends since he isn't from here."

"Keep thinking," I said. "If you think of anyone, please give me or the sheriff a call."

"Okay," she agreed. "But, Major, after what you've just told me, I have to tell you and Sheriff Statton that Louie could be very dangerous."

"Yes," I said. "I think we'll heed your warning."

Chapter Twenty-Three

WHEN WE WERE BACK IN Lisette's car, I said, "I think we're getting close but not close enough. I wish we could find Wyatt. Maybe we could learn something from him."

"Maybe," she said. "But so far he's been pretty elusive."

"And that woman, the one I spoke to at the protest, I need to see if I can find her," I said.

"How will you do that, Major?"

"There are a couple of things I can do. For one, I could look around town, try to find anyone whose face I recognize from the protest and ask them," I said. "And while I'm doing that, I could watch specifically for her. She's got to be around here somewhere."

"Jarbi saw her too, right?" Lisette asked.

"Yes, she did," I agreed.

"Then I'll have her look too. Between you, maybe you can find her," she said, looking hopeful.

I had one more idea, not one I relished but one that was worth mentioning. "If that doesn't work, I think I'll try to talk to Earl Bassinger. He was at the protest for a while, and he and Louie Fagan obviously knew each other. From the look that passed between them, I'd say it's more than an acquaintance. If that's true, he probably knows who this other woman is."

Lisette looked doubtful. "I think that's a long shot, but if you think he'll talk, I'll go along with it. In fact, if you want me to, I'll talk to him myself. Or I could go with you."

"Thanks, Lisette," I said, reaching across the seat and placing my hand on hers. "If you give me a ride back to my office, I'll start searching."

She smiled at me, a smile I was really coming to enjoy. "I'll have Jarbi call you, and the two of you can coordinate your efforts."

* * *

Jarbi and I both worked for several hours without results. We worked separately but kept in constant contact. We did talk to several people we'd recognized, but they all denied knowing the woman we described. We didn't quit until ten that night. By then we were both exhausted.

Crystal's car was home, but she was not. At least this time I knew where she was. She had a date that night with Jarrett Bloom. I was beginning to wonder just how long I would have someone to share the rent on this really nice house. I was just getting ready for bed a little after eleven when headlights struck the blinds to my bedroom. I peeked out and watched just for a moment as the two of them strolled arm in arm around the house toward the basement stairwell.

I was so exhausted that it didn't take me long to fall asleep. I had really looked forward to a long and deep sleep that night. I didn't get it. An alarm went off and woke me with a start, my heart pounding. A quick glance at my clock showed it was just past three in the morning.

I grabbed my pistol from the nightstand and hurried to the back door. It was another dark night, but I'd left my porch light on so there'd be some light near the helicopter. I could see a shadowy figure moving near my Jet Ranger. I eased the door open as quietly as I could and stepped onto the porch. Whoever was by the helicopter wasn't paying attention to the house. Whoever was out there was not a pro, I thought as I slipped across the grass.

Suddenly, he turned toward me, gasped, and lit out, running for the yard gate to the east. I'm not the fastest runner in the world, but with the aid of an adrenaline rush, I moved pretty quickly. I tackled the intruder several feet short of the gate. He began swinging at me, but he didn't stand a chance. One blow to his cheek put him down for the count.

I dragged him back to my porch, slipped cuffs on his arms and leg irons on his ankles, and removed a long folding knife from his pocket. I soon had my captive seated on a chair. Then I doused his head with cold water and waited for him to regain consciousness. By the time he began to mumble, I heard a sound behind me. Crystal said, "What's going on, Corbin?"

"I caught a trespasser," I said. I asked him his name. He refused to give it, so I dug into his pockets again and pulled out a wallet and handed it to Crystal. My eyes didn't leave the man. "You may just as well cooperate. What exactly were you planning to do to my helicopter?"

"Nothing, I swear, mister. I was just curious and wanted to look at it," he said, his voice trembling. He was young, Hispanic, and quite small in stature.

"At three in the morning?" I asked. "You don't really expect me to believe that, do you?"

He didn't answer, not that anything he could have said would have convinced me he was telling the truth.

"His name is Juan Lopez," Crystal said. "He is sixteen and lives here in Moab." She had his wallet open and was reading his ID.

I took a deep breath. "Mr. Lopez, you're not leaving here until you tell me exactly what you were doing and who sent you."

"I ain't saying nothing," he said stubbornly.

"Crystal, keep an eye on him while I go get a light and have a look around my chopper, would you please?" I asked.

"Of course. Would you like me to call the cops?" she asked.

"Not yet," I said. "They might not approve of the way I get him to answer my questions." I gave him a hard look.

"You can't make me say nothing," our young captive said. "You touch me, and I'll sue you."

"They learn young, don't they?" I rolled my eyes and looked at Crystal. "They think if they threaten to sue it'll make anyone tremble, and all the troubles they've brought on themselves will go away." I leaned close to his face. "Juan, that won't work with me. Anyway, I have cameras covering everything we're doing, and in case you weren't paying attention, I have a No Trespassing sign on the gate."

"I didn't see no sign," he said.

"That's because you were so intent on doing damage to my helicopter that you weren't paying attention. Now, Juan, I don't intend to hurt you, but you will answer my questions."

I went inside, got the flashlight, and came back out. It didn't take me long to find the small bag of wrenches he'd dropped beside my helicopter. I looked a little longer but didn't find anything else. I carried the bag back over to where Juan was sitting. I knelt down in front of him and said, "Tell me what you were going to do with these wrenches."

He stubbornly shook his head.

I said, "Do you have any idea what it's like to sit in a jail cell day after day after day?" He looked at me with a stubborn set to his jaw. "It's not fun," I told him. "In fact, it's terrible. You would hate it, but that's exactly what's going to happen if you don't tell me what you were going to do."

He glanced down at one of his front pants pockets, and he moved his handcuffed hands to cover the opening.

I looked up at Crystal and smiled. "I think he just told me something."

"I didn't say nothing," he protested.

"But you told me something just the same. Stand up."

With Crystal's help, he was soon on his feet. I reached for his front left pocket. He struggled and tried to keep his hands over it, but I easily reached and pulled out a small, folded piece of paper.

"Hey, that's mine!" he screamed. "You got no business reading that."

I ignored him as I unfolded the paper and stepped directly beneath my porch light to read. The handwritten note was addressed to Juan. It was a clearly diagrammed set of instructions that, if followed in exactness, would have caused my Jet Ranger to have serious trouble sometime in flight. The trouble would have been serious enough to cause a crash, one that would almost certainly have proved fatal.

I had just averted another cold and calculated effort to destroy my Jet Ranger—and me in the process. My face must have reflected my anger because Crystal asked, "What does it say, Corbin?"

"Call the sheriff," I said, gritting my teeth. "This young man is to be charged with conspiracy to murder."

He jerked away from Crystal's grasp and tried to escape off the porch—as if he could go anywhere with those handcuffs and leg irons. All he succeeded in doing was tripping and falling face forward down the steps to the sidewalk. "Get the sheriff," I said again. "This young man has something he needs to tell me."

I lifted him up, clear off his feet, quickly inspecting him for injuries. His nose was bleeding slightly, but other than that he appeared unhurt.

I held him nose to nose with me, his feet dangling and kicking. "Who gave you these instructions?" I asked, my voice a growl.

"I can't tell you," he said weakly.

"You may be sixteen, but this note could land you in prison for the rest of your life, Juan. Is that what you want?"

"Put me down," he begged.

"I will when you give me the name of the person you're working for. Otherwise I'll string you up by your feet on that tree over there," I said, glancing toward a large elm tree in the corner of the fenced yard.

He twisted his neck to look at the tree. He must have decided that I might really do what I had just threatened because he spoke the name in a frightened voice. In anger, I let go of him. He fell six inches to the sidewalk, lost his balance, and went over backward onto the grass.

I knelt down beside him, aware of Crystal watching us. "How much did he pay you?"

"A hundred dollars," Juan said through quivering lips.

I stood back up and said to Crystal, "Well, at least I know how much my life is worth—not very much."

I helped Juan sit up, steered him back onto the porch, and sat him gently in the same chair he'd been in before. My anger at Juan dissipated into the cool night air. A poor Hispanic kid, he was nothing more than a pawn to people with a terrible, deadly agenda, people who would destroy anyone who interfered in any way, including Juan. And they did it with no regard for innocent people who might get hurt or die as the killers pursued their nefarious goals.

Crystal went inside for a wet cloth to sponge Juan's face, and I stood there beside him, feeling nothing but pity for him now. I said, "Hey, kid, don't get me wrong. I'm sorry you got caught up in a mess that wasn't yours. I'm sure you were told that no one would get hurt, and I'll make sure the sheriff knows that."

Lisette showed up a few minutes later, fully dressed, unlike my cousin and me. We were in our pajamas, but I was too upset to be embarrassed.

"Major," Lisette cried as she came running into the yard. "What happened? Crystal said someone was trying to kill you."

She stopped at the base of the steps and looked at Juan, who was still sitting in handcuffs and leg irons. "This kid tried to kill you?" she asked. "That's Juan Lopez. He's just a little shoplifter. He's never done anything worse than that before."

"He was suckered into earning a hundred bucks," I told her. "The kid had no idea what he was doing."

* * *

Two hours later, after the sheriff had taped a full statement from Juan, in the presence of his parents, he was released to them. Frankly, I think he may have been better off in juvenile detention. His father was irate. Both of the parents thought the boy had been home in bed. They thanked me a dozen times and assured me, to Juan's obvious discomfort, that he would never do such a thing again.

The sheriff warned them to keep him out of sight because of the danger he could be in when word got around that he had failed. "If I were you and he was my kid, I'd get him out of town for a while."

Both the sheriff and I were dead tired. Sleep just didn't seem to be something we got a lot of lately. But the three hours I'd had were sound ones, and I was too wide awake and wired to try to go back to bed. Besides, we had someone to find and arrest before another attempt was made on my life. I liked my life, and I was extremely anxious to preserve it.

From the way the sheriff hugged me after Juan and his parents left, I got the feeling she was anxious to keep me alive as well. That made me feel warm all over.

At eight o'clock we were in her office planning our next move when Jarbi and Ev joined us. We quickly brought them up to speed on the events of the night, and then we went looking for the author of Juan's deadly note.

By noon, we had failed to find our suspect or any of the others we believed might be involved as well. The woman from the protest proved to be as elusive as the others. Frustrated, Lisette assigned three of her deputies to spend the afternoon keeping an eye on locations where those key players might show up, then she went home to take a nap. I did the same.

Chapter Twenty-Four

BELIEVE IT OR NOT, I got another three hours of sleep before a phone call sent me running for my truck. By the time I passed the sheriff's house, she was also in her vehicle and headed for her office. We had a suspect, a woman, who had been picked up by one of the deputies. Both the sheriff and I were anxious to talk to her—if she would talk.

Her name was Desiree Keefe, and she was not at all happy to see us. She was the protester I'd spoken to at the rally. She appeared to be in her midthirties. She was a plain woman, slender, about five four, with gray eyes, no makeup, and long, dishwater-blonde hair. She was still dressed in the flowered dress she'd worn at the protest. It looked like she'd slept in it, probably more than once, since it'd last been washed.

"Do you know why you're here?" Lisette asked as she and I sat down across a small conference table from Desiree.

"I guess because I was at the rally yesterday, but that was all legal, so you have no right to hold me," she said, her scowl not doing anything for her already plain face.

"No, you're here because we need to talk to you about your friend, Louie Fagan," Lisette said.

Miss Keefe eyed the sheriff darkly, gray eyes full of disgust. Then she turned those eyes on me. "You were at the rally," she said. "Whose side are you on, anyway?"

"The same side I've always been on," I said. "Tell us how you know Louie. You told me yesterday how much you admire him, but I need to know what your relationship with him is."

"Am I charged with something?" Desiree asked, turning those scornful eyes back on Lisette.

"No, but we need you to tell us more about Louie and some of his friends," the sheriff responded.

"I've known Louie for about five years," she said. "He's my boyfriend. Now you know, so I'll be going."

She got to her feet, but Lisette said, "Not so fast, Desiree. We need to talk to Louie. Where is he?"

"I don't know. I haven't seen him since the rally yesterday."

The shifting of her eyes told me that she was lying. I threw out a question. "When did you talk to Wyatt last?"

"I haven't seen him—" She caught herself. "I don't know who you're talking about." Those gray eyes were shifting all over the place now.

"How do you give orders to those men if you never see them?" Lisette asked.

The surprise on Desiree's face was, I believed, genuine. She was clearly part of the gang, but its leader? I wasn't totally convinced. Then again, maybe her surprise was because we knew about her rather than because it was not true. I threw out a couple other names, and as before, she shifted her eyes while she denied knowing them.

I tried another trick. "Lonnie says you give the orders. How do you explain that?"

"Lonnie doesn't know anything. If you believe anything he says, you're more stupid than I thought, and that's saying something," she said with a curl on her lips.

"So you do know him," I said flatly. His was one of the names I'd already mentioned.

"I didn't say that," Desiree said, fingering her long, stringy hair.

"You didn't need to," I said. "I already know it."

The next ten minutes were more of the same. We asked questions; she dodged them or outright lied to us. She might not be the brains of the operation, but she was part of it all. Then again, she could be the one in charge. I just didn't know. However, I had decided that I would treat her as though she wasn't and consider other women. Lonnie had said it was a woman, and I believed him. But who that woman was, if not Desiree Keefe, I had no idea.

Or did I?

After we reluctantly let Desiree go, I said to Lisette, "I think it would be a good idea to have someone keep an eye on that woman."

"My thought exactly," she said, and she gave the order over her phone.

When she was finished, I asked, "Would you be opposed to me having a talk with Mrs. Yost?"

She scrunched her eyebrows. "Surely you don't think she's the mastermind?"

"If it's not Miss Keefe, and I realize it could be, but if it's not, then who else could it be? I think a few questions might convince me either that it is or isn't Desiree or Mrs. Yost."

A few minutes later, I sat across from the mother of the now infamous Yost brothers. I spent a total of ten minutes with her. When I had the officer take her back to her cell, I knew two things for certain. First, she was not the woman Lonnie had alluded to. Second, Mrs. Yost was totally supportive of whatever her two sons wanted to do. She was, because of them, a criminal. And so was her husband. Their sons had pretty much destroyed them. But Mrs. Yost was no criminal mastermind.

I asked to talk to Lonnie Summers again. When he came in, he sat down morosely. The depth of trouble he was in seemed to be settling into his sluggish brain.

"What do you need to know?" he asked, sounding resigned.

"I need you to tell me about Desiree Keefe," I said.

He didn't even flinch. "She's Louie's girl," he said, not telling me anything I didn't already know.

"Besides that," I said.

"She's creepy. I don't like her."

I didn't either, but that didn't get me any closer to solving the mystery of who the woman leader was. "What else?" I asked.

"Nothing," he said.

"Is she the woman who gives the orders to Louie and Wyatt?"

"No. She's not smart enough," he said.

I should have asked him that first. It would have saved me some time. But now that I had him, I decided to see if I could somehow jog his memory into giving me something that would help me figure out who the woman was.

I tried several questions. None of them got me any closer, and finally I said, "When was the last time you heard Wyatt or Louie mention the boss woman?"

He scrunched his eyes, shook his head slowly from side to side, and then he told me. His answer was like a light coming on. I knew who the woman was. I didn't just suspect it. I knew! I gave him the name. He shook his head, but that didn't change my mind. Maybe he didn't know the name or remember it, but I knew.

I tried my conclusion out on Lisette a few minutes later. She smiled, kissed my cheek, and said, "Major, you are a genius. Let's get over to her house right now."

We never got there. A call came through from one of the oil rigs to the dispatcher, and we raced for my house. In a few minutes, we were streaking through the sky in my Jet Ranger.

We could see the billowing smoke from miles away. The only information we had was that there had been an explosion followed by a raging fire. When we got closer, we could see that the rig had folded. It was the rig that Devan Rish and Bill Grady worked on. I feared the worst. From Lisette's eyes, I could see that she did too.

"I wish I could believe this was an accident," she said as I circled once around the rig before landing a hundred yards or so away.

I was relieved to see two men come running toward us as we climbed to the ground. Devan Rish was the first one to reach us. He was covered with black, and he was bleeding from a small cut on his forehead. "We need an air ambulance," he shouted. "Bill Grady's hurt real bad."

Lisette began working on the request as I asked, "Is he the only one?"

"Yep, that's all. One guy must be dead. We can't find him. The others are okay. I mean, you know, we all got hurt, but we'll be okay," he said. "Follow me."

He took me to where Bill was stretched out on the ground, two men kneeling beside him. Looking at him reminded me of the wars I'd fought in. One hand was gone. His face was disfigured, and it looked like he was bleeding from a dozen wounds. It could have been from a land mine or a car bomb or any number of other weapons that our enemies had used.

I didn't panic. This was familiar territory. I had both received training and experienced this type of thing firsthand in the army. The men beside Bill had already succeeded in stopping the bleeding from his stump. They'd tied a rag just above the end of what was left of his arm. They had a first-aid kit there, but I told Devan to get the one from my helicopter. I told him where it was stored, and he obediently ran toward the chopper.

"Bill, it's Major Daniels," I said. "You're going to be okay. I know what I'm doing." I was a trained and certified EMT. I'd actually been an ambulance paramedic for the first couple years after I'd left the army.

"Major," he said so quietly I had to lean close to his mouth to hear him. "It wasn't an accident."

That was as I had feared. But he was too weak, in too much pain, and too deep in shock to get details from him at this point. What he needed was a hospital. For now, I'd do the best job I could. "Be calm. I'll give you something for pain in a moment."

"My hand hurts awful bad," he said, waving his bloody stump. Both his eyes were swollen shut, so he couldn't see.

"I'll help you," I said, not about to tell him that he didn't have a left hand anymore.

"Help is on the way," Lisette announced as she knelt beside me. "A life-flight helicopter is coming from Grand Junction."

"Good, I'll see if I can't stabilize Bill before they get here."

"What about the other men?" she asked as I slit Bill's pant leg open from hip to ankle, exposing a nasty wound that needed attention.

"One's missing, almost undoubtedly dead," I said. "The others will be okay, according to Devan."

"Do you need my help with Bill?" she asked. "Not that it isn't pretty obvious that you've done this kind of thing before."

"No, I've got this. You check on the others," I suggested. "Devan can help me here."

Lisette moved quickly in the direction of the burning rig just as Devan came running up with my first aid kit. I opened it as Bill moaned and groaned in pain. The first thing I did was give him a shot of morphine. Then I disinfected and put a dressing on the deep gash in his leg. After that I turned my attention to his arm. I cleaned the wound at the end as well as I could and then replaced the rag with a sterile dressing.

The morphine did its work, and Bill calmed down. After a few minutes, he seemed to be asleep. With Devan's help, I worked on one wound after another. Bill would survive, but he would never be whole again. I was filled with anger as I worked on his battered and bloody body.

"Is he going to live?" Devan asked after a half hour or so.

"I think so. He's lost a lot of blood, but I think he'll be okay until they get him to the hospital and give him more. They'll have IV fluids that will help a lot once he's on the life flight," I said. "The biggest danger is infection. And that's true of you as well. As soon as we finish patching him up, let me give you a hand and disinfect the cut on your face."

All of the men gathered around Bill when the life-flight helicopter arrived. Before he was loaded in, one of the scenic-tour helicopters from Moab arrived with Ev and Jarbi on board. Special Agent Warner and the same agent that had been with him before also landed about the time Bill was being loaded into the life flight.

One of the men on the medical helicopter asked who had attended to Bill's wounds.

"The major did. He's done this sort of thing before," Devan said.

I was told that I'd done a great job, and then they were off. I began cleaning and patching a variety of wounds on the other men while the officers conducted interviews and surveyed the scene. There was no sign of the missing worker.

"He was closest to where the explosion occurred," Devan said. "He's gone, I'm afraid."

"What caused the explosion?" Agent Warner asked.

"Bill spoke to me while I was treating him. He told me before he lost consciousness that it wasn't an accident," I reported.

Devan and the others felt the same way, but no one really knew what had happened.

"Could someone have brought a bomb onto the rig?" I asked. "Have you had any visitors?"

"No, there's only been us since all of you left after the thing with Bean on Monday," Devan said.

It was hard to believe that Jordan's attempt to kill me had been only two days ago. A lot had happened since Monday morning, and yet it was only Wednesday afternoon. If this rig explosion had anything to do with Louie Fagan or Wyatt Mortell, the group had acted fast since being rebuffed by the county council just the day before. I said as much to Lisette. She looked back at where the rig lay in a pile on the ground and flames, and smoke shot from the center.

Finally, she turned to Devan and asked, "Could a bomb have been dropped from the air?"

He shrugged his shoulders. "I don't know. None of us saw a plane fly over, but we were busy, and it's really noisy on the rig."

"When Bill spoke to me, he seemed very sure. He seemed to know something the rest of you didn't," I said.

"You need to talk to him then," Devan suggested.

"Not until he's stable. He's probably going to be kept in a drug-induced coma for a while, possibly even a few days," I said.

"What about Bill's wife?" Devan asked. "Does she know yet?"

Lisette answered, "The chief of police talked to her. A neighbor is driving her to the Grand Junction hospital."

Based on what Bill had said, the oil well location was considered a crime scene and treated accordingly. Lisette had more deputies come to the scene by car; it took a long time to get to the rig from Moab that way. The oil company flew in its own investigators and said that more were on the way. A crew to extinguish the fire would need to be flown in from Texas.

The body of the missing man was assumed burned, possibly to the point that nothing of the body could ever be recovered. I wasn't needed there anymore, so I pulled the sheriff aside. "I'll come back for you when you're ready to leave," I said. "In the meantime, there are some things I think I'd like to do in Moab."

"You go then, Major," she said. She gave me a hug and a kiss on the cheek and then went back to her work.

After fueling up at the airport, I parked my Jet Ranger behind the house, checked in with Crystal, grabbed a bite to eat, and then got in my pickup. I sat in my driveway for a while thinking. Then I began to drive around town. Frankly, I hadn't expected to see Wyatt or Louie, and my expectations were right on. I drove by Earl Bassinger's place after checking to see if his Jet Ranger was parked in its usual place, which it was. It was time to talk to Earl. I rang his doorbell and waited. Then I knocked. Still no answer. I tried again with the same result.

A third time brought his wife to the door. I'd never seen her before. She was a mousy little woman, messy hair, no makeup, fingernails chewed to the quick, and eyes that had no luster. I told her who I was, and she began to shake her head. She told me to go away. I told her I needed to speak with her husband. She told me he was out of town. When I pointed out that his Jet Ranger was right here in Moab, she told me he'd taken his truck. I asked her where he'd gone. She told me it was none of my business and shut the door in my face.

I walked back to my truck and started the engine; then I sat there and stared at the Bassinger house. I wanted to confront the man, have it out with him. My gut told me he was inside but didn't have the guts to talk to me. The thought even crossed my mind that I could probably force my way in and have a talk with him, but then I might have the city police after me, and that would not be helpful. I drove away, disappointed and annoyed.

I spent another hour checking for Louie and Wyatt at all the bars in the area. I had the same results as before.

It was getting late. I wondered when the sheriff would call. She didn't until nine, and then she said, "Major, you don't have to fly out again. Denzel says there's room for me in the FBI helicopter, and he plans to spend the night in Moab anyway. So I'll ride back with him."

Chapter Twenty-Five

I DROVE HOME AND THOUGHT about going to bed, but at the last minute, I decided I wasn't going to take a chance on someone trying to tamper with my helicopter again. Knowing who had hired Juan the night before, I had every reason to believe that another attempt might be made tonight. I needed sleep, but at the moment I was far from sleepy.

I called downstairs to Crystal, told her what I had in mind, then flew to Grand Junction. I got a hotel room near the airport and slept until ten o'clock the next morning. After breakfast, I drove to the hospital. I knew I might not be able to talk to Bill yet, but I was determined to be there if he did wake up. And besides that, I felt like I should support Asher.

Lisette didn't call me, which was probably a good thing, yet it was also disappointing. I didn't really want her to know that I had jumped the gun in coming to Grand Junction. On the other hand, I wished she'd call just because she wanted to hear my voice the way I wanted to hear hers. I missed her, and I hoped she missed me.

Feeling just a little down, I entered the hospital. I inquired about which room Bill Grady was in and was told that he was in intensive care. I had expected that, of course. I asked them to call and see if his wife would come down and talk to me.

They agreed, and in about five minutes, Asher appeared in the lobby. The moment she saw me she ran to me and collapsed in my arms in tears. It seemed like an eternity before she finally drew away. "They tried to kill him. Trace's friends tried to kill my husband. They blew his hand off. He's a cripple now. He never did anything to anybody. He was just working so he could support our family."

She once again collapsed against me. It was hard to know how to comfort her. I was not practiced in such things. I felt stiff and awkward. Once again she drew away, rubbed mascara all over her face, and said, "Can you catch them, Major?"

"If it was the guys I think it was, and if they really did cause that explosion, then yes, Asher, I will not rest until I get them," I said. I suppose that was a rash thing to say, but I meant it, nonetheless.

"Thank you," she said. "That won't give Bill his hand back, but at least we might get a little bit of justice."

"Tell me, Asher, how it is that you know someone caused the explosion?"

She told me that Bill was awake for a little while and had told her what had happened. "It was hard to understand him, but I think I got the main idea."

"Tell me what you think he said," I prompted.

She told me as much as she could. I slammed one fist into the other. If I'd been a swearing man, I would have done so then. It took me a moment to cool my rage. Finally, I took a deep breath. "Do you think Bill can talk to me if they let me come up? I need to make sure I have this all straight."

"You can come up. And you can wait until he wakes up again."

I wasn't sure she would get her way with the hospital staff, but she was on the fight now. The tears had dried up, and she wouldn't take no for an answer. At last I was allowed to go up and sit beside the bed of Bill Grady, waiting for the next time he woke up. It wasn't long before his eyelids blinked and then opened. Much of the swelling had gone down, and I could see his pupils through the narrow slit of his eyelids. He tried to focus for a minute, and he finally said, "Major. You came."

"Yes, I came," I said. "Can you tell me what happened at the rig when you got hurt?"

"Yes." His voice was hoarse and weak.

I flipped on my recorder, held it close to him, and said, "Okay, go ahead." What he said next was pretty much what Asher had already told me, but I was able to clarify a few things until I was sure I had it all straight.

I shut off the recorder and sat with Asher and Bill for a few more minutes. Bill fell asleep again after moaning about losing his hand. I finally stood up and said, "Asher, you take care of your man. I'll be back," I said.

As I drove back to my helicopter, I felt like I was ready to go into battle. It was a feeling I'd had countless times before. I was not going to fail. I had promised to get the people who had caused so much death and suffering, and that's what I intended to do—or die trying.

As I was driving into the car rental place, I remembered that I'd shut off my phone while I was with Bill. I had been so deep in thought about how I was going to find the people who had done this that I hadn't even given my phone a second thought. All I could think about was getting back to Moab and taking up the hunt.

I pulled into the lot, but instead of turning my car in, I let the engine idle while I pulled my iPhone out and turned it on. I had a bunch of missed calls. Two were from Crystal, a half dozen from Lisette, and one from Special Agent Warner.

I decided to make my calls before I returned the car. I started with Crystal.

"Hi, Corbin," she said. "I just wondered how it's going."

I told her and then said, "I'm just turning in my rental. Then I'll go get my helicopter and be on my way back."

"Corbin," she said. "I know you want to get them, but please, please be careful. These are dangerous people."

"I'm an old veteran of war," I told her lightly. "I can handle myself in battle."

She didn't like the way I put it and again warned me to be careful. I thanked her and hung up.

After debating with myself for a minute, I made the next call to Denzel Warner. "Hey, Major, where are you?" he asked.

"I'm just getting ready to fly to Moab. I'm in Grand Junction."

"I wondered if that's where you were. So how is Bill Grady doing?"

I briefly described Bill's condition, then I said, "He told me what happened at the rig; that the explosion wasn't an accident. He was very clear about it and provided me with some details."

"Good work, Major," he responded. "I'll be back in Moab in a day or two, but right now I've got to go to Denver. We've got a big problem up there, and they say they need me. I told them I need to be here, but my boss doesn't care. He sets the priorities, and if they differ from those of us in the field, well, too bad for us. So I'm sorry, but I have to go now even though it's so late."

"I wish you could be here, but I guess we'll just have to do the best we can without you," I said. "I'll see you when you get back."

After he'd hung up, I realized he hadn't asked the details of what Bill had told me. But that was just as well, I thought. I wanted to be the one to end this thing, and if he told his supervisor, the man might have a change of heart and let Denzel stay. Of course, there was no guarantee this would be over by the time Denzel came back. After all, these people had proved to be elusive so far.

My last call was to Lisette. "Hi," I said, trying to sound lighthearted, even though I felt anything but that. "Have you made any progress on the rig explosion?"

It was silent on the other end, and I had a feeling the sheriff was not happy with me. She finally said, "When I tried to call you an hour or so ago, I didn't get an answer. So I drove over to your house. And what do you think I found?" I didn't say anything, wondering what I could do to curb her anger. Finally she spoke again. "Nothing, that's what I found, Major. Well, not quite nothing. Your truck was there. But you and your helicopter were not. Why haven't you answered my calls?"

"I'm sorry, it wasn't intentional," I said.

"Where are you? Grand Junction?" she asked.

"Yes."

"I would have gone with you if you'd have given me the chance," she snapped, but she sounded more hurt than angry. I suspect she was both, and I honestly didn't blame her.

"I decided to leave on the spur of the moment," I said. "I didn't want to leave my chopper exposed again. I felt it would be safer here. You were still with the FBI and your deputies. I knew you were busy, but I wasn't, so I came alone. But now I'm ready to come back, and I need your help. Or maybe I should say, you need mine—I hope."

"Did you talk to Bill, or is he still in a coma?" she asked, sounding a little more like herself.

"Yes, I talked to him. And I know what happened."

"Will you tell me?"

"Of course, but first let me explain why my phone was off," I said. "I kept hoping you would call, but it was like pulling teeth getting them to even let me talk to Bill. They made me shut my phone off before I was allowed to accompany Asher up to his room. Then, after he woke up and told me what had happened, what he'd seen, I didn't feel like I could just leave him and Asher. When I did leave the hospital, I was so angry and frustrated that I simply focused on getting back to Moab and what I needed to do when I got there. I honestly forgot to turn my phone back on until I was pulling in to return my rental car."

"Okay," she said. "That's a reasonable excuse, or rather, excuses. So are you going to tell me what you learned?"

"On one condition," I said.

"What is the condition?" She was sounding a little angry again.

"That you forgive me," I said. "Please."

"Oh, Major, of course I forgive you. Now tell me before I burst my girdle," she said.

I chuckled at that. "Now unless I'm really stupid, I'd say you don't wear a girdle."

"It's a figure of speech," she said, finally laughing lightly.

I told her.

From her reaction, I decided it was good she wasn't wearing a girdle because she would have busted it she was so angry. Finally she said, "Surely you don't plan to come back tonight. You must be really tired. It'll worry me if you try to fly tonight."

I thought about that for a moment, knew she was right, and said, "I am tired, and my helicopter really is safer here than at home. So, okay, I'll stay, but I'll be back fairly early tomorrow."

"I'll be waiting," she said. "Call me when you're ready to leave."

* * *

I flew back to Moab the next morning, refreshed and ready. I fueled up at Canyonlands Field and then landed in the sheriff's parking lot as she had requested when I'd spoken with her that morning. She was waiting as I climbed out of the Jet Ranger. I was glad she wasn't still mad, for I probably wouldn't have gotten the tender hug that I did.

"Let's figure out what to do," she said, directing me inside. Once we were seated in her office, she said, "I've been thinking about this since I talked to you last night."

"As have I," I told her.

"The first thing I did this morning was send Jarbi, Ev, and three other officers out looking for our suspects. The chief has some officers helping as well. We both told our people to lean as heavily as they could on any of the known radicals they could find and see if they would cooperate. It's my thinking that some of them know where Louie hangs out. And if Wyatt happens to be in the area, I think they might know where he is as well."

"Good," I said. "I wonder if we should go out and join the search. I'm in the mood for war, and when I'm in that kind of mood, I don't do well sitting around twiddling my thumbs. I'd like to specifically look for Desiree Keefe. With what we know now, I think there's a good chance I can get her to talk."

"I have another idea," Sheriff Statton said. "I'd like to go find our ringleader. Which should we do first?"

"Let's check out a couple of places where Ms. Keefe could be hanging out," I said. "It won't take long."

We hadn't even gotten to the bar where I wanted to look before we heard a radio call from Jarbi. "I am in pursuit of a silver SUV." She was excited and talking rapidly. "I'm not sure of the make. But it's being driven by Louie Fagan, and there is a woman with him."

Jarbi gave her location and direction of travel before she got off the air. The dispatcher began to direct other officers to the area to assist. Lisette sped that way as well, but we were far from the chase, and they were heading away from us.

"Lisette," I said as I made a sudden decision, "we're closer to your office than to Jarbi. Let's get my chopper. If they don't get the van stopped, at least we can keep track of it from the air."

She didn't speak, just applied her brakes, spun her vehicle around, and sped toward her office. We were almost there when Jarbi's voice came over the radio again. "They're shooting at me! My car's been hit!"

"Are you okay?" the dispatcher asked urgently.

"I'm fine, but I'm out of the chase. My car's spewing some kind of fluid all over the place."

Other officers chimed in. One city officer had the vehicle in view, but he was also being shot at and had to back off. Lisette raced into the parking lot and screeched to a stop, and we both leapt from her car. I felt a rush of adrenaline as I ran for my Jet Ranger. I turned back to Lisette. "You get your shotgun, and I'll get this thing running."

She spun around without a word, and a moment later, she returned, carrying the shotgun, a handheld radio, and a box of twelve-gauge shotgun shells. "I've got some slugs here," she reported as she climbed in beside me.

"And I have a rifle in the backseat," I said. "I put it in before I left Moab. It's just a thirty-thirty, but it's light and easy to handle. I also have extra ammo."

I had decided, after all that had happened the past few days, that I was not going anywhere unarmed. Besides the rifle, I had my 9mm pistol on me. I was ready to fight.

We'd barely gotten into the air when we learned that Louie and the unidentified woman had gotten into a helicopter.

"Let's go get them," Lisette said over the headset.

I had a sudden flashback, and my gut twisted in agony.

Chapter Twenty-Six

THE LAST TIME I HAD flown into battle with a woman beside me had been in Afghanistan. My fiancée, Angie Brower, had been my copilot in a Black Hawk. The pain of that memory almost blinded me. "I can't do this," I suddenly said as I backed off on the speed.

"Major, you've got to," the first woman I had allowed to get close to my heart since the death of my beloved Angie shouted. "We've got to get them."

"I can't chase them with you on board," I said as I fought with my demons.

"I'm not getting off," she said. "This is my fight as much or more than yours."

"The last time—" I began.

"Don't think about what happened to your fiancée, Major," she ordered. "Let's get these people. We can't let them get away."

"It's too dangerous." I was losing altitude.

"Major, don't do this. I need your help. Others are arranging support on the ground. Our job is to keep them in sight," she pleaded.

"Yeah, like when I was chasing Trace. And look how that turned out."

"Major, please. Don't lose nerve now. This is it. We can get Louie and Earl and the woman and the guy in the other chopper. It could be Wyatt."

I looked over at her. "I have the nerve, Sheriff," I said. "Don't question my courage. It's you I'm worried about."

"I have the courage too." She was nearly shouting through my headphones. "Now go. We're in this together. Please, Major."

I knew what I had to do. She was an officer of the law. A client of mine had suffered terrible losses because of the people in that other Jet Ranger. I had a duty, even as Lisette had a duty. Even as Angie and I had had a duty. Dear, dead Angie.

Without another word, I changed my heading, urged all the speed I could out of my Jet Ranger, and began a pursuit that I dreaded yet knew I could never live down if I backed off now.

"Where's Bassinger now?" I asked as I felt a determined focus settle over me. This was indeed war, and I was ready. Earl Bassinger had dropped a bomb that had killed a man and maimed my client's husband for life, and now I was quite sure that he had also sent her father to his death from that very helicopter we were now in pursuit of.

Lisette told me which direction the helicopter was flying, and I adjusted my heading a little. "We can catch him," I said as we flew over the wild and rugged terrain west of Moab. "We're running at an angle to him. We can cut him off as long as he doesn't change course. And we have an advantage. We know where he is. He doesn't even know we're in the air."

A few minutes later, Lisette shouted, "There they are!"

And there they went. The moment we were spotted, Earl Bassinger headed straight away from us. I coaxed the Jet Ranger to go faster, wishing I was flying a Black Hawk again. But at least my chopper was newer and appeared to be faster than Earl's.

I closed in until I was right on his tail, and then I stayed there. Before long, I got a call on my aircraft radio. I had support in the sky, but it was a small plane without the speed of my Jet Ranger, so it wasn't going to be able to catch up, not that it could do anything more than I could anyway.

In fact, it could only have done less, I realized as Earl suddenly dropped rapidly until he was flying through a twisting canyon with towering walls. I stayed right with him. He tried several evasive maneuvers, but he couldn't shake me. I was in my element now. And he was clearly out of his.

Suddenly, he took a sharp turn to the right and began to climb. I let him climb past me.

"That looks like Wyatt Mortell, Earl, and Louie, and they all have rifles. I didn't get a good look at the woman," Lisette said.

I didn't say anything. I was totally focused on the chase. I followed him up out of the canyon and let him get a little bit of a lead. Then once again, I closed in, just to let Earl and his passengers know who had the faster aircraft. He was flying east now, in the general direction of Moab.

We continued that direction for about five minutes, which was enough time that the pilot in the fixed-wing aircraft was able to reach us. However, he was flying much higher and spoke to me on the radio, letting me know he would stay up there and observe. I thanked him while keeping a close eye on the helicopter.

Earl must have thought he could lose me by dropping into a canyon because that's exactly what he did again, cutting sharply back to the west again and dropping dangerously. I followed him down, keeping fairly close. Almost in unison, Earl and I raced up the canyon. It had some sharp corners. I backed off just a little. If he messed up, I didn't want to be close enough to clip him. That would bring us both down, and at the speed we were going, there would be no survivors.

For the next hour, we kept up the dangerous game. Most of the time, we were flying in canyons, sometimes going in one direction and sometimes another. I had no idea how much fuel Earl had, but I could keep this up for a long time yet. I didn't relish the thought. I kept hoping he'd finally land somewhere and give up.

By going back and forth the way he was, Earl had allowed more aircraft to fill the skies above us. Lisette reported that another helicopter was even in the area now. There was very little chatter coming over our radio from the other aircraft. However, there was enough that I was able to identify the other helicopter as being from the FBI. The pilot made it clear that he was only in the air to help us when we landed; he wasn't into the kind of evasive maneuvers and fancy flying that was taking place. He made it clear he would keep out of our way. I was grateful for that. He also told us that Special Agent Warner was with him.

Lisette and I looked at each other briefly. "I thought he couldn't be here," she said.

I shrugged as I watched Earl and his helicopter. I didn't speak on the radio any more than I had to—I was too busy concentrating on my flying—but I was grateful to know there were others in the vicinity, especially Warner. I had confidence in him.

Earl's flying seemed to be getting a little bit erratic. I was feeling the strain myself, but I was younger and likely more experienced in flying under tense and dangerous circumstances. I hoped that gave me an edge.

We were flying up a deep canyon that suddenly turned sharply to the right. The canyon walls on both sides closed in on us. I backed off a little bit more, not sure Earl was going to successfully navigate the gap. He made it, but his rotors had come within inches of the canyon wall. Once through the narrow gap, the canyon opened up considerably.

We flew on for only a short distance before Earl suddenly slowed down and began to rapidly descend. I backed way off, expecting him to pull up, but he didn't. His aircraft continued downward until it struck the valley floor. A huge cloud of dust puffed up, and I expected it to be joined by flames and smoke, but that didn't happen.

Lisette was clearly thinking along the same lines. "Surely it's about to explode."

I circled back over the wreckage, hoping to see how bad it was. "He must have run out of fuel."

Suddenly, my own helicopter shuddered. "Someone's shooting at us!" Lisette cried.

I couldn't respond, because she was right, and we were going down. We had plenty of fuel, so if I couldn't control the crash, Lisette and I would go up in flames along with my aircraft. I had to fight off the memory of the last time I'd been shot down—with Angie on board and the enemy waiting for us on the hot Afghanistan desert floor. I willed the memory away, resolved to not let this end tragically like it had that time.

It took every ounce of my strength and all the skill I possessed to guide my damaged chopper down. We hit with a gentle thump. We were lucky but not lucky enough. Another bullet hit my helicopter. Lisette and I threw open the door and scrambled to get out. She took the shotgun and extra shells. I took the rifle and extra shells. Another shot rang out as we ran away from the crash, ducking low and weaving back and forth, seeking some kind of protection.

All that we found was a mound of rocky dirt; we threw ourselves across and to the other side. There we lay panting, hugging the ground, and watching dirt spray up around us as a couple more bullets struck dangerously close.

Finally, after we'd both caught our breath, I stated the obvious, "Someone made it out alive."

I could hear the thumping of another helicopter and turned my head so that I could see up. The FBI helicopter was not too far away, but when another shot rang out and no dust kicked up near us, I knew it was being shot at too. It flew quickly out of range. For the moment, we were on our own.

The next bullet nicked my shirt sleeve. Too close, I thought as I suddenly imagined that I could feel the scar on my face from another bullet at another time. "Fire a round in their direction," I told Lisette. "But don't raise yourself up. I'll jump up and try to get an accurate shot off."

She nodded her agreement, and a moment later there was a loud boom from the twelve gauge. I rose swiftly to my feet, located the shooter forty or fifty feet from the wrecked chopper, and flinched when another round from the shotgun went off. Then I fired. I knew as I dropped back down beside Lisette, jacking in another round, that my shot had been accurate, for I'd heard the plopping sound that was all too familiar—the sound of a bullet hitting flesh.

"It was Louie," I said. "He's down beside a large rock. Stay here, and cover me; I'll see if he is still a danger to us." Before she could protest, I rose and darted to the right. Nothing happened so I kept going, my eyes shifting rapidly back and forth between where Louie lay and Earl's wrecked chopper. Running like a dodging jackrabbit, I reached the injured man out of sight of the chopper. Feeling no immediate threat from that direction, I gave my full attention to Louie.

He was lying very still, and I could see blood coming from one leg. His rifle lay just beyond his reach. For a moment, I thought he was unconscious, but then I saw a finger twitch on his outstretched left hand. The other hand was out of sight across his body from me. Suddenly, springing like a cat, he came at me with a knife gleaming in his right hand.

I reacted instinctively, using my rifle as a club. I hit his hand, and the knife flew away, landing in the sand beyond the rock. Louie kept coming. I dodged aside, he stumbled, and I struck him again with the rifle. He fell in a heap.

"I'm coming," Lisette called. But before I could tell her to wait until I had a chance to check out the helicopter, another shot rang out. I watched as Lisette stumbled and then fell face forward on the ground.

I left Louie where he lay, and with a cry of anguish, I made a desperate dash toward Lisette. My heart threatened to break out of my chest. As I dropped beside her, I saw a movement at the crashed chopper, and there was another shot. I didn't feel anything. I didn't care anyway. If I got shot, I got shot. All I wanted to do was help Lisette.

I heard running footsteps as I picked Lisette up and held her, tears streaming down my face. "Not again," I cried aloud. "Please, not again." I heard myself repeating, "I love you, please don't leave me," over and over again.

The footsteps stopped beside me, and I looked up, expecting to be peering into the barrel of a rifle. But what I saw was the concerned face of Special Agent Denzel Warren. "I got him," he said.

I could only nod and hold the woman I knew, despite all my effort, I had fallen in love with. It was just too much.

"Let me help you," I heard Denzel say.

"It's too late. He shot her," I cried in anguish. I'd been transported back in time, and in my mind I was holding Angie, the vibrant person she had been, snuffed out like a candle.

Denzel knelt beside me and gently pried Lisette loose from my hold. "She's alive, Major. Help me here."

Those words brought me out of my stupor, and I turned toward where he was now laying Lisette on the ground. Instantly, I could see what had to be done. She had a serious wound in her stomach, and it was bleeding badly, but she was breathing. Together we cut her shirt back, and then Denzel said, "We need to cover this and put some pressure on it."

"I'll get my first aid kit," I said and ran to my crippled Jet Ranger. When I got back, I already had the kit open and was pulling out a large bandage. "Use this," I said. I became aware of the distinctive thumping of a helicopter.

I helped Denzel and his pilot load my beloved sheriff into the FBI chopper. "You go with her," Denzel said. "There's a medical helicopter coming from Grand Junction. When they transfer her, you go with them if they'll let you. My pilot will come back here."

I sat in the backseat and held Lisette as we streaked above the rugged landscape. We met the life-flight chopper, and Lisette was soon being attended to by competent medical personnel. I begged to go with them but was told there simply wasn't room. So with a string of prayers, we flew back to where our little war had ended. We landed beside my Jet Ranger, and I got out wearily.

Denzel brought me up-to-date as we waited for more help to arrive. Louie, though injured, was conscious and cursing. Denzel had him tightly bound so he wasn't a threat. His wounds had been attended to, and despite his angry cries to get him to a hospital, we ignored him. The others were all deceased. Earl Bassinger, who had stupidly run his helicopter out of fuel, was dead at the controls. Behind him, also dead from the crash, was Desiree Keefe. Lying within a couple of yards of the chopper was Wyatt Mortell. He had died of a bullet fired by Special Agent Warren. But Denzel said, "He would have died anyway. Just look at his injuries. I wonder how he was even able to fire that rifle."

"He was aided by pure hatred," I said. "It has never ceased to amaze me how hate can cause a person to do things that seem impossible."

* * *

After some of the sheriff's deputies arrived, Denzel volunteered to stay and help them while his pilot flew me to Grand Junction. Louie was being taken to the same hospital that Lisette was at now and where Bill Grady was having to adjust to the loss of his hand.

I walked up to the hospital and stopped outside the entrance. I bowed my head, offered a short prayer, and then stepped through the doors.

Chapter Twenty-Seven

MY HEART ALMOST LODGED IN my throat when I stepped into the room where Lisette, only an hour out of surgery, was lying. Tubes ran everywhere, monitors reported the state of her condition in various lines and numbers. A nurse stood over her, doing whatever it was she was doing. I focused on Lisette's face. Her eyes were closed and her skin pale, but when one eyelid twitched, I felt a surge of hope. I made myself as comfortable as I could in the chair beside her bed, determined not to move until I was sure she'd be okay.

It was sometime in the middle of the night when I heard her stir. "Major," she said in a barely discernible voice.

"I'm right here," I said as I leaned close.

"Was it me you were talking to or was it her?" she asked.

"When?" I asked, but then I remembered.

"You know, when you said, 'I love you.'"

I felt myself redden in the semidarkness of her room. "It was you."

"I love you too," she responded. "Thank you for saving my life."

"I didn't," I confessed. "That was Denzel."

"He helped, but not until you saved me," she said. "I was dying when you said those words. I had given up. Your love brought me back. Your love made me fight to stay alive."

Tears coursed down my face, across the scar of that long-ago battle, while I thanked my God for the miracle that was this woman.

A few hours later, as I sat beside Lisette, she said, "We need to wrap this case up. Will you help Jarbi and Ev get it done?"

"I don't want to leave you alone," I said.

"It's okay. It won't take you long, I'm sure."

"But I would rather—" I began.

A gentle finger touched my lip. "Go, my love," she said tenderly. "I have a duty, and I need you to help me complete it. Please."

There was nothing else I could do. I kissed Lisette, expressed my love to her, and left the room. Minutes later, I was with Bill and Asher Grady.

"What are you doing here?" Asher asked. "Did you get them?"

"Yes, we got them," I said. "But there are a couple of loose ends we need to tie up. I need your help to do that, Asher."

"First," her husband said from his bed, "tell us how you did it."

I told them, including the fact that the sheriff now lay seriously injured just a few rooms away. "I misjudged her," Asher admitted.

I nodded. "Your uncle is also here. Will you come with me to talk to him?"

"I hate him!" she said vehemently.

"I understand, but I still need your help. He can tell us how your father died and who is responsible," I said.

"In that case, yes, I'll come with you."

For some reason, I wasn't surprised when I was greeted outside the door of Louie's room by Trooper Stone. He grinned as Asher and I approached. "Same place, different suspect," he said. "I'll be glad when I get some seniority. But at least I was cleared of any wrongdoing in the last incident. I guess I'm just glad to be here."

"Sorry you have to pull bad duty," I said. "But I'm happy to see you. This is Asher Grady. Trace Jones was her brother. The man in this room is her uncle. We need to speak with him."

"Of course," he said. "Whatever you want, Major." He turned to Asher, his face grave. "I'm sorry about your husband. I hear he is a good man."

"Unlike my brother and my uncle," she said, but somehow, on her crazily painted and bejeweled face, she managed a smile.

We got no smiles from the man inside the room. "You," he said, pointing a finger at me. "You did this to me." He pointed at his bandaged leg. That was only one of a number of injuries, but I guessed it was the worst one.

"And you tried to shoot me," I reminded him. "But we're not here to talk about who the best shot is. Your niece and I want to know who killed her dad, why, and how."

My hand was in my pocket, and I smoothly turned on the little recorder, just in case he said something of importance. To my surprise, he did. "Johanna was my sister," Louie said. "I respected and honored her."

"And obeyed her?" I asked, not daring to look at Asher when I asked that question.

"Yes, I obeyed her. When Edward acted the fool and tried to unravel our plans to stop the drilling, Johanna told me and Wyatt to take care of him. So we did." He shrugged.

I heard a gasp from beside me, but I still didn't dare look at Asher. I asked, "Who gave him the shot to sedate him?"

"My sister."

"And then what did you and Wyatt do?"

"I think you know. Earl took us and Edward for a helicopter ride."

"Who pushed Edward out?" I asked.

"Wyatt did," he said. "Satisfied?"

Before I could say anything, Asher, her voice scarcely more than a whisper, asked, "Who threw the bomb out of the helicopter, you know, the bomb that blew my husband's hand off?"

"I know you want me to say that I did," he said with an evil grin. "Well, it so happens that I did not. That was Wyatt. Sorry, niece. You can't hang it on me."

"But you were there," I stated flatly.

"Of course I was there. After Trace so carelessly killed Johanna, that made me the boss. I needed to make sure it was done and done properly," he said.

Now I looked at Asher. Her face looked tortured. "My mother started all this? This stuff against Bill's job?" she asked.

"She sure did. Why do you think she and your dad were having so much trouble? She felt strongly about what was happening. She asked me to help her. So I did," he said. "And I'd do it again in a heartbeat." He looked back at me. "As for you, Major Daniels, I'll get you yet, you interfering—"

"Let's go, Asher," I said as I took her gently by the arm. "I've got it all recorded. Louie will spend the rest of his miserable days in prison."

Louie was spewing something as I led her out the door, but I didn't pay any attention to it. In the hallway, Asher fell into my arms again and sobbed. "My mother did all that," she said, still in shock. "Did you know that, Major?"

"Not until just now, but I suspected it. According to Trace, she told him to shoot me that day in front of his house. I had a bad feeling about her from the moment I heard that," I said. "I didn't really believe Trace, but then I was told that a woman was calling the shots with this violent little group."

"I'm sorry," she said softly as she let go of me. "I'm sorry for what happened to so many innocent people. If I had only known, maybe I could have stopped her."

I shook my head. "I don't think so, Asher. Your dad tried, and look where it got him."

She tearfully shook her head, gave me another hug, and headed for her husband's room. I spoke to Trooper Stone for a moment, explaining what Louie had just admitted. "I hope he won't be here long," the trooper said.

"I don't think he will be," I said.

When I returned to Lisette's room, Ev and Jarbi were there. Lisette looked just like she had when I'd left. She was lying very still, looked very sick, and was beautiful beyond my comprehension. I told her so, the beauty part, I mean, and she smiled. And in case there was any question about how things were between me and her in the minds of her two deputies, she settled it when she said, "I love you, Major."

"And I love you," I, the formerly confirmed bachelor, said. "Now, let's get down to business." I pulled the digital recorder from my pocket. "I think you might be interested in the conversation Asher Grady and I just had with Louie Fagan."

* * *

The only person left to prosecute was Louie, but the sheriff wanted to make sure that when she officially closed the case, there would be no loose ends and, insofar as it was possible, no unanswered questions.

To that end, Jarbi, Ev, and I performed another search of the home of Edward and Johanna Jones, with Asher's written permission. We were looking for different kinds of things than we had been when it was searched before. And we found those different things. Johanna had kept a written record of the orders she'd given. To the unsuspecting eye, they looked like a box full of old letters. They had been glanced at and discarded the first time through.

Those documents proved to be very incriminating. The fact that Johanna was the mastermind and driving force behind the violent protesters was confirmed. Those documents also pointed accusing fingers at all of the Yosts as well as Trace, Wyatt, Louie, Desiree, and Earl. The order for her own husband to be executed was clearly documented.

A subsequent search of the wreckage of Earl's Jet Ranger did even more to backup what Louie had told us. Fingerprints as well as a small smear of Edward's blood were found inside the chopper. Despite being sedated, he had apparently struggled some, knocking the suitcase with the pamphlets out the door and cutting himself slightly before taking his fatal plunge.

Officially, my case with Asher Grady was over. So was my case with Dayna Simonson. The other protestors, those of a less violent nature, seemed to melt away. The drilling went on, and peace returned to the area.

Epilogue

AFTER MY HELICOPTER WAS REPAIRED, I took the sheriff, Lisette Statton, for a ride in it. She was still on the mend and not back to work yet, although she was directing her department from home.

That day we flew, not for business or in the interest of finding criminals. Rather, we flew on a personal sort of mission. Up there, high above some of the most beautiful scenery in Grand County, Utah, I asked her to be my wife.

Believe it or not, she accepted. That evening, with the help of my ever steady and dependable assistant, I fixed dinner for her at my home. We actually had four people for dinner that night, two future married couples. Besides my wonderful fiancée, I also enjoyed the company of Crystal and her fiancé, Jarrett Bloom.

Part of Crystal's reason for moving with me to Moab had been fulfilled. She had found the long-sought-after man of her life. I, on the other hand, had failed in mine. I had made the move with the intention of staying happily single the rest of my life. I am so grateful for my failure, and Lisette tells me she is too.

About the Author

CLAIR M. POULSON WAS BORN and raised in Duchesne, Utah. His father was a rancher and farmer, his mother a librarian. Clair has always been an avid reader, having found his love for books as a very young boy.

He has served for over forty years in the criminal justice system. Twenty years were spent in law enforcement, ending his police career with eight years as the Duchesne County Sheriff. For the past twenty-plus years, Clair has worked as a justice court judge for Duchesne County. Clair is also a veteran of the US Army, where he was a military policeman. During his time in the Military Police, Clair became very well acquainted with two accused killers. In law enforcement, he has been personally involved in the investigation of murders and other violent crimes. Clair has also served on various boards and councils during his professional career, including the Justice Court Board of Judges, the Utah Commission on Criminal and Juvenile Justice, the Utah Judicial Council, the Utah Peace Officer Standards and Training Council, an FBI advisory board, and others.

In addition to his criminal justice work, Clair has farmed and ranched all of his life. He has raised many kinds of animals, but his greatest interests are is horses and cattle. He's also involved in the grocery store business with his oldest son and other family members.

Clair has served in many capacities in the LDS Church, including full-time missionary (California Mission), bishop, counselor to two bishops, young men president, high councilor, stake mission president, Scoutmaster, and high priest group leader. He currently serves as a Gospel Doctrine teacher.

Clair is married to Ruth, and they have five children, all of whom are married: Alan (Vicena) Poulson, Kelly Ann (Wade) Hatch, Amanda (Ben) Semadeni, Wade (Brooke) Poulson, and Mary (Tyler) Hicken. They also have twenty-three wonderful grandchildren. Clair and Ruth met while both were students at Snow College and were married in the Manti temple.

Clair has always loved telling his children, and later his grandchildren, made-up stories. His vast experience in life and his love of literature have contributed to both his telling stories to children and his writing of adventure and suspense novels.

With this book, Clair will have published over two dozen novels. He would love to hear from his fans, who can contact him by going to his website, *clairmpoulson.com*.